D1431113

PRAISE FOR LARISSA REINHART

PORTRAIT OF A DEAD GUY
A Cherry Tucker Mystery

Finalist for 2012 Daphne Du Maurier finalist, The Emily, and a winner of the 2011 Dixie Kane Memorial, Night Owl Reviews Top Pick

"Reinhart is a truly talented author and this book was one of the best cozy mysteries we reviewed this year." – *Mystery Tribune*

"It takes a rare talent to successfully portray a beer-and-hormone-addled artist as a sympathetic and worthy heroine, but Reinhart pulls it off with tongue-in-cheek panache. Cherry is a lovable riot, whether drooling over the town's hunky males, defending her dysfunctional family's honor, or snooping around murder scenes."— *Mystery Scene Magazine*

"*Portrait of a Dead Guy* is an entertaining mystery full of quirky characters and solid plotting. Larissa Reinhart writes with panache and flair, her colorful details and vibrant descriptions painting a vivid, engaging picture of a small Southern town…Highly recommended for anyone who likes their mysteries strong and their mint juleps stronger!" — Jennie Bentley, *NY Times* Bestselling Author of *Flipped Out*

"The story moves at a rapid pace taking you on a curvy road with a disastrous funeral, crazy ex-boyfriends, and illegal high stakes gambling... Portrait of a Dead Guy is pure enjoyment, a laugh out loud mystery with some Southern romance thrown in. Five stars out of five." — Lynn Farris, National Mystery Review Examiner at Examiner.com

"Laugh-out-loud funny and as Southern as sweet tea and cheese grits, Larissa Reinhart's masterfully crafted whodunit, *Portrait of a Dead Guy*, provides high-octane action with quirky, down-home characters and a trouble-magnet heroine who'll steal readers' hearts..." — Debby Giusti, Author of *The Captain's Mission* and *The Colonel's Daughter*

"A fun, fast-paced read and a rollicking start to her Cherry Tucker Mystery Series. If you like your stories southern-fried with a side of romance, this book's for you!" — Leslie Tentler, Author of *Midnight Caller*

A Composition In Murder (#6)

"Anytime artist Cherry Tucker has what she calls a Matlock moment, can investigating a murder be far behind? A Composition in Murder is a rollicking good time." – Terrie Farley Moran, Agatha Award-Winning Author of *Read to Death*

"Boasting a wonderful cast of characters, witty banter blooming with southern charm, this is a fantastic read and I especially love how this book ended with exciting new opportunities, making it one of the best book in this delightfully endearing series." — Dru Ann Love, *Dru's book musings*

"This is a winning series that continues to grow stronger and never fails to entertain with laughs, a little snark, and a ton of heart." – *Kings River Life Magazine*

The Body In The Landscape (#5)

"Cherry Tucker is a strong, sassy, Southern sleuth who keeps you on the edge of your seat. She's back in action in *The Body in the Landscape* with witty banter, Southern charm, plenty of suspects, and dead bodies—you will not be disappointed!" – Tonya Kappes, *USA Today* Bestselling Author

"Anyone who likes humorous mysteries will also enjoy local author Larissa Reinhart, who captures small town Georgia in the laugh- out-loud escapades of struggling artist Cherry Tucker." – *Fayette Woman Magazine*

"Portraits of freshly dead people turn up in strange places in Larissa Reinhart's mysteries, and her The Body in the Landscape is no exception. Because of Cherry's experiences, she knows that— Super Swine notwithstanding—man has always been the most dangerous game, making her the perfect protagonist for this giggle-inducing, down-home fun."— Betty Webb, *Mystery Scene Magazine*

Death In Perspective (#4)

"One fasten-your-seatbelt, pedal-to-the-metal mystery, and Cherry Tucker is the perfect sleuth to have behind the wheel. Smart, feisty, as tough as she is tender, Cherry's got justice in her crosshairs." – Tina Whittle, Author of the *Tai Randolph Mysteries*

"The perfect blend of funny, intriguing, and sexy! Another must-read masterpiece from the hilarious Cherry Tucker Mystery Series." – Ann Charles, *USA Today* Bestselling Author of the *Deadwood* and *Jackrabbit Junction Mystery Series*.

"Artist and accidental detective Cherry Tucker goes back to high school and finds plenty of trouble and skeletons...Reinhart's charming, sweet-tea flavored series keeps getting better!" – Gretchen Archer, *USA Today* Bestselling Author of the *Davis Way Crime Caper Series*

Hijack In Abstract (#3)

"The fast-paced plot careens through small-town politics and deadly rivalries, with zany side trips through art-world shenanigans and romantic hijinx. Like front-porch lemonade, Reinhart's cast of characters offer a perfect balance of tart and sweet." – Sophie Littlefield, Bestselling Author of *A Bad Day for Sorry*

"Reinhart manages to braid a complicated plot into a tight and funny tale. The reader grows to love Cherry and her quirky world-view, her sometimes misguided judgment, and the eccentric characters that populate the country of Halo, Georgia. Cozy fans will love this latest Cherry Tucker mystery."– Mary Marks, *New York Journal of Books*

"In HIJACK IN ABSTRACT, Cherry Tucker is back—tart-tongued and full of sass. With her paint-stained fingers in every pie, she's in for a truckload of trouble."– J.J. Murphy, Author of the *Algonquin Round Table Mysteries*

Still Life In Brunswick Stew (#2)

"Reinhart's country-fried mystery is as much fun as a ride on the tilt-a-whirl at a state fair. Her sleuth wields a paintbrush and unravels clues with equal skill and flair. Readers who like a little small-town charm with their mysteries will enjoy Reinhart's series." – Denise Swanson, *New York Times* Bestselling Author of the *Scumble River Mysteries*

"The hilariously droll Larissa Reinhart cooks up a quirky and entertaining page-turner! This charming mystery is delightfully Southern, surprisingly edgy, and deliciously unpredictable." – Hank Phillippi Ryan, Agatha Award-Winning Author of *Truth Be Told*

"This mystery keeps you laughing and guessing from the first page to the last. A whole-hearted five stars."– Denise Grover Swank, *New York Times* and *USA TODAY* bestselling author

The Maizie Albright Star Detective Series
15 MINUTES

"Hollywood glitz meets backwoods grit in this fast-paced ride on

D-list celeb Maizie Albright's waning star—even as it's reborn in a spectacular collision with her nightmarish stage mother, her deer-pee-scented-apparel-inventing daddy...and a murderer. Sassy, sexy, and fun, 15 Minutes is hours of enjoyment—and a wonderful start to a fun new series from the charmingly Southern-fried Reinhart."
— Phoebe Fox, author of *The Breakup Doctor* series

"I was already a huge fan of Larissa Reinhart's "Cherry Tucker" series, but in her new mystery series, FIFTEEN MINUTES, she had me at the end of the first line: "Donuts." Maizie Albright is the kind of fresh, fun, and feisty "star detective" I love spending time with, a kind of Nancy Drew meets Lucy Ricardo. Move over, Janet Evanovich. Reinhart is my new "star mystery writer!"— Penny Warner, author of *Death Of a Chocolate Cheater* and *The Code Busters Club*

"Child star and hilarious hot mess Maizie Albright trades Hollywood for the backwoods of Georgia and pure delight ensues. Maizie's my new favorite escape from reality." — Gretchen Archer, *USA Today* bestselling author of the *Davis Way Crime Caper* series

"I love Larissa Reinhart's books because they are funny but they also show the big heart of the protagonist. Despite the movie star background Maize is down to earth and cares about everyone and justice. I strongly recommend this book and look forward to the next in this series. Five stars out of five." —Lynn Farris, *Hot Mystery Review*

PORTRAIT OF A DEAD GUY

A CHERRY TUCKER MYSTERY

LARISSA REINHART

Past Perfect Press

PORTRAIT OF A DEAD GUY

A Cherry Tucker Mystery #1

Second Edition

Published by PAST PERFECT PRESS

Copyright © 2017 by Larissa Reinhart

Library of Congress Control Number: 2017912591

ISBN: 978-0-9985484-2-5

Author Photograph by Scott Asano

Cover Design by The Killion Group, Inc.

All rights reserved. No part of this book may be used or reproduced in any manner whatsoever, including Internet usage, without written permission from Past Perfect Press, except in the case of brief quotations embodied in critical articles and reviews.

Original Copyright © 2012 by Larissa Reinhart

Original Publication date: Henery Press; 1 edition (August 23, 2012)

This is a work of fiction. Any references to historical events, real people, or real locales are used fictitiously. Other names, characters, places, and incidents are the product of the author's imagination, and any resemblance to actual events or locales or persons, living or dead, is entirely coincidental.

Printed in the United States of America

ALSO BY LARISSA REINHART

A Cherry Tucker Mystery Series

Novels

PORTRAIT OF A DEAD GUY (#1)

STILL LIFE IN BRUNSWICK STEW (#2)

HIJACK IN ABSTRACT (#3)

DEATH IN PERSPECTIVE (#4)

THE BODY IN THE LANDSCAPE (#5)

A COMPOSITION IN MURDER (#6)

Novellas

QUICK SKETCH in HEARTACHE MOTEL

THE VIGILANTE VIGNETTE (also in MIDNIGHT MYSTERIES)

A VIEW TO A CHILL (also in THE 12 SLAYS OF CHRISTMAS)

Audio

PORTRAIT OF A DEAD GUY

STILL LIFE IN BRUNSWICK STEW

Maizie Albright Star Detective Series

Novels

15 MINUTES

16 MILLIMETERS

NC-17

Novellas

A VIEW TO A CHILL (also in THE 12 SLAYS OF CHRISTMAS)

To keep up with Larissa's latest releases, contests, and events, please join her newsletter: http://smarturl.it/LarissasBookNews & receive a free short story

Note: Larissa will not share your email address and you can unsubscribe at any time.

Thank you!

.

Dedicated with love to Larry Reinhart, who partly inspired my story, and to Trey, Sophie, and Luci, who support me at my craziest.

ONE

IN A SMALL TOWN, there is a thin gray line between personal freedom and public ruin. Everyone knows your business without even trying. Folks act polite all the while remembering every stupid thing you've done in your life. Not to mention getting tied to all the dumbass stuff your relations — even those dead or gone — have done. We forgive but don't forget.

I thought the name Cherry Tucker carried some respectability as an artist in my hometown of Halo. I actually chose to live in rural Georgia. I could have sought a loft apartment in Atlanta where people appreciate your talent to paint nudes in classical poses, but I like my town and most of the three thousand or so people that live in it. Even though most of Halo wouldn't know a Picasso from a plate of spaghetti.

Still, it's a nice town full of nice people and a lot cheaper to live in than Atlanta. Halo citizens might buy their living room art from the guy who hawks motel overstock in front of the Winn-Dixie, but they also love personalized mementos. Portraits of their kids and their dogs, architectural photos of their homes and gardens, poster-size photos of their trips to Daytona and Disney World. God bless them.

That's my specialty, portraits.

But at this point, I'd paint the side of a barn to make some money. I'm this close from working the night shift at the Waffle Hut. And if I had to wear one of those starchy, brown uniforms day after day, a little part of my soul would die.

Actually, a big part of my soul would die because I'd shoot myself first.

When I heard the high falutin Bransons wanted to commission a portrait of Dustin, their recently deceased thug son, I hightailed it to Cooper's Funeral Home. I assumed they hadn't called me for the commission yet because the shock of Dustin's murder rendered them senseless. After all, what kind of crazy called for a portrait of their murdered boy? But then, important members of a small community could get away with little eccentricities.

I was in no position to judge. I needed the money.

After Dustin's death made the paper three days ago, there'd been a lot of teeth sucking and head shaking in town, but no surprise at Dustin's untimely demise from questionable circumstances. It was going to be that or the State Pen. Dustin had been a criminal in the making for twenty-seven years.

Not that I'd share my observations with the Bransons. Good customer service is important for starving artists if we want to get over that whole starving thing.

As if to remind me, my stomach responded with a sound similar to a lawnmower hitting a chunk of wood. Luckily, the metallic knocking in the long-suffering Datsun engine of my pickup drowned out the hunger rumblings of my tummy.

My poor truck shuddered into Cooper's Funeral Home parking lot in a flurry of flaking yellow paint, jerking and gasping in what sounded like a death rattle. However, I needed her to hang on. After a couple of big commissions, hopefully, the Datsun could go to the big junkyard in the sky.

My little yellow workhorse deserved to rest in peace.

I entered the Victorian monstrosity that is Cooper's, leaving my portfolio case in the truck. I made a quick scan of the lobby and headed toward the first viewing room on the right. A sizable group of Bransons huddled in a corner. Sporadic groupings of flower arrangements sat around the narrow room, though the viewing didn't start until tomorrow.

A plump woman in her early fifties, hair colored and high-lighted sunshine blonde, spun around in kitten heel mules and pulled me into her considerable soft chest. Wanda Branson, step-mother to the deceased, was a hugger. As a kid, I spent many a Sunday School smothered in Miss Wanda's loving arms.

"Cherry!" She rocked me into a deeper hug. "What are you doing here? It's so nice to see you. You can't believe how hard these past few days have been for us." Wanda began sobbing. I continued to rock with her, patting her back while I eased my face out of the ample bosom.

"I'm glad I can help." The turquoise and salmon print silk top muffled my voice. I extricated myself and patted her arm. "It was a shock to hear about Dustin's passing. I remember him from high school."

I remembered him, all right. I remembered hiding from the already notorious Dustin as a freshman and all through high school. Of course, that's water under the bridge now, since he's dead and all.

"It's so sweet of you to come."

"Now Miss Wanda, why don't we find you a place to sit? You tell me exactly what you want, and I'll take notes. How about the lobby? There are some chairs out there. Or outside? It's a beautiful morning and the fresh air might be do you good."

"I'm not sure what you mean," said Wanda. "Tell you what I want?"

"For the portrait. Dustin's portrait."

"Is there a problem?" An older gentleman in a golf shirt and khaki slacks eyed me while running a hand through his thinning salt and pepper hair. John Branson, locally known as JB, strode to his wife's side. "You're Cherry Tucker, Ed Ballard's granddaughter, right?"

I nodded, whipping out a business card.

He glanced at it and looked me over. I had the feeling JB wasn't expecting this little bitty girl with flyaway blonde hair and cornflower blue eyes. My local customers find my appearance disappointing. I think they expected me to return from art school looking as if I walked out of 1920s' bohemian Paris wearing black, slouchy clothes and a ridiculous beret.

I like color and a little bling myself. However, I toned it down for this occasion and chose jeans and a soft orange tee with sequins circling the collar.

"Yes sir," I said, shaking his hand. "I got here as soon as I could. I'm sorry about Dustin."

"Why exactly did you come?" JB spoke calmly but with distaste, as if he held something bitter on his tongue. Probably the idea of me painting his dead son.

"To do the portrait, of course. I figured the sooner I got here, the sooner I could get started. I am pretty fast. You probably heard about my time in high school as a Six Flags quick sketch artist. But time is money, the way I look at it. You'll want your painting sooner than later."

"Cherry, honey, I think there's been some kind of misunderstanding." Wanda looped her arm around JB's elbow.

"JB's niece Shawna is doing the painting."

"Shawna Branson?" I would have keeled over if I hadn't been at Cooper's and worried someone might pop me in a coffin.

Shawna was a smooth-talking Amazonian poacher who wrestled me for the last piece of cake at a church picnic some fifteen years ago. Although she was three heads taller, my scrappy tenacity and love of sugar helped me win. Shawna marked that day as a challenge to defeat me at every turn. In high school, she stole my leather jacket, slept with my boyfriend, and brown-nosed my teachers. She didn't even go to my school.

And now she was after my commission.

"She's driving over from Line Creek today," Wanda said. "You know, she got her degree from Georgia Southern and started a business. She's very busy, but she thinks she can make the time for us."

"I've seen her work," I said. "Lots of hearts, polka dots, and those curlicue letters you monogram on everything."

"Oh yes," said Wanda, showing her fondness for curlicue letters. "She's very talented."

"But ma'am. Can she paint a portrait? I have credentials. I'm a graduate of SCAD, Savannah College of Art and Design. I'm formally trained on mixing color, using light, creating perspective, not to mention the hours spent with live models. I can do curlicue. But don't you want more than curlicue?"

Wanda relaxed her grip on JB's arm. Her eyes wandered to the floral arrangements, considering.

"I have the skill and the eye for portraiture," I continued. "And this is Dustin's final portrait. Don't you want an expert to handle his precious memory?"

"She does have a point, J.B," Wanda conceded.

JB grunted. "The whole idea is damn foolish."

Wanda blushed and fidgeted with JB's sleeve.

"The Victorians used to wear a cameo pin with a lock of their deceased's hair in it," I said, glad to reference my last-minute research as I defended her. "It was considered a memorial. When photography became popular, some propped up the dead for one last picture."

"Exactly. Besides, this is a painting, not a photograph," said Wanda. "It's been hard. I wanted to be closer to Dustin. JB did, too, in his way. And then Dustin was taken before his time."

I detected an eye roll from JB. Money wasn't the issue. Propriety needled him. Wanda loved to spend JB's money, and he encouraged her. JB's problem wasn't that Wanda was flashy; she just shopped above her raising. Which can have unfortunate results. Like hiring someone to paint her dead stepson.

"A somber representation of your son could be comforting," I said. Not that I believed it for a minute.

"Do you need the work, honey?" Wanda asked. "I want to do a

memory box. You know, pick up one of those frames at the Crafty Corner for his mementos. You could do that."

"I'll do the memory box," I said. "I've done some flag cases, so a memory box will be no problem. But I really think you should reconsider Shawna for the painting."

"Now lookee here," said JB. "Shawna's my niece."

"Let me get my portfolio," I said. Pictures speak louder than words, and it looked like JB needed more convincing.

I dashed out of the viewing room and took a deep breath to regain some composure. I couldn't let Shawna Branson steal my commission. The Bransons needed this portrait done right. Who knows what kind of paint slaughter Shawna would commit. As far as I was concerned, she could keep her curlicue business as long as she left the real art to me.

My bright yellow pickup glowed like a radiant beacon in the sea of black, silver, and white cars. I opened the driver door with a yank, cursing a patch of rust growing around the lock.

Standing on my toes, I reached for the portfolio bag on the passenger side. The stretch tipped me off my toes and splayed me flat across the bench.

"I recognize this truck." A lazy voice floated behind me. "And the view. Doesn't look like much's changed either way in ten years."

I gasped and crawled out.

Luke Harper, Dustin's step-brother.

I had forgotten that twig on the Branson family tree. More like snapped it from my memory. His lanky stance blocked the open truck door. One hand splayed against my side window. His other wrist lay propped over the top of my door.

Within the cage of Luke's arms, we examined each other. Fondness didn't dwell in my eyes. I'm never sure what dwelled in his.

Luke drove me crazy in ways I didn't appreciate. He knew how to push buttons that switched me from tough to soft, smart to dumb. Beautiful men were my kryptonite. Local gossip said my mother had the same problem. My poor sister, Casey, was just as inflicted. We would have been better off inheriting a squinty eye or a duck walk.

"Hello, Luke Harper." I tried not to sound snide.

Drawing up to my fullest five foot and a half inches, I cocked a hip in casual belligerence.

"How's it going, Cherry?" A glint of light sparked his smoky eyes, and I expected it corresponded with a certain memory of a nineteen-year-old me wearing a pair of red cowboy boots and not much else. "You hanging out at funeral homes now? Never took you for a necrophiliac."

This time I gave Luke my best what-the-hell redneck glare. Crossing my arms, I took a tiny step forward in the trapped space. He stared at me with a faint smile tugging the corners of his mouth.

If I could paint those gorgeous curls and long sideburns — which will never happen, by the way — I would use a rich, raw umber with burnt sienna highlights. For his eyes, I'd mix Prussian blue and a teensy Napthal red. However, he would call his hair "plain old dark brown" and eyes "gray."

But, what does he know? Not much about art, I can tell you that.

"I thought you were in Afghanistan or Alabama," I said. "What are you doing back?"

"Discharged. You still mad at me? It's been a while."

"Mad? I barely remember the last time I saw you." I wasn't really lying. My last memory wasn't of seeing him, but seeing the piece of trash in his truck. And by piece of trash, I mean the kind with boobs.

"You were pretty mad at the time. And I know you and your grudges."

"I've got more to do than think about something that happened when I was barely out of high school."

"Are you going to hold my youthful indiscretions against me now?" He smiled. "I'm only in town for a short time. You know I can only take Halo in small doses."

"If you're not sticking around, I can't see how my opinion of you matters. Not like you asked me about your sudden decision to join the Army and clear out of dodge."

"That's what you're mad about?"

Dear God, men are clueless. Why He didn't sharpen them up a bit has to be one of life's greatest mysteries.

"There are a number of things you did. But I'm not about to print you out a list."

"We had some good times, too."

"Which you sabotaged with your idiocy."

"You're one to talk," he mumbled.

I took another step forward, but Luke didn't move. His eyes roamed from my face to my boots. My irritation grew.

"Do you mind? I need to get back to Cooper's. I'm working." I shoved him out of the way, dragging my unwieldy portfolio bag behind me.

"Just trying to put my finger on what about you changed."

I clamped my mouth shut as an unwelcome blush crept up the back of my neck.

"I know," he continued. "Your boots are plain old brown. Where're those red cowboy boots?"

I stomped toward the funeral home. "At home with my Backstreet Boys albums. I don't have time to play catch up with you. I've got stuff to do."

"How about playing catch up later, then?" I glanced back to see a glimmer of a smile. "Don't you think it'd be fun to stroll down memory lane? Does everybody still hang out at Red's?"

The sunlight played with the auburn highlights in his dark curls and the tips of his long, black eyelashes.

Lord, why does he have to be so good looking? It was incredibly unfair how easily beauty weakened me. Gave suffering for art a whole new meaning.

"It was seven years ago," I said before I could stop myself.

"What?"

"Not ten years," I corrected. "But a lot has happened in seven."

"I bet."

I FOUND Wanda shredding a tissue in the viewing room, watching JB bark orders at the assorted non-nuclear Bransons who then cowed and scurried as if he were the king of Forks County. He owned many businesses that supported most of the Branson clan, including the big Ford dealership, but he had inherited the Branson patrilineal power seat.

Ironically, the two Bransons who never bowed to JB were his son, Dustin, and stepson, Luke. And that was where the similarities between Dustin and Luke stopped.

Luke and Dustin were never close. Luke loved his mother and put up with Dustin when she remarried. However, Luke got out of Halo as soon as possible. Couldn't blame him, with a cold stepfather and a mother pouring her attention into rehabilitating an emerging sociopath. But poor Wanda had her hands full.

Made me wonder, though. With Dustin out of the picture, was there now more room for Luke? Interesting that Luke left the Army right when his step-brother got offed.

Hating that ugly thought, I hurried over to Wanda. "I just ran into Luke," I said, giving her shoulder a quick hug.

"I'm glad to see he's here to help you through this."

"Yes, it is a blessing. Served his time, you know, and of course, he won't tell me his plans yet. But that's Luke. Doesn't like to worry me."

"Keeps his cards pretty close to his chest, does he?"

"Look at him," Wanda waved at her son. "I've never been able to tell what he's thinking. Just like his father, God bless him. Maybe it was losing his daddy so young. He just keeps everything clammed up inside."

Spotting his mother's wave, Luke wandered into the viewing room. He had always been a wiry guy, displaying his strength in high school on the wrestling team and fighting behind the Highway 19 Quik Stop with the other boys carrying boulder-size chips on their shoulder. He still seemed dangerous, yet more settled and confident.

There was no softness about him. Luke was all hard edges.

"Oh, I don't know," I murmured. "I lost my daddy young, too, but I've always been an open book."

"Well, boys and girls are different," said Wanda.

"Don't I know it." I swung one palm to my hip but waved my other in casual deference to Luke's arrival. "Let's go sit, and you can take a look at my portfolio. While you're looking at my samples, I'll sketch some ideas I have for Dustin."

"What's this?" Luke asked. "Ideas for Dustin?"

"I'm having Dustin's portrait done," Wanda explained.

"I'll hang it next to the painting of him as a child. That one's thirty-by-forty. I'd like them to be the same size."

Holy cow, that's a big picture of a dead guy, I thought but nodded my head as if it was the most reasonable idea in the world.

"That's downright morbid." Although he directed the statement to his mother, the accusation lay at my feet. "I swear you haven't changed Cherry, with all the nutty art stuff."

I felt like telling Luke, "this is your mother's crazy notion, not mine." Instead, I responded in my most proper aren't-you-an-idiot drawl, "Your momma is just dealing with this horrible tragedy the best she can, God bless her. It's a memorial."

"A memorial for Dustin? You don't know what Dustin was mixed up in, Mom. Death doesn't turn a sinner into a saint. God knows you tried your best. More than his father did."

"Come on, Miss Wanda," I tugged on her arm. Between Luke and Shawna, I was going to lose this commission. "I'll get you a cup of tea, and you can look at my paintings. It'll get your mind off things for a minute, anyway. I've got a real cute one of Snug, Terrell Jacob's Coonhound."

Wanda beckoned JB, and they conferred for a moment. With a shrug, he followed her out of the viewing room.

Luke shoved his hands in his pockets. "You spent all that money on art school to paint pictures of dogs?"

"I spent all that money on art school to become a professional artist," I said. "It's early days yet. For now, I take what I can get."

"Including painting the departed?"

"You ever heard of a still life?" I shot back and stalked out of the viewing room, swinging my portfolio bag behind me.

I followed Wanda and JB into a little room crowded with a table and chairs. Unzipping the large bag, I pulled out a binder of photographs of my college works and a sheaf of plastic-encased photos of my newer stuff. Snug the dog, a horse named Conquering Hero, and a half-dozen kid portraits. I much preferred animals to children as subjects, something you don't learn in school.

Getting a four-year-old to sit still is damn near impossible. However, you take a well-trained dog in the right pose, and you've got the perfect model. Snug the Coonhound sat better than most people. We had an easy working relationship, what with Snug's deferential silence. No need for forced conversation with that subject.

Of course with this job, I couldn't expect any conversation either. I could make do with photographs.

But first I needed to get the job.

"I don't know why you're wasting my time looking at pictures," said JB. He tossed the portraits of Snug and Hero on the table.

"This one is just beautiful, Cherry," said Wanda, holding up a Sargent inspired painting. The model wore a sheet draped like a toga, but the effect was tasteful with wonderful folds to show depth and shadow.

"I'm glad you pointed out that one. Don't you love the light on her face? You might not be able to tell, but that's not an oil painting. I had a tight schedule, so I used acrylics. They dry quickly, and I didn't have to varnish the painting immediately. Someone mentioned you displaying the portrait at the funeral service? Oils wouldn't dry fast enough to get the painting done without messing up the color."

"I was fixing on making a photo display for the service when I realized we didn't have many of Dustin after he passed a certain age." Wanda's face colored and she cast her eyes away from JB. "I've just been in a tizzy, not knowing what to do with myself and not sleeping. That's when I got the idea for the memory box. Started gathering stuff Dustin left in his old room. Then I remembered the family portraits we had done at our wedding and thought maybe a new painting would be a nice tribute."

"Let her have what she needs," said JB. "A picture's not bringing him back, but if it makes Wanda feel better, she can have it."

"I totally agree, sir," I said. "That's why you should let me have the honor of painting this portrait. You can see what quality I can produce. You don't want a final memorial done by an amateur."

"What about Shawna?" he said, eyeing me. "Although Shawna did set a pretty hefty price for painting my son."

I squirmed, caught between a rock and a rattlesnake. JB would sell out his niece for a lower price. But probably wouldn't help me underbid her, either.

"A portrait lasts for generations." I began with my salesman pitch. "My paintings are heirloom quality and will be around long after…" Since the subject was dead, I stopped before my mouth ate my foot. "Anyway, a portrait is priceless."

"Priceless? You talking free?" JB leaned back in his chair.

"Of course a professional artist would base the price on other features. Number of people. Intricacy of the clothing, jewelry, and props. Complexity of the background. And of course, the size." I could not get over the size.

"How complex is a coffin?" He steepled his hands under his chin. "And we don't need background details."

"JB, don't be cheap," said Wanda. "Like Cherry said, we're talking heirloom quality."

"Who in the hell wants to inherit a picture of Dustin in a coffin, Wanda?" JB said. "Even if little Dustins start crawling out of the woodwork, and God help us if that happens, I'm sure none of them will want this painting. We can cut some corners, here."

"Coffin portrait?" I said, swallowing hard. My mouth went dry, and I had trouble getting my tongue to form intelligible words. "I thought you'd want me to work from snapshots or something. Dustin standing in a field, looking off to heaven, that sort of thing."

"Oh no," said Wanda. "That would be phony. Dustin never would have stood in a field unless he was hunting, and I doubt he thought about heaven much."

She cast a quick look at her husband. "I want him as he is now. And realistic. None of that abstract stuff."

I gulped. "As he is now." The man was murdered. An abstract would be easier to stomach. Not like anyone would enjoy looking at David's *The Death of Marat* in their TV room. "All right. Uh, do you want me to create a pose, or do you want the whole, um, coffin?"

"Could you paint it like we were looking down at Dustin? Like angels gazing?" Wanda's moist blue eyes stared off into the distance, and I shivered.

I grabbed my notebook and made a quick sketch. "Something like this?" I showed her the rough illustration of my idea.

"Oh, it's just perfect," she said, grabbing the sketchbook to shove at JB. "Let's give Cherry a chance, honey. I want this view. Shawna said she has an allergy to formaldehyde so she couldn't paint Dustin this way."

"Tell you what." JB leaned forward, hands flat on the table. "I'll give you a shot. I want Wanda to be happy after what all she's endured with Dustin. He was my son and I owe her that."

"Yes, sir," I said, although my skin still prickled from the word formaldehyde.

"But," he said, "you got to have the painting done for the funeral. The whole she-bang. Wanda can choose between you and Shawna, so you better make it good. She likes quality."

"After the funeral, I'm done. Wanda can hang up his picture

and look at it all she wants, but I'm putting this whole blasted deal out of my mind. I'm paying off his creditors right and left, dealing with folks' complaints, and living through the embarrassment of the way he went. Do you know what they are saying about him?"

I knew, but I sure wasn't going to say. Folks thought a bad drug deal or payback from a robbery ring. Or someone just got tired of Dustin's mouth and went postal on him.

Hard to say with Dustin. There were so many crimes to choose from.

"I'll work up a contract," I said. "Thank you for this opportunity. I'll get cracking right away, and I'll also do the memory box."

"We'll have Cooper set out the body for you then." JB didn't smile, but I did see a flash of teeth. "Got to admire your tenacity, Cherry. I hate to say it, but stories I heard about your family made me question your reliability."

A shot of heat worked its way from my toes to my scalp. People always bring up my family's history over the years, but it never got any easier.

"My reputation is important to me. I am judged by my actions as well as those that surround me. You know how people like to talk."

"Yes, sir."

He looked at me evenly. "I'm glad we agree on this issue. As a businesswoman, you have your reputation to protect and a lot of history to overcome."

A million comebacks crossed my mind, but none were appropriate for a bereaved father sitting in a funeral home with a large check that could have my name on it.

I swallowed my pride and tried not to choke. "I'll bring that contract by tomorrow."

He had better keep his end of the bargain because, after that humiliation, I sure as hell wasn't working for free.

TWO

I HUSTLED out of the cramped conference room to find Cooper. Walking down the dim hallway, I glanced in the first room on the right. The wooden door rested open showing an office filled with oversized mahogany furniture and misty paintings of sunrises or sunsets. I'm never sure which they're supposed to be.

I waved at Cooper who chatted with Will Thompson, our county coroner and sheriff, and one of my favorite men on the planet. But that's a pretty short list.

"How are you, girl?" Will was a good friend of my grandpa. Will was about thirty years younger, a hundred pounds heavier, and a million times nicer than Grandpa, but they paired up better than sausage and biscuits.

"Hey, Uncle Will. How are you, Mr. Cooper?" I waltzed into his serenity-blue office to hug Will.

"What are you doing here, Cherry?" asked Cooper. "Get a time wrong for a visitation?"

"I'm here for the Bransons. And I need a favor. Did you hear about the painting they want?"

Cooper nodded.

Will leaned back in a well-padded armchair and settled folded hands over the mounded expanse of his belly. Will had been a tackle for Georgia back in his prime. It worked to his advantage as sheriff, but I knew him as a big teddy bear.

"Did the Bransons talk to you about making the body available?" I asked.

Cooper pursed his lips. He almost perfected the art of masking his emotions except for the occasional tic that managed to escape.

"Why would the Bransons need the body available today?" Will questioned Cooper while watching me. "Visitation is tomorrow, isn't it? Is your girl even done making him up?"

"She is," said Cooper. "Originally, I assumed they wanted to spend extra time with the deceased. Happens occasionally. Then they started talking about having a," Cooper coughed quietly into his hand, "memorial painting made."

"Memorial painting?" said Will.

"Portrait of Dustin," I said. "In his coffin."

Bug-eyed, Will turned from Cooper to me. I rocked back on my heels, doing my best to keep a straight face. It wouldn't do to have a Branson walk into the office with us hooting about their strange choice of commemorating their son.

Will pulled himself together, but for a half a second I was sure he was going to fall out of his chair. "Good Lord."

"Mr. Cooper. How's this going to work? Please tell me I don't have to visit your basement. I'm still shaking with the heebie jeebies as it is."

"I can bring Dustin upstairs," said Cooper. "His room is ready. But, honey, I thought some Branson was coming to do his picture."

"I convinced Wanda and JB to let me try." I couldn't help a little smirk at competing for the job with Shawna. She was going to throw a big hissy. And I hoped I got to see it.

"Well, if you say so." Creaking, Cooper rose from his wooden desk chair. "It's your funeral." He dry heaved a few chuckles. "That's a little mortuary humor, hon."

A whoop of laughter burst from Will.

"Good one," I said and pulled the curl out of my lip.

Cooper ambled out the office, heading for the basement morgue.

"You best get yourself together, Sheriff Thompson," I said to Will and made a quick pivot to speed out of the office.

"Hang on a minute." Will swung his considerable body around to face me. "Where're you going?"

"I've got some sketching supplies in my truck."

"I'll walk with you. Let's go out the back door."

He rose, towering over me, and placed a large hand on the back of my neck. Like a dog on a leash, Will guided me through the hallway until we reached an arched doorway. After a glance down the hall, he hustled me through the door and into a kitchen.

I shook free of his grip and crossed the room. Leaning my back against a Formica counter, I waited for Will to say his piece.

"Just spit it out, Uncle Will," I said. "I'm not walking clear around this house looking like you're ready to shove me into a police car. Obviously, you got something to tell me."

"You doing all right?"

"I'm okay. What's going on?" I crossed my arms and met his look. Will didn't usually worry about me. My siblings, Casey and Cody, were a whole different kettle of fish, though.

Some days it felt like their good decisions were the exception to a lifetime of dumb moments.

"I mean for money." Will shoved his hands into his pockets. "Why are you taking a crazy gig like this? Miss Wanda is a nice woman, but she has some different ideas about decorating. Did you hear about her having all those bushes cut like animals?"

"That's topiary. What's the big deal about that?"

"She had clothes made for them, too. What kind of woman dresses up hollies?"

"Don't worry about me." I relaxed off my previous attitude. "But every dollar helps. Art school wasn't cheap. Although I'm glad to not live at the farm, Great-Gam's house is a money pit. Today I found something oozing through the plaster in the living room wall. And you know about my truck. Besides, this portrait means doing what I really love, painting pictures of people. Even if the guy's not breathing."

"I'd help you if you'd let me."

"Thank you, but I'm plenty old enough to take care of myself." And if Casey and Cody heard I borrowed money from Will, they would forever be knocking at his door looking for handouts. "Grandpa didn't raise me to take charity."

Will grunted in affirmation.

"Now tell me about the murder." I spied an electric kettle and a box of tea bags on the countertop. "You want some tea? It'll take Cooper a minute to bring up Dustin."

"No thanks, hon." Will ran a hand over his thick salty-brown buzz. "I'm leading the investigation, of course. Still don't have a number on what happened to him. That's between you and me, now."

"You got some suspects? Murder weapon?"

He stared at me stone-faced.

"Come on, Uncle Will. Give me something."

"Girl, you know better than to mix our personal relations with my job."

"That's no fun." I twisted around to lean over the counter, hunting for a mug in the cupboards. "For once, I'd love to be the first one to report some exciting news to Grandpa."

"By news you mean gossip." He reached over my head, snatched the mug on a shelf just out of my grasp, and slid it onto the counter. "You kids are getting a little old to compete for Ed's attention like that."

I shrugged and dropped a tea bag into the mug. "Speaking of gossip, what's the deal with Dustin's step-brother coming back in town?"

"Who, Luke Harper? You sound like it's unreasonable for him to come to a family funeral." He eyed my fake nonchalance. "What's wrong with you?"

"Me?" I turned my back to Will and checked the kettle.

"I'm just asking. He hasn't been home in seven years. I'm just wondering what you heard about his plans now that he's out of the Army."

"Luke Harper's plans?" Will chewed on that idea for a moment. "I know what this is about. It's his looks, isn't it?"

"Good Lord, I'm not a boy crazy teenager anymore." I spun around, color rising in my cheeks. "Give me some credit. I used to know him. I just wondered is all."

"You lost your credit with that fiasco in Vegas." Will winked, referring to my dumbest moment in twenty-six years.

"Todd cannot keep his mouth shut," I muttered. "We did not get married. I don't care what he says. And why would anyone believe him over me? I've had more intelligent conversations with Snug the Coonhound than Todd McIntosh."

"Thereby proving my point. All I'm saying is know your weaknesses and avoid them."

"Man. You can't get away with anything in this town."

"Remember that. It'll keep you in line." Will squeezed my shoulder as the steam blew. "There's your kettle. You best get your skinny behind to work. If something's oozing through your walls, that'd be a plumbing issue. You want to get rich, marry a plumber."

"I'll work on that."

"I'd rather you work on marrying a plumber than doing crazy jobs like painting Dustin Branson's picture." He faked a shudder to accompany his wink. "Just thinking about painting a guy in a funeral home is enough to give me the willies."

I THREADED my way through the back maze of Cooper's to the front lobby, intent on grabbing my sketching supplies from my truck bed. Now that I competed for the commission with Shawna, I realized the craziness of the situation. Wanda and JB compartmentalized their feelings like crime scene veterans. Of course, I wasn't privy to the private goings-on of the Bransons. There was probably some perfectly good psychological explanation for wanting a coffin portrait of a son you didn't seem to like very much. I had bigger worries.

Like spending some quality time with a dead guy.

And avoiding Luke, I thought, as Wanda flagged me down. Luke hovered next to her.

The portfolio case I had snagged from the conference room bumped against my back, keeping time with my steps. As I threw him an eye roll, my toe hit a seam in the carpet, and I stumbled. The long case strap twisted beneath my arm and the oversized bag flipped forward. A hard corner smacked me in the gut. With a mostly silent grunt, I fixed the strap, flipped the case back, and looked up.

A dimple glimmered in Luke's cheek and went out.

"Cherry, where did you get to?" asked Wanda. She pointed to a large red shopping bag at her feet. "I've got Dustin's mementos here for you. I had them in my car in case I got a chance to pass by Crafty Corner."

"Great." I slung the portfolio bag onto my back, picked up the bag, and supported the sagging weight under one hand.

Luke's dimple, hovering somewhere beneath his hardened jaw, threatened to re-emerge as he watched my struggle.

"I'd get the door for you," he said, "but I'm sure you'll be fine seeing as how you're a businesswoman and all. You probably got used to getting your own doors in the last seven years. I was raised a gentleman, but I'm not going to tread on your independence."

Wanda nudged him. "Honey, you help Cherry. Stop teasing her. She might not know what a joker you are."

"Don't worry, ma'am," I said. "I find it hard to take him seriously."

"Give me the bag," he said.

I eyed Miss Wanda. Considering my overburdened arms and my rush to get started, my protests would seem ridiculous.

"Fine." I set the bag on the floor and yanked off my portfolio case. "Take this to the viewing room. I'll be back in a minute with my sketching stuff."

I didn't want to chance getting stuck in my truck with him. Memories of Luke and my truck were starting to trickle back. Although they weren't as bad as memories of Luke and his truck. His truck had been much more comfortable than mine.

I jettisoned to the Datsun and back to find Dustin ready and waiting in the viewing room. JB's minions had cleared out. Wanda and JB had also disappeared, although their Lincoln MKT still sat in the parking lot. So did a black Ford Raptor pickup.

Someone with a stepdad in the auto industry had recently received a shiny new truck.

The man with the penchant for black pickups had dropped the portfolio case on a chair in the viewing room and disappeared. I blew a sigh of relief and used the solitude to get accustomed to my first literal still life.

"Hey Dustin," I whispered. "I'm sorry about your passing. At least the way you went. No one deserves to have their life taken from them like that."

Footsteps approached the doorway, and I realized the family probably hadn't spent time with Dustin yet. I grabbed my sketchbook and slid into a back corner chair, where a grouping of floral arrangements kept my presence unobtrusive. Luke, Wanda, and JB strolled in with Cooper.

"Oh my," said Wanda, walking directly to the coffin. She closed her eyes in prayer for a moment. "You did a nice job, Cooper."

"I got a new girl," said Cooper, "she's pretty good. Keeps forgetting her keys, though, and leaving them in the kitchen."

"Hard to train new staff," said JB gruffly. He and Luke hung back to stand at right angles to the casket. "The coffin looks good quality. I didn't think we needed top of the line, but a lot of people are going to see it, I suspect."

From behind a palm frond, I watched Cooper nod. "You should have a good turnout for the visitation and the funeral. I've been taking calls all day."

"Heard from Virginia yet, JB?" Luke asked.

"Surprisingly, no," said JB. "Any normal woman would have scooted up here as soon as she heard her son was dead."

He ran a hand through his thinning hair. "As if I could take any more embarrassment over this fiasco. Now I'll have my crazy ex-wife up here stirring up trouble. She's probably postponing the visit on purpose."

"What purpose?" Switching his stance to face JB, Luke placed himself in line with me.

I hunkered over the sketchbook, pretending to draw, and prayed the Bransons were too preoccupied to notice me. I didn't want to lose the commission over something as dumb as being in the wrong place at the wrong time. Shawna would love that.

"Who knows with Virginia?" JB uttered a disgusted grunt. "Probably trying to figure out how to get some money out of this. You know she tried to sue me for child support after she abandoned her own kid?"

"She didn't abandon Dustin," Wanda said.

"I don't know what else you call leaving a kid to run around like a cat in heat." JB turned his back on the coffin.

"Not like you were a saint at the time," Luke said. "I wonder if Daddy Branson hadn't told you to straighten up or lose the family business, you might still be carousing with Virginia. Were you ever going to do the same with Dustin? Call him on the floor before delivering the empire?"

"Luke," Wanda said, hurrying to JB's side. "Don't talk to JB like that."

"It's the truth, Mom." He crossed his arms and stole a glance at Cooper. "Sorry, Cooper. Don't mean to air the Branson dirty laundry in front of you."

Cooper gave a noncommittal cough and shuffled to the casket, putting some space between him and the family.

"I'd say I've had enough time in here," said JB. "Come on, Wanda."

"We should go over the service if you're ready," said Cooper.

He patted the casket and faced the Bransons. "We can go to the conference room or my office."

"Let's get it done," said JB. "I want to get to the office and check a few things."

"Can't you get Ronny to do that for you?" Wanda tucked her arm inside JB's, slowing his pace to exit the room.

"We're expecting more people today." Cooper trudged after them, looking like he barely survived World War III. Which for Cooper meant a couple of extra lines furrowing his brow.

"Did you get all that?"

I looked up from the little dog I doodled in my notebook.

Luke faced me, his stance wide and arms crossed.

Scrambling up from the chair, I scooted around a flower arrangement.

"I was already in here and didn't want to disturb you," I said. "But yeah, I heard. We've all got skeletons in our closets. No big deal."

Luke scowled. "Knowing I'm going to encounter Virginia always puts me in a bad mood. She's a couple of fries short of a Happy Meal. Dustin didn't have much of a chance with that DNA combination."

"Well, I know something about mothers who choose a love life over their kids."

"Yeah." Luke wandered over to my pile of supplies and picked up a portable easel. "Me, too."

There wasn't much more to say unless someone put a Loretta Lynn song on the jukebox and handed out shots of Jack.

I let Luke futz around with my easel while I took another tour of Dustin. There was no "angel viewing" angle with my height. Cooper had the coffin jacked up unnecessarily high. I held my sketch pad under one arm and stood on my toes peering over the coffin. Dustin looked pretty good. The police hadn't revealed how he had been killed, but there was no obvious injury to his face, thank the Lord.

"I could lift you up so you can see more than the coffin handles," said the soft baritone hovering above my head.

"That's original. A joke about my height." I resisted the urge to turn around. "You want to give me a little space? I don't know Dustin well enough to get this friendly with him."

Luke stepped back but shifted to my side instead of leaving. His hands dropped to rest on the coffin's edge. "He would have liked to know you're hanging all over him now. Harassing his parents to get a chance to spend time with him."

"Wasn't going to happen while he was alive, so I guess I can give him some attention now."

Luke tried to crack a smile, but you could have bounced a penny off those tight shoulders.

"Do you know how he died?" I asked.

"Somebody smacked the back of his skull with something heavy." Luke stared at his step-brother. "Probably walked up to him and beamed him in one blow."

"How could someone do that?"

"Easy. I could've knocked you a good one. Hidden something in my pocket or picked something up in the room. You knew I was here and didn't turn around. I stood right…"

The hair rose on the back of my neck. "Yeah, I know where you were standing, and you've done it a few too many times today." I looked at him askance. "I don't like my personal space violated."

"That's not what I remember…"

"You can stop right there, Hugh Hefner. Let's get something straight. I'm all grown up. I'm not, nor was I ever, some piece of trash you could get drunk on Boone's Farm, have your way with in your truck, and leave at the Waffle Hut with an unpaid check."

"Man, that was a long time ago. You really do hold a grudge."

"You did it more than once!" I tossed my sketchbook to the floor. Placing my hands on my hips, I took a step closer and flung my chin up.

"Hell, you're just mad because you wanted me so bad, you let me get away with it."

"You want to try that again?"

"You know I'm right."

"You are a..." I struggled for appropriate words to use in a funeral home. "Pig! I've news for you, Luke Harper."

He edged closer.

I resisted retreat and took another step forward until we stood inches away. I glowered and poked a finger into his chest.

"You start messing with me, you're gonna end up with a behind full of buckshot. Not only do I still have that piece of crap yellow truck, I also have my daddy's shotgun, and I know how to use it."

Snatching my hand, he folded the offending finger to rest within his palm. "And if you don't keep your fingers to yourself, you're going to lose one." He released my hand.

I stepped back and retrieved my sketchbook from the floor. "It's time I got back to work. Now that I'm done with SCAD, I've crazy student loans to pay off, not to mention a few other bills. Make yourself useful. Ask Cooper how to lower this table so I can get a good view."

He stared at me a beat, then left the room.

I scrambled through my tackle box looking for a good piece of charcoal. Quality art supplies were expensive, and I tried to balance the line between conservation and cheapskate. I opened a larger pad of heavier bond, luxuriating in the feel of the soft, bumpy surface on my fingers. Flipping through the pages, I found a blank sheet, set the sketchpad on the easel with the charcoal, and waited for the return of Luke with Cooper.

No Luke or Cooper.

I eyed the oak-paneled casket. As usual, a discussion with Luke spun me away from reality. Had we just gone another round while a dead body lay before us like a pitcher of beer and plate of nachos? I needed to refocus on the reason I stood in a funeral home with a sketchbook and empty pockets. This time when I peered over the side of the oak paneling, I wanted to see Dustin as his mother would. Or stepmother, in this case.

Dustin usually had stringy blonde hair, worn long and unkempt, but Cooper had his beautician brush and trim it. Now the smooth, blonde locks fell gently, pillowing his head. Death softened his face, hiding the angry lines that held a scowl and a scornful set to the eyes. Dark eyebrows relaxed above blonde eyelashes tipped in brown, permanently closed.

I sighed, trying to imagine Dustin singing with angels. Too hard. More than likely a giant pitchfork poked him right about now.

My eyes drifted over the blue suit to the clasped hands. The long fingers had a beautiful shape and an undisclosed strength. I'd be willing to bet they would have been skilled at fine arts and crafts. Such a waste to have those beautiful hands and not the mind to match them. I wanted to capture the slight turns and creases of the knuckles, the long digits that portrayed an artistic suppleness. Even the nails appeared smoothly squared and buffed.

Of course, the nails looked nice. He just had the manicure to end all manicures. Literally.

I took a deep breath and gave myself a mental shaking. I had my focal point. No need to get all artsy-fartsy. I turned away from Dustin and walked to the doorway in search of living beings. Glancing around the empty reception area, I took a right down the hallway. Voices murmured from the kitchen. I quick-stepped through the hall and stopped in the archway.

Intent on their heated discussion, Luke and Uncle Will didn't notice me. Their voices remained low and tense. Will used his bulk to tower over Luke. He gestured with one hand; the other rested on his holster. Luke stood ramrod straight with arms crossed and chin high.

I didn't guess they were arguing about baseball since the Braves only had a few games under their belt. The Bulldogs still had about four months until their first game. NASCAR wasn't that controversial. That left me out of ideas. I backed out of the doorway and got my nose out of their business.

THREE

MINUTES LATER COOPER and I cranked the portable table to lower Dustin. I stood over the coffin pleased with my lofty angelic view. Cooper watched while I lugged the easel closer to the casket.

Pinching the sooty stick between my thumb and pointer finger, I let the charcoal glide over the paper. Glancing back at Dustin, I noted the sharp jut of his chin, the shadow in the corner of his eye, and the slight depression under his cheekbone. I refocused on the paper, and the charcoal flew over the rough surface.

I skimmed a look back to Dustin's hands. The knuckles appeared too large in my drawing, the thumbs too short. Rubbed a gummy eraser over the problem lines and tried again. I stepped back, cocked my head, and compared the real body with the picture.

"Dang, Cherry. That's a God-given talent you got there. I never saw anyone draw that fast. Looks pretty much like him." Cooper hovered behind my shoulder. The scent of lemon sours and formaldehyde enveloped me.

"Guess we can't all be brain surgeons, so I'll take the gift I got."

Together we stared at the drawing. Two art critics at a gallery show wouldn't have examined the sketch so solemnly.

Cooper continued to gaze while I squirmed. After a long moment, I flipped the page.

I picked up the charcoal and winced. A toxic lemon cloud drifted up my nostrils. Pivoting, I almost bumped into Cooper's chest.

"Hey there, Mr. Cooper. Didn't realize you were right behind me."

"I think his nose was too wide in the last picture. And the eyes weren't quite right."

"Alrighty. Thanks so much."

"Glad to be of help. I know bodies pretty well, you know."

"I'm sure you do." I refused to think about the context of that statement.

Cooper nodded and let his eyes drift back to Dustin.

I tapped my foot, rolling the charcoal between my fingers.

Cooper rocked back on his heels.

I folded my arms and bounced on my toes while Cooper remained in position in front of the easel. I cleared my throat.

"Uh, sir. I kind of need to get back to work."

"Go right ahead, hon."

I fought my eyeballs from circling their sockets and my urge to tell this patient, soft-spoken man as-old-as-the-hills to back it up. I took a deep breath and swallowed a mouthful of pickled lemon. I fought my urge to gag. And then I was tired of fighting with myself.

Patience isn't a virtue when you're in a hurry. But I had to be sweet.

"Mr. Cooper. Sir. I know you want to watch me, but I really need to work alone. I can concentrate better, and I kind of need to get a move on. So if you don't mind…" I flapped my hand.

He grunted, gave me the old undertaker nod, and began to shuffle toward the doorway.

"Don't forget the nose!" he called with a final glance over his shoulder.

Everyone's a critic.

Turning back to Dustin, I reexamined the nose and eyes of my failing. The florescent lights overhead brightened his pallid face to a shine.

He looked a little too dead.

I skipped over to the light switch, cut off the florescent, and turned the dimmer knob. The harsh lighting vanished, leaving the room murky. Frustrated, I walked back and peered into the coffin. Dustin looked less antiseptic, but the raised coffin lid shaded half of his face.

"Looking for a more romantic ambiance?"

I jumped and banged my hip against a metal handle on the coffin. "Would you quit doing that?"

Luke hung over my shoulder, squinting at Dustin. "You have him on the kid's table now. Just your size."

"Funny. You need to get out of my way. I'm still working."

"So you keep reminding me." Luke retreated to an unlit corner, grousing about the darkness under his breath.

Reapplying the charcoal to the paper, I cast heavier shadows this time. I softened the tip of Dustin's ear peeking behind his hair and the recess below his Adam's apple. His lips developed. By whisking small lines for the creases of the bent fingers, strong, agile hands emerged. I stepped away from the easel.

"Pretty good. His hair is too dark, though." Luke's voice glided over my left shoulder.

"It's charcoal. I'm going to paint with color," I snapped.

"His eyebrows aren't thick enough." I spun toward the open door. Uncle Will strode to the easel. "You should put some decorations on his tie, too. Liven it up a bit."

Decorations on his tie? "Now just a minute…"

A beep interrupted my protest. A scratchy voice lost in a cloud of hisses and pops followed. Will drew his radio and answered the call.

Luke tensed as the radio crackled a string of numbers and letters followed by an address.

Will murmured, concurring his response to the dispatcher. His eyes swept across Dustin, then back to Luke and me.

Luke watched Will replace the radio in its holder. Even in his stillness, I felt nervous energy rippling through him.

"That's Dustin's apartment, isn't it? Someone broke in?" Luke asked.

"Gotta go. Have fun with your doodling, honey." Will placed his large paw on my shoulder and squeezed. He pointed his other hand at Luke. "And you. I know better, son. I'm checking on you. Better hope all your skeletons have been cleaned out."

I turned to face Luke. "What's he talking about? What skeletons?"

Shrugging, he shifted his stance. Luke ran a finger along the edge of the drawing. "How long are you going to stay here?"

"'Till I'm done." I wondered why his sudden appearance after seven years warranted a background investigation.

"Why would someone break into Dustin's apartment?"

"Probably looking for something."

"You know anything about that?"

"Why would I know anything about that?" Luke lifted his finger and examined the smudged tip. "How late?"

He took a step closer. Luke's proximity always created a visceral reaction that didn't please me. Didn't please the thinking parts of me, anyway.

His subtle smile toyed with me.

It always had. It was a great smile. I recalled that smile spreading across his face like warm butter on hot toast whenever I climbed into his truck. Even showed a little dimple. I salivated over those dimples.

However, hindsight taught me the devil lay in little dimples, and it was best to stay clear.

Luke studied my distracted expression and flashed the dimple again.

Catching myself, I jerked my conscious back to the top quarter of my body. He was playing me.

Again.

"I'll be very late if you keep this up." I grabbed the sketch pad and flipped the page.

"Remember what they say about all work and no play." Luke broadened the grin.

"Sorry to disappoint but when I'm ready to play, it's not going to be with you." I stepped around him and picked up the charcoal. My hand raced over the paper. Dissatisfied, I flipped the page and tried again.

"Is that a threat or a dare?"

"Luke, are you in here, honey?" Wanda tapped on the open door.

Luke and I jerked like two fish on a line.

"Yes, ma'am." Luke slipped his hands behind his back, squeezing his shoulders into rigidity.

"Cherry, how's it going? Is Luke bothering you?"

I hesitated, and she didn't wait for me to answer.

"Come in here, Shawna. It's okay. You don't have to look." Wanda stepped into the windowless room and shivered. "It's so dark." She leaned toward the wall and flicked on the florescent lights.

Preparing for battle, a few unpleasant words drifted through my mind and I laid the charcoal on the edge of the easel. But Wanda and Shawna stayed in the doorway. Maybe the formaldehyde allergy continued to work in my favor. I leaned over, fishing a wet wipe from the tackle box on the floor.

Luke dropped to a crouch next to me.

"Don't say anything about Sheriff Thompson to my mom," he whispered.

I cocked an eyebrow.

"I don't want her upset any more than she already is."

We stood as Wanda coaxed Shawna into the viewing room. Massive waves of auburn hair spilled down her back. Slender by no means, she held her weight well and in the right places on her tall frame.

I instinctively compared her bounty to my inadequacies and winced. I sensed Luke preparing his dimple and smoking up his gray eyes.

Not one to let Amazons throw me off my stride, I strutted across the beige carpet and extended my hand.

"How's it going, Shawna?"

Shawna's line of sight skipped over me and bounced right onto Luke. The pupils of her blue-green eyes enlarged, and her hands ran down the sides of her dress, smoothing the material over her curves.

"Luke, Shawna had volunteered to paint Dustin's picture even though she has an allergy that doesn't allow her around the deceased," said Wanda. "That's why we're letting Cherry try, too. Wasn't that nice of Shawna, though?"

"Very nice," remarked Luke. "Haven't seen you in a while. Didn't you go to Georgia Southern?"

"I did indeed. Go Eagles." Shawna beamed at Luke while I stood like the village idiot with my outstretched hand still floating in mid-air.

"Good to see you again, Shawna." I shoved my hand into hers and pumped. "Glad to know you're going to be a sport about this," I said, without a hint of sarcasm.

Sometimes I amaze myself.

Shawna popped her eyes off Luke to incline her head toward me. "Sorry. Didn't see you down there, Cherry. I was surprised to hear you're still painting. I thought for sure your little studio would have gone under by now. It's so hard to make a living doing outdated forms of art."

She pulled out a pink card and handed it to me. "On the other hand, I'm so busy I can barely see straight. Did you see my website?"

"I have not," I said, glancing at the business card covered in curlicue letters and polka dots.

"I'm so sorry." Shawna laid a hand on her bountiful chest. "You might need a high-speed connection and you probably can't afford it. My site's all in flash. Maybe try the library to look at it."

"I've got a pretty good idea what your website looks like. I doubt your repertoire has diversified that much. Still a big fan of glitter glue and chocolate pudding finger paint?"

"You can joke, but you're about to face some serious competition in the art world. I've got an idea about using a snapshot and making it look like a painting. I'm going to sell Paintographs hand over fist in Forks County." She waved a jeweled hand before me. "Check out my new bling."

I admit to salivating a bit over the baseball-size rock on her finger. Even that sized Cubic Zirconia would cost a mint.

"Paintographs." The word dumped off my tongue. "Sounds like color by number. Or an infomercial product."

"Much better," she said. "But enough shop talk. You'll see a Paintograph at Dustin's funeral. I'm going ahead with my plans, Aunt Wanda. The way JB explained it, I doubt Cherry can finish Dustin's portrait the old-fashioned way. It's so quaint she's trying so hard. However, I'd hate for you to be disappointed. I know how much you want a beautiful tribute to Dustin. You just need to rustle me up a photo."

"Old-fashioned? I'm using acrylics. That's a modern technique. I can't see how you can make a beautiful tribute by coloring in a photo. What do you use? Magic Markers?"

"Acrylics. You're so cute," she cooed. "Just like your name. Named after a fruit. Isn't she cute, Luke? So cute I can barely stand it."

Only Shawna or my siblings knew how much I hated the word cute. It fell in with perky and spunky. Not a short girl's friend when you want to be taken seriously.

"Don't you worry about me getting the painting done on time." My eyelids narrowed until I could barely see anything but lashes. "We'll see who's cute. My Flemish Renaissance-inspired acrylic or your Paint-by-Number dealio. By the way, if you use smelly markers, you could add a scratch and sniff element."

"I didn't know you were an artist, Shawna." Luke eased between us, nudging me to the side.

"She's not," I muttered.

"Were you named after a fruit? I thought Cherry was short for something else." Wanda ping-ponged between us, trying to keep up with our conversation.

"Not exactly, ma'am. My sister, Casey, couldn't say Cherrilyn when she was little, and it stuck." I didn't know which name was worst. Cherry suited me, but you can imagine the liberties taken with a name like Cherry. Fourteen-year-old boys seemed particularly creative. And hateful girls like Shawna.

A spiteful grin unfurled from Shawna's glossy lips. She returned her long-lashed gaze to Luke. "I swear that story makes Cherry even more adorable."

"Cherry, adorable?" Luke shoved his hands in his back pockets. "That's not the word that comes to mind."

"I can be adorable. When I feel like it. Which is not now."

"I'll leave y'all to get reacquainted," said Wanda. "I forgot to ask Cooper something. After this, we'll head back to the house. More Bransons coming this afternoon. The house is filling to the rafters with people and food."

"Do you need help?" Luke asked.

Shawna took the opportunity to sidle toward my easel.

I hopped forward and closed the sketchbook.

"No, JB is in the lobby with Ronny Price. I don't know why Ronny insisted on coming with us. JB would be happier if he stayed at the dealership and watched over things."

"He's worked for JB a long time, Mom. Maybe Ronny thought he could offer y'all some help. People don't always know what to do in these situations."

"I guess you're right," said Wanda. "Shawna, why don't you stay in here with Luke and Cherry? They're getting ready for another viewing in the other room, so it'd be best if you stay out of the lobby."

Just what I needed. Shawna watching me draw. I wondered if she'll find my sketches of Dustin's dead body cute.

Or adorable.

"What about your allergy, Shawna?" I asked. "Don't want you foaming at the mouth."

She shot me a look that would have killed a weaker woman. Lucky for me, my family is well versed in the evil eye. Grandpa's house might as well have been a dojo for casting slitty-eyed looks.

"Hon? You coming?" JB strode into the room, circling his gaze and snapping it back before resting on Dustin.

Ronny Price followed. Ronny's shiny forehead matched the sheen of his eggplant silk shirt and purple striped tie. He mopped a white handkerchief across his face, shoved it in his pocket, and ran both hands methodically over his gleaming brown pompadour.

Shawna's brow creased, and she slunk closer to Luke.

Feeling more out of place, I edged toward my easel unsure what good manners dictated in this situation. One thing was for sure; I wasn't getting much sketching done.

"JB, do you have the little sack I want to bury with Dustin?" said Wanda.

All eyes fixed on Wanda as we collectively wondered what items could necessitate burying with Dustin. A childhood toy that somehow survived Dustin's abuse?

You know the pyromaniac kid who lops off the heads of his action figures and burns them in effigy on the backyard grill? That was Dustin.

And I now had a shopping bag of these treasures in my truck. The memory box project promised to be interesting work. Hopefully, Miss Wanda didn't choose anything too freakish for display. My stomach did an unsettling flop at that idea.

JB handed her a small cloth pouch. "Just shove them in his pocket or something." Glowering, he pivoted on his heel and left the room. Wanda grasped the gray flannel bag in her hand, a wrinkle of unease forming between her eyes.

"I'll take that for you, Mom." Luke reached for the bag, but Wanda whisked it into her purse.

"No, no. I'll have Cooper do it." She trailed after JB.

Ronny considered the group left in the room. Smoothing his coiffure, he studied Shawna who returned his appreciative glance with an unbecoming lift to her lip. He turned his attention to Luke and me. "Good to see you, Luke. Been a long time. What're you doing here, Cherry?"

I glanced at the coffin. "Miss Wanda wants Dustin's final portrait painted."

"I'm doing it, too," piped in Shawna. "Except I'm making a Paintograph. It's cutting edge."

"Say what?"

I smirked, hoping I'd hear that response a lot in the next few days. Ronny moved to a safer subject. "Still got the Datsun? Is that thing still running? Ready to trade it in?"

"Still running. Not quite ready to give her up."

Luke sniggered, and I glared back. We couldn't all have a stepdad who provided gleaming black pickups to keep the family peace. Unfortunately, JB couldn't do the same for his biological son. Dustin sold the vehicles and pocketed the cash.

Ronny nodded. "You come see me when you're ready. I'm surprised that truck's still holding together. The Japanese know how to build them, don't they?"

"Yes, sir." I shuffled my feet and edged back. "Guess I should be getting to work."

My stomach rumbled low and long, reminding me I had not fed it breakfast. A quick glimpse at my watch showed it far past lunch.

"And what are you doing here, Luke?" said Ronny. "Going to stay here all day? Your momma wants everyone back at the house soon."

"Maybe," Luke grumbled. "Just taking a break from all the company."

"Remember I'm company, too," said Shawna, giving Luke a playful push.

I groaned aloud and tried to cover the sound with a cough.

"Of course, I didn't expect Shawna to be at the house," Luke snuck a hard look at me while directing his answer to Ronny. "When did I last see you, Shawna?"

"Oh goodness me," said Shawna, "I can't rightly say. Years and years ago."

I slapped a hand over my mouth, but the snort ripped through me anyway. I mean, who talks like that? If Luke fell for that kind of crap, he had changed a lot more than I thought.

I returned to the easel. Ronny slipped to the far wall after me. He gripped the edge of the coffin, riveted on Dustin. I laid a hand on Ronny's back.

"Are you okay, Mr. Price? I guess you've known Dustin since he was little. This must be hard for you."

"Thank you, hon'," he said. "It's hard to believe." Slipping out from under my hand, he sped out the room.

"Poor guy," I said, turning back to Luke and Shawna. With a disgusted grunt, I snatched my drawings from Shawna's light fingers.

Oblivious to Shawna's snooping, Luke stood with his arms crossed, watching Ronny's retreat.

It seemed Dustin's troubled character made his death as difficult as his life. This commission positioned me on the edge of the Branson-Harper mire. I had my own family bogs to wade through, and they weren't much prettier than the Bransons'.

But other people's problems are sure a lot more interesting than your own.

THIRTY MINUTES later I gave up my attempts to sketch.

Shawna and Luke found my last nerve and worked together to snap it, standing in a corner, reminiscing about Eagle football victories between Shawna's catty comments on my ability to capture Dustin's likeness on paper.

Besides, I was starving.

I packed up my tackle box, grabbed my sketchbook, and strode out the door. Luke followed though we didn't speak.

When I pulled out of the drive, I glimpsed him leaning against his pickup, watching me. A shiver ran through me, and I squashed it.

I had no business thinking about Luke or his dimples. The whole Dustin situation didn't sit well with me. He acted the teeniest bit odd.

My stomach gurgled, drowning the blast of the radio. I turned off the main road onto Highway 19 toward my family's farm and checked my rear view for the large grill of a black truck.

I'd be lying if I said memories of Luke hadn't crossed my mind a time or two over the years. However, after the Las Vegas fiasco, I vowed to abstain from men.

Luke made me stupid, and I hated stupid. Todd was temporary insanity and harmless.

Luke was dangerous.

I scrunched my face and eased the accelerator until the engine knocking quieted. I detested restrictions. Even self-imposed ones.

He might be dangerous, but Luke didn't scare me.

Therein lay the problem.

FOUR

PULLING into the farm could be trickier than holding onto the bottom lane at Bristol Motor Speedway. With the right signal blinking, the Datsun idled before the gravel turn. I scanned the rutted drive and weedy foreground with its smattering of chewed forsythia. Searched the split in the lane leading to a rusty roofed barn.

Empty.

The other fork led to a little ranch house with a tacked-on screened porch and crumbling flower beds. The house hid behind a thick ancient oak and an overgrown Bradford Pear flush with white blossoms.

I craned my neck, but couldn't see past the limbs of the oak still clinging to last season's dead leaves. I revved my engine, but that trick never worked.

Whistling wouldn't work either.

A clump of half-chewed hollyhocks grew by the fence post. A grunt of disgust escaped my lips. I adored those hollyhocks. Wasted half a day adding manure to the Georgia clay to coax them into growing. I loved their colors: dark purples, brilliant reds, and pinks with tips pale as blush and deepening to dark magenta centers.

However, even the tenacious hollyhocks had become victim to the farmyard terror.

Behind the fence, three of the neighbor's horses pulled at the long weeds lining the road and watched me.

"Yeah, it's me," I called to them. "He only does this to me."

Or maybe it was the Datsun. Another reason to get this paycheck and toss the clunker.

I drummed my fingers on the steering wheel. Bleating floated through the open window, but the cries came from the far pasture behind the shed. My stomach protested the prolonged wait with a clamorous rumble that would have given a thunderstorm a run for its money.

Maybe I would get lucky.

My yellow truck accelerated down the lane, churning clay and gravel in its wake. The object of the game was to get to the house before Tater saw me. Either that or I'd have to endure a long walk with him nudging and nibbling me the entire way. I'd be covered in goat muck before reaching the house.

Why couldn't Grandpa have kept the cows? He never let them roam the yard. Heck, he treated Tater better than his grandkids.

My thoughts stopped short at the site of a massive white billy goat trotting out from behind the Bradford Pear. Chewing his cud, he studied the yellow truck barreling down the drive. The buck shook his beard, pawed the dirt, and lowered his horns.

Much as Tater drove me crazy, I didn't want to hit him. He'd probably wreck my truck.

I pounded the brakes.

Tater galloped along the drive like he was Secretariat in the last quarter turn of the Derby while I scrambled to pull the keys from the ignition and open the door. The latch popped as Tater darted around the grill of the Datsun to my side. I squeezed out the cracked door, shoved it shut with my butt, and locked it.

"You are not getting in my truck again. I have important stuff in there."

Tater cocked his head, evaluating my words. His cud swished from cheek to cheek. Evaluation over, he butted me in the stomach, thrusting me against the truck.

Goat spittle and dirt speckled my orange tee.

"Dangit, Tater!" I pushed back. "I hate goats. Has that not occurred to you yet?"

"YOU AGAIN. I thought you didn't live here anymore," said Ed Ballard, glancing over his shoulder at the slam of the screen door.

"Nice to see you, too, Grandpa." I bent over and pecked his raspy cheek. "You know that old goat stopped me again. Why don't you put him in back with the others?"

I could feel the tremor of a smile, but it disappeared by the time my lips left his cheek. He sat with crossed legs at the rattan table set bought thirty years earlier for the bright yellow kitchen. His small frame appeared delicately old and grizzled, yet the denim britches and work shirt hid muscles as tough and stringy as an overcooked chicken, something you were not likely to find in the Ballard house. A folded newspaper lay on the table next to an empty plate and half-drunk glass of tea.

"Anybody else here?" I said.

"How would I know? This place is a revolving door for you kids."

"I'm right here, old man." Casey stepped onto the faded linoleum in bare feet. Her toenails sparkled with glittery purple polish and an inch of flesh peeked between her t-shirt and low-rise jeans. "You'd think I hadn't just cooked you up a fierce dinner."

"Fierce dinner?" I licked my lips.

Casey and Grandpa ignored me.

"I don't need watching by rude children. What I want is some peace." Grandpa tapped his hand on the paper and eyed me. "Sister, fix her a plate. I only see Cherry when she's hungry, but that's often enough."

I slid onto the chair next to him and smiled. "You want to know what I've been doing?"

Casey plopped onto a chair opposite and leaned her elbows on the table.

"Wha'ch you been doing?" She tossed her long brown hair over a shoulder, her brown eyes sparking with interest.

Casey lived for gossip and excitement. Gossip was easy to find, but excitement a bit harder in Halo. That meant Casey made her own excitement, which often resulted in more gossip.

"I've got a chance for a new commission," I said.

Casey delivered me a blank look.

"A new customer to paint. It's Dustin Branson."

"Uh-uh. He's dead."

"I know. The Bransons hired me to paint him dead. Can you believe it?" I turned to Grandpa. "Saw Uncle Will at Cooper's. The Sheriff's Office is investigating. What do you know about it?"

"Well," he pulled on the word while arranging himself for a lengthy answer. Half the information would be factual and the rest supposition, but I might learn something. I hopped up to pour a glass of sweet tea while Casey picked at her nails.

"Dustin was found in the auto bay of Mather's tire shop. That's where he worked when he bothered showing up."

He shook his head, discontented with Dustin's work habits. "It was after closing, so the front door was locked. Curtis Mather found Dustin face down under the lift with drained oil dripping on him and his head smashed in. Probably used one of the tools in the garage, maybe a tire iron? That's my guess, now. Will wouldn't tell me the murder weapon."

"What was he doing there after hours?"

"Dustin was working on his car." Grandpa tapped his chin. "An old Malibu. He worked on rebuilding it after work sometimes."

"How'd you know that?"

"Got my sources. I wonder if JB's going to sell that Malibu. Cody's mighty interested. Been busting to ask Branson next time he's in the dealership garage. I told Cody to wait and see. The man just lost his son. That boy's got no sense of decorum. Anyway, that's all I need is another vehicle on blocks in my barn."

"Knowing my brother and cars, he'll wrangle that Malibu somehow. It'll be sitting in the barn within the month guaranteed," I said.

"He better sell some of his other junk first. There ain't room. What's the point of spending all his money on cars if he can't afford the parts to fix them?"

I set down the tea and walked to the fridge. A plate of cold chicken sat wrapped in plastic on the shelf. A roar from my stomach accompanied a touch of drool.

"That chicken's for supper," Casey called without looking up.

I ignored Casey and grabbed a leg of chicken before sitting at the worn table again.

Grandpa glowered. "Don't be eating my supper now, Cherry."

"It would've been my supper, too. I'm just eating my share since I'm going back to Cooper's tonight." I bit into the succulent chicken and sighed. "Casey, you could put Chicken D'Lite out of business if you'd open your own place."

"You keep saying that. And I keep telling you waiting tables at Red's is more than enough for me."

"Why would I want her to open a restaurant?" asked Grandpa. "Then somebody else will eat her chicken and not me."

"Don't you want to be successful?" I studied Casey as she leaned over to peer at her toenails. Casey couldn't find ambition if it drew her a map and hired a sherpa.

"Not if it means slaving away for a bunch of people who don't give a rat's ass about me."

I skipped over her implication at my constant scramble for commissions. "I care about you. So, you have anything to go with the chicken? I'm starving."

"You're always starving. You got Gam's house, and I know it

has a kitchen. Why don't you learn to cook for yourself?" She stretched from her seat with deliberate indolence, our squabble already forgotten.

"Why should I when you do it so much better? Who wants to eat ramen noodles when I can eat this?"

"As I was saying." Grandpa cleared his throat. "Now, the papers read that Dustin was dealing drugs out the back of the tire shop. Witnesses saw people going in and out that back door late at night from time to time. He could've been dealing drugs, wouldn't put it past him, but I know something else that goes on there."

"What?" Casey and I responded together.

She laid a plate of reheated butter rolls, okra, and green beans before me. My eyes dilated. I shoveled Casey's cooking into my mouth, chewing quickly to hear Grandpa's reply.

"Sam McGill's poker group. Got 'em going on all over town."

I swallowed a half-chewed bit of roll and swished it down with tea. "If there was a poker game, wouldn't someone have seen him dead and reported it?"

"It weren't there that night. Will says it was at the Tan-N-Go a few nights before. But if folks were seeing people at odd hours in the garage, had to be poker. If it were drugs, they would've been sneakier. Maybe Dustin would've hidden the drugs with the tires. You think that would work? Maybe on the wheel under the hubcap?"

Grandpa leaned back, imagining the clandestine workings of a hubcap drug ring.

"Why don't they play poker in their houses like normal people? I think you'd be more comfortable in your house." Casey plopped into her chair with a bottle of florescent orange polish. She opened the bottle and spread one hand on the table.

"Because of the wives, of course. That's how it started anyway. Sam's wife didn't want him playing poker, and his friends' wives would've told her if he played at their houses. Sam don't have that wife anymore, but they still play in the businesses for the hell of it."

"Who's involved in those games?" I asked.

"Not the crowd I'd hang out with, I'll tell you that. Can't see Dustin or his group playing with them neither."

"Who else works at the tire shop?"

Grandpa rubbed the short whiskers on his chin with one hand. "Can't say. Don't get my tires there. I go to the Walmart in Line Creek."

"Any younger guys in that poker group?"

"Wondering about anyone in particular? Ain't seeing drummer boy again, are you? I never understood your fascination with that one. He's got less sense than Cody. And a gambling problem to boot."

Casey laughed. "Todd may be dumb, but he's awfully pretty, Grandpa. There's your fascination. And he worships Cherry."

"That shows you how dumb he is," said Grandpa.

"Thanks. You and Casey do wonders for my self esteem."

"Speaking of awful pretty, Luke Harper's back in town for the funeral. You seen him yet?" Casey glanced up from her nails to check my scowl. "Which do we need to lock up? You or Daddy's gun?"

"That was a long time ago. And I was young."

Grandpa grimaced. "What are you talking about? Are you in trouble, Cherry? You girls are going to be the death of me."

"Everything's fine, Grandpa. Cody will be the death of you, not me."

"Cody's not the one who tried to run away and get married."

"I didn't run away to get married. Todd won a contest to go to Vegas, and I went along for fun. The wedding was annulled before anything happened, thank you, Jesus. It was a momentary lapse in judgment."

"Call it what you want. Should've locked you up then, too," remarked Casey.

"You're one to talk."

"That's my own business."

"That's not an answer."

Grandpa shoved his chair back and stood up. He placed his hands on the table, flexing the gnarled muscles in his thin arms. "I'm going to talk to my goats. They have more sense than the two of you." He pushed off the table and snapped his arm, waving us off. "Y'all are just like your mother. You better watch yourselves."

Casey and I stared at each other with raised brows.

That was the one line that could always hush us up.

I WENT BACK to Cooper's Funeral Home, but Cooper kicked me out. Told me to come back in the morning when it was less hectic. He failed to understand, even after a mostly patient explanation from yours truly, that I needed to start painting tonight. I couldn't spread my tarp and lay out my paints within hours of the visitation. And even as fast as acrylics dried, I still needed to use glazing to get the look of an oil painting. Glazing took time.

Nothing would stop me from getting this painting perfectly executed and delivered to that funeral. Not even a little thing like locked doors to an empty funeral parlor. In a creaky, old house probably riddled with ghosts.

And if Cooper didn't want people showing up after hours, he needed to have strong words with his beautician who left her keys in plain view on the kitchenette counter.

Unlocking the side door, I slipped in under the hazy orange glow of a security light. I chuckled at the simplicity of creeping in after hours. It reminded me of sneaking into the high school art room after dark. I was finally caught by a late-night janitor, but until then, I had done some of my best work in the empty building. Taught me to clean up well, too.

And how to pick locks on closets with a paperclip.

Not that working in a funeral home after dark was my idea of a good time, but at least Cooper wouldn't lurk over my shoulder asking questions. And I wouldn't choke on undertaker fumes either.

I used my flashlight to find my way along the dim hallway. At the entrance to the lobby, my hand hovered over the light switch. Passing car lights shone through the glass front doors, spotlighting my still form. Some nosy biddy would surely notice lights on at Cooper's after dark and call Mr. Cooper. Or the sheriff.

I left the lights off and stole into the Branson viewing room.

"Hey there, Dustin," I whispered. After adjusting the dimmer, I dumped my bag and tackle box on the floor and crept out. Several minutes later, I returned with a primed canvas and another larger tackle box. I spread a thin plastic sheet under the easel and kicked off my boots and socks.

I surprise myself sometimes. I'm not known for being shy or cautious, but I never imagined hanging out with a dead guy. Yet here I stood next to a coffin, bopping along to the music on my headphones while I brushed on Dustin's underpainting in bold strokes.

"Looking good," I sang to my painting.

My head beat along to the throbbing chords ringing from my earbuds. The purplish base color, mixed from alizarin crimson and ultramarine blue, would provide a cooler tone to Dustin's skin and the shadowy background. I had snapped some photos of Dustin in case I needed to work at home, but using a live subject is always preferable.

Or dead, in this case.

Taking a break for the first coat to dry, I covered my palette of mixed paints with a wet paper towel and grabbed a Coke from my bag. I took a deep swig, wiped my mouth with the back of my hand, and sighed.

Painting made me happy.

Getting paid for it made me downright ecstatic.

A beer would perfect the moment, but I sucked on the Coke instead. Breaking into a funeral home to paint the deceased was bad enough. Somehow cracking into a six-pack pushed the crime into redneck realm.

Wandering over to the coffin, I took another swig and stared at Dustin. Something looked different. I scanned him again and spotted the incongruence. The pocket flap on the far side of his suit jacket was folded inside itself, a minor detail that would bug me. I should fix it. But no, thank you.

Though I wouldn't actually have to touch Dustin. Just his pocket.

I twitched my nose. But every glance from the easel to Dustin would zone in on that stupid pocket flap.

That's a lot of glances.

A light flashed in my periphery, and the hairs on my arms rose. I craned my neck toward the door but saw nothing.

My head bobbed to the throbbing music while I fixated on the pocket flap. A light flashed again. This time I pivoted toward the darkened doorway and ducked.

Still nothing.

Perfectly reasonable to have jitters standing next to a dead man in a coffin in a dark funeral parlor. I also suspected my mind was playing tricks on me so I could procrastinate touching that pocket. The flash was a car light or something. Probably some reflection thingy I didn't understand because I didn't pay attention in physics.

Taking a deep breath, I turned back to the coffin. My hand hovered over the body. I reached into the coffin and tugged the edge of the flap. It caught on something.

I plunged my hand into the pocket feeling for the obstruction. The flap flipped up, and I pulled out a small gray bag. Tiny hard misshapen objects rolled between my fingers through the soft pouch.

"Eew!" I dropped the bag, shaking my hand free of the heebie-jeebies. What would feel like that?

I took another swig of Coke and grabbed hold of my nerves. Just as I lectured myself to stop messing around, a beam of light slid across the wall before me, then swung toward the ceiling.

That's no car light. That's a flashlight.

The hairs on the back of my neck prickled. I began to turn.

One crack to my skull and the headphones popped out of my

ears. My knees buckled. The Coke foamed and splashed as my body dropped.

Intense, bright colors exploded in my vision.

Cad red.

Titanium white.

And finally, Mars black.

FIVE

"WAKE UP, CHERRY."

The loud voice crashed through throbbing pain. I ignored it, searching for the pillow of nothingness that slipped away a moment ago.

"Cherrilyn Tucker, come on now. Time to get up, hon'."

The voice bounced inside my head like a pinball on steroids. This had to be the worst hangover I'd ever felt. I snarled a reply to the visitor.

"Whoa. She'll be fine boys. Hold off on the gurney."

The throbbing beat a tattoo in my head. Gurney? I blinked one eye open and focused through the haze of pain. I lay face down on a wrinkled plastic sheet. My hands were speckled purple, my face sticky wet. I groaned and felt a remnant of drool dribble off my lips. Wiping my chin on my shoulder, I considered the owner of the voice. A slice of panic cut through me, but I rolled over anyway.

Uncle Will 's face loomed above mine. I began to push myself up on my elbows. He shoved me down.

"What in the hell is going on?" I struggled to sit up, but the sheriff kept a firm hand on my shoulder. "What happened?"

"You tell me."

I glanced around the viewing room, careful of my aching head. My easel and paints were strewn over the floor. The coffin lay almost tipped on its side, Dustin's body half dumped on the table. His jacket and pants looked dark in spots.

My breath pulled tight in my chest. "Is that blood?"

Will knelt next to me on the plastic sheet, his hand draped over my shoulder. He glanced behind him and shook his head. "No. I think it's Coke. There's a bottle on the floor."

I groaned again and gingerly felt the lump on the back of my head.

"Are you okay, Cherry? What are you doing here?"

"I don't know. My head hurts. I think somebody hit me." I shuddered. Dustin looked like a Halloween prop. "I don't know how his coffin tipped. This place is a mess."

I turned from the dumped corpse to my overturned easel and paints. "Hell, all that paint I mixed. Dammit, look at my canvas. There's spilled paint on it. I'm going to have to stretch another one."

"Cherrilyn, I'm going to ask you again. What are you doing at Cooper's?" Will looked past me toward the door.

I pushed up on my elbows to follow his gaze. Lights blazed in the lobby as two deputies chatted in the doorway.

This wasn't good.

"Painting?" I squeaked.

"And how did you get in?" Will asked, faking patience.

"With a key," I said, staring at the ceiling. The heat creeping into my face made me woozier.

"A key given to you by...?"

"Am I going to need a lawyer?" I closed my eyes. The droning wail of a siren grew louder. "I don't need an ambulance. I can't afford an ambulance."

"How do you know it's for you?"

My eyes snapped open.

"It's for you," said Will. "First we'll take you to the ER to get your head checked. Then you'll get a little trip to the station."

"Uncle Will," I shot up despite the weight of his hand on my shoulder and nearly passed out. "The station? Seriously? That's all the way in Line Creek. Think of your budget. Do you really want the taxpayers footing the bill to haul me to jail? I just came in to paint Dustin."

"Let's see," Will tapped his chin. "I'm looking at destruction of property. Breaking and entering. Battery. Can't tell if there's been a robbery yet. Trespassing at the very least."

"Oh God," I said, burying my face in my hands.

"Praying is always good at times like these." His thick fingers tentatively searched my hair for a lump. "That's a nice goose egg right there. I should have put on gloves."

He wiped his fingers on the tarp, leaving a smear of purple.

"What's this?" he said, pointing to something beneath my bent legs. "Just a minute, don't move."

He pulled a pen from his pocket and used it to drag the object from under the shadow of my body. The little gray bag slipped out.

"Ugh," I shuddered. "There's the whole reason for this mess."

Will's head jerked up, and he cornered me with a sharp gaze. "Explain."

"I was trying to fix Dustin's pocket because that bag was inside, when someone walloped me."

I grabbed Will 's arm and started to babble. "I just came in here to paint, honest, Uncle Will. I'm trying to get a jump on the project, so Shawna doesn't collect the commission money. She wants to color over a picture and call it a portrait. We're not talking Andy Warhol silk screen stuff. It's not even Photoshop tinting. If the Bransons choose her painting over mine, everyone will follow their lead. It's going to ruin my business and ruin the craft. She can't be allowed to call something like Paintograph art."

Rolling his eyes, he scooped up the pouch in his hand.

"I need an evidence bag," he called to a deputy behind him.

"What about fingerprints?"

"If I could pull prints off a cloth bag," he said, "whose prints do you think I'm going to find?"

"Dammit."

"Exactly. What's in here anyway?" He rolled the bag in his hand. "Feels kind of nasty."

He pulled open the drawstring and sprinkled some of the contents into his hand. Small, yellow objects rolled within his palm.

A shiver ran through me.

"You missing any teeth?" he said.

"I DON'T SEE why we have to eat here," I said, stirring my cheese grits. "I have bad memories from the Waffle Hut. And now I'm going to associate hash browns with getting sucker punched in the head."

"Just eat your food and stop your whining," said my brother, Cody. "You said you were starving, and where else could we go?" He pointed with his knife and resumed sawing his rib eye. "I mean, look at you. You look like you dunked yourself in a paint bucket."

My clothes looked like a Jackson Pollock experiment. Globs of plasticized purple stuck in my fine hair. The paint matched the doorknob sized bump on the back of my head.

"I don't think you look too bad," said Todd. "If you pushed your hair up into a Mohawk and ripped your t-shirt, we could drive up to Atlanta and find a punk club."

"Why did you bring him?" I asked Cody.

"He was at Red's when I got your call." Cody pulled off his battered Braves cap and scratched his shaggy blonde hair.

The brown eyes danced over the grinning studmuffin sitting next to me. Cody's mouth drew into a smirk. "I figured if you needed bail money, your husband could put it up. You know I'm broke."

"I was not arrested, and Todd is not my husband," I shoveled a spoonful of grits into my mouth and glared across the table. "This was just a big misunderstanding."

"A big misunderstanding that landed you in jail."

"It was just questioning!"

"I believe you, baby," said Todd. "If you were going to rob a dead guy you would have been much sneakier."

"Thank you." I studied him from the corner of my eye.

The tall, blonde Adonis — worthy of a Botticelli fresco or at least a Calvin Klein underwear ad — stretched his arm across the back of our booth. Drumsticks poked out of the carpenter pocket of his cargo shorts. Somewhere beneath the table, slot-machine cherries tattooed one calf.

"What's with the new tattoo? I saw it when we walked in."

"You like it?" He beamed. "I did it for you. Because your name is Cherry."

"Yeah, I got that," I said. "I don't think it's a good idea for you to permanently ink references to me on your body."

"You're my wife." He corrected himself. "My first wife."

"Stop saying that." I stabbed a piece of sausage. "We weren't hardly married. Filling out the annulment papers took longer than the wedding."

"I actually don't remember getting unmarried, only getting married."

"That can be blamed on tequila. You also didn't remember me after the wedding." I gazed at the solid forearms and broad shoulders with regret. "I spent my so-called honeymoon searching the casinos for you."

"That's Vegas, baby. What can I say?" He shrugged. "We could try it again."

"You're delusional."

"That's the nicest thing you've said about me in a long time." Todd hooked a piece of sausage from my plate. "I think you're growing sweet on me again."

I sighed.

Cody snorted. "I think you make a great couple. I don't care what people say about y'all."

The bell above the door tinkled. Our attention swung toward the entrance to check out the newcomer. Late night Waffle Hut always brought in an interesting crowd.

We watched a lanky man with curly dark hair and fierce gray eyes push through the door. I hunkered over my plate, finding sudden fascination in my cooling grits and link sausage.

"I guess grave robbing worked you up an appetite," said Luke, ambling up to our table.

I muttered a string of choice words not quite under my breath. "I wasn't robbing Dustin. I was painting."

"Sheriff said they found Dustin's effects on your person."

"That's stretching it. They found that little bag under my person. I don't think I'd go to all that trouble to steal baby teeth."

"Baby teeth?" said Todd. "Who would want to steal baby teeth?"

"Who knows," said Luke. "Maybe some flaky artist wants to make some crazy art doo-dad with them."

"I don't do assemblage. I paint. And I'm not flaky."

"Going to a funeral home to paint a dead body in the dark isn't flaky?"

"Sounds flaky to me." Cody leaned back in the booth and adjusted his cap to study Luke. "Who are you? You make my sister cuss like that, gets me pretty curious."

"You must be Cody. Mind if I sit?" Luke slid into the booth next to him. "I'm Luke Harper. You were a young 'un last time I met you. I've been gone a long time."

"I'm Todd McIntosh." Todd extended his hand across the table. "I'm Cherry's husband. Sort of."

Luke's eyebrows rose a notch. "I didn't realize she was married."

"I'm not. Todd's mistaken."

"How can you be mistaken about that?"

I looked up from my bowl. Todd's wide-eyed, open face

greeted Luke's shuttered countenance. They reminded me of Lassie meeting Cujo.

"You'd have to know Todd better," Cody said.

Todd nodded in acquiescence.

"He's a great guy though," Cody added, sidling a look toward Luke.

"I'm a drummer," said Todd.

"A drummer," Luke drawled.

"My band is called Sticks. You know, because I'm a drummer."

"Good one."

"Okay, enough with the get-to-know-you." I tossed my fork on the table. The cold grits had congealed, and Todd had eaten all my sausage. "I've got to get home and stretch another canvas."

"What are you doing here?" Cody turned toward Luke, ignoring me.

"Sheriff Thompson told me you were going to the Waffle Hut. My family got the call about the breaking and entering at the funeral home."

Luke stopped me with a look when I started to protest. "I went down to the Sheriff's Office as a representative of the family to decide if we'd press charges. I didn't get a look at Dustin, but it didn't sound like much harm was done other than the coffin tipping. And the teeth weren't successfully stolen."

"I didn't try to steal those teeth. Somebody else tried to rob Dustin. I've got a gigantic headache to prove it."

"So tell me what happened," said Luke.

I stumbled through my explanation of painting and seeing the flashlight.

"Where were you guys when this happened?" He looked at Cody.

"The County Line Tap. Heard on Red's scanner there was a break-in at Cooper's, then got the call Uncle Will hauled Cherry off in the paddy wagon."

"I didn't get hauled off in the paddy wagon." I slammed my cup on the table, sprinkling my hand with lukewarm coffee. "You better not tell Grandpa that. Uncle Will drove me to the hospital in the Crown Vic."

"Who was at Red's?" Luke said, ignoring me.

"The regulars," Todd muttered and blushed.

"Wait a minute, it's Wednesday night. The County Line isn't open this late on a weekday." I shook my finger. "Were y'all playing cards at Red's? You're going to get Red in a lot of trouble if his place gets busted."

The blush flared. "Now, baby. I'm not really playing. We wouldn't do that to Red. It was for fun. Pennies. Nothing big."

"Are you talking about poker?" Luke asked.

Todd shrugged. "Yeah. I like to play."

"He's like the idiot savant of poker," said Cody.

"Cody." My voice hummed with warning. Todd wore the dumb blonde look well, but I sometimes wondered if the act was real or a game that amused him. He really did play poker like a pro. And I sort of found myself married to him for a minute.

"Thanks, Cody." Todd beamed. "Yeah, I'm pretty good. I did so good in an online league that I won a contest to play in Vegas."

His hands slapped the table in a happy rhythm. "Cherry went with me."

"Lucky you," Luke said to me.

"Lucky Todd." Cody snorted.

"Hush, Cody. That reminds me. Grandpa told me Sam McGill's got a traveling poker group that met in Mather's tire shop. You know anything about that?" I winced at my insensitivity. "Sorry Luke. You probably don't want to be reminded of Mather's."

"No, actually I'd like to know what happened. Go on, Todd." Luke leaned back in the booth. "Is it high stakes?"

"McGill's boys? Nothing higher than a twenty in that group. It's for fun. And the guys are old." Todd's fingers tapped the underside of the table. "You looking for a high stakes game?"

"Can I find that around here?" Luke asked.

Cody glanced at me. I shrugged.

Todd folded his arms on the table and leaned toward Luke. "If you were looking, I could probably get you in."

"Todd," I said. "You told me you don't do that. It's illegal."

He waved off my complaint. "I didn't say I did it. I just know about it."

"So you know some of the guys that do?" Luke continued with a look of exasperation at me.

"Sure. They all want me to play poker with them. Old guys even."

"Nobody believes how good he is until they play him," said Cody.

"Did you know my step-brother?" said Luke. "Dustin Branson?"

"Sure. He was friends with my roommate, Pete."

Todd's fingers crept on top of the table and strummed the surface. He turned to me. "Not Jackson. You liked him. Pete's the one you don't like."

"Yeah, Creepy Pete." I stuck out my tongue and made a gagging noise.

"Pete's not in the band," Todd explained to Luke. "But he plays poker, too. He got Dustin his gig with Mr. Max's outfit."

"What do you mean by gig? Who's Mr. Max?"

"I can't pronounce his last name, so we call him Mr. Max. He heard about my poker wins and wanted to meet me. I couldn't understand him so I asked Pete to talk to him." Todd stopped to take a bite of waffle.

"And?" I prompted.

Todd lifted his brows.

"Don't keep us hanging. What happened after you introduced Pete to Mr. Max?"

"Oh. Pete started hanging out with him. Mr. Max's got a big house with a lot of acreage east of here but he also lives in Atlanta. Or Florida. Or somewhere else. Anyway, Pete started doing odd jobs for him, like bartending, while Mr. Max and his buddies play poker."

Todd's words ran together, and his fingers tapped a quick

cadence on the wooden table. "Pete said Mr. Max runs the games real fancy because it's a massive pot. Like ten thousand just to get in. They do it over a long weekend with everybody staying there. Some of the folks are important. Like politicians and athletes. I bet some musicians, too. Pete waits on them while they play poker. Just like Vegas."

He broke his story with a sigh and leaned toward me. "Wouldn't that be fun, baby?

"That's going on in Halo? I can't believe it. Who is this Mr. Max? Uncle Will needs to know about this. He should be hunting this guy down instead of wasting his time questioning me."

Luke rapped his finger near Todd's plate. "Go on with your story."

"Pete introduced Dustin to Mr. Max. Dustin doesn't play poker, but he started doing other work for the guy. More important than bartending."

"Like how important?"

"Dustin was his right-hand man. Heard him talking about it to Pete once. But I don't know what that means. Your brother was kind of secretive."

"Step-brother." The word popped from Luke's mouth, but his thoughts roamed elsewhere.

"You can be sure Dustin was proud of working for Mr. Max," Todd continued. "He and Pete did fight about it some. Pete thought Dustin was getting too big for his britches."

"I bet," muttered Luke. "Do you know anything more about this Mr. Max?"

"I do if I know the house you're talking about." Cody slipped forward in his seat, eager to be part of the conversation. "I don't know the name, but some foreign guy called the dealership. Needed a mechanic for on-site oil changes and maintenance. Must be nice. Dude has a ten-car garage. Hummer, Maserati, Corvette, Escalade."

Cody's eyes gleamed. "Even a '57 Chevy. I think he moved here about a year ago."

"Why haven't I heard about him?" I said.

"Probably too busy with your trip to Vegas." Cody smirked. "Anyway, Ronny Price went out there, too. Like he's going to sell that guy an F-150."

Cody rolled his eyes. "I guess Mr. Max is a big time collector. Ronny said he's really into Civil War stuff. He even has a cannon on his front lawn."

"What does he do to have that kind of money?" I said. "Can you get that rich from playing poker?"

"Ronny didn't say." Cody tipped his hat back and scratched his head. "Just kind of bragged about his collections, like Ronny's special for seeing them. Mr. Max needs a better security system. Ronny's such a tool."

Cody glanced at Luke. "Sorry. I guess you know Ronny pretty well because of your dad owning the dealership. He's not real popular in the auto-bay."

"Stepdad." Luke shrugged. "Whatever."

"I need to get home. Can you drive me back to Halo now?" I nudged Todd. "I have a ruined canvas to replace. I don't even have a deposit to pay myself back for the supplies."

The men pushed out of their seats and wandered to the door. The night was clear and cool, reminding me of the late hour. I hadn't touched the memory box collection, and I was back to square one with the painting. It was going to be a long night.

"Dude, is that your truck?" Cody pointed to the black Raptor gleaming under the parking lot light.

Luke tossed him the keys. "Go ahead and give it a spin. But if you're not back in five, I'll call the sheriff."

"Come on, Todd. Let's see what she can do." Cody trotted to the truck.

Todd followed, glancing over his shoulder.

"Don't worry about me. Not like I'm in a hurry or it's the middle of the night," I said, leaning against Todd's little, red hatchback. There was no deterring my brother from checking out any kind of vehicle. I'd have better luck teaching a cat to swim.

Luke stopped before me, pushed a dusky brown curl off his forehead, and stretched into a yawn.

My eyes skimmed over the muscles in the upraised arms, down the firm chest, and found a spot of exposed flesh between his jeans and raised t-shirt. Darting a glance back to his face, I realized he caught me looking.

He lowered his arms and smoothed his t-shirt over his jeans.

"So what did the sheriff say about the break-in?" Luke asked. "Does he have any suspects?"

"Uh." The parking lot light buzzed and dimmed overhead. His eyes darkened, reminding me of flint. Shadows filled his dimples and carved his cheekbones. He'd make a good pen and ink study tonight.

A nude life study would be nice.

I shook myself awake. "What?"

He maneuvered into my personal space again, placing a hand on the car roof. "What did the sheriff say?"

Oh man, I thought. Luke Harper needs to stop draping his body around me. Resisting temptation was not this girl's forte.

"Uncle Will wasn't happy with me. Doesn't want me to keep painting, either." I blew out a sigh, thinking about the commission. "But I'm going to do it anyway. I'll use the photo I took. I need the money and the recommendation if your mom and JB like it."

"JB's not going to be too happy with you, that's for sure." Luke's free hand slipped behind my head to search for the bump.

"How's your head?" His fingers caressed my skull.

I closed my eyes and thought about pushing him away. At my moan, the nimble fingers crept to massage the muscles at the back of my neck.

"Um, it's okay." I took a deep breath, and the fingers kneaded my shoulders. My knees buckled, and I slid a few inches down the door.

Luke's knee against my thigh stopped my decline.

"Oh, that feels so good." I hoped I wasn't drooling.

"So when the sheriff questioned you about what happened, did he offer some opinions on the perp?" Both hands massaged my shoulders now.

I gripped the handle with one hand. The other hand seemed to have slipped to Luke's waist without permission.

Oh Lordy. No love handles on this guy. He was all smooth muscle. I struggled to think of an answer to his question.

"He thinks I forgot to lock the back door behind me. Could be anyone."

My hand slid to his back and pressed him closer. The other clutched the door handle like a life preserver.

"You'd tell me if you learn anything else, right?"

"I guess so." I sighed.

Luke's hands skated from my shoulders to my face. "You always liked being in the middle of things." A finger stroked my cheek.

"What kind of middle you talking about?" I lifted my face.

A truck roared into the parking lot, brakes squealing as Cody spun a donut in the empty lot.

I sensed Luke inching closer. Taking a deep breath, I waited for a second and cracked my lids. A kiss glided to my forehead. His hand covered mine to pop the handle. My feet stumbled as he yanked open the door.

"Better hop in. Getting chilly out here."

I landed butt-first in the back seat, and the door thumped back in place. Scrambling around to peer out the back window, I caught Luke's long-legged stride retreating from the Civic.

"What in the hell was that?" I moaned. "I can't believe I fell for it."

Flipping around, I slumped in my seat. Todd jerked open the driver door and slid inside with a quick glance into the backseat. "You doing okay, hon?"

"Just peachy." I crossed my arms and tossing up my chin. "Take me home. I've got a kick-ass portrait to paint. I'll show those Bransons."

SIX

MORNING CAME TOO EARLY for me, but others in Halo bustled with spring enthusiasm. I waved to my neighbors as my Datsun shambled along Loblolly Avenue. If I hadn't moved into my Great Gam's abandoned cottage on Loblolly, Magnolia Avenue — the other main street from Halo's whistles-top heyday — would have been the better choice for a business.

Of course, at this point, I couldn't afford a free bungalow on Loblolly, let alone a house on Magnolia. Great Gam's place was just fine.

Rounding the square, I headed north to the outskirts of town where new subdivisions of larger homes flanked Halo. A thirty-by-forty canvas, stretched, gessoed, and painted in the wee hours of the morning rode shotgun. A form of Dustin lying peacefully in his coffin had been roughly established over the underpainting.

If the rudimentary portrayal met the Bransons' approval, I'd be able to whisk it back home to finish. A corner of Wanda's red shopping bag peeked from under the frame where I shoved it in my bleary-eyed haste this morning. I hadn't peeked in the bag yet, but Dustin's memory box was next on my list.

After I got the contract signed.

Dustin's portrait and I breezed through Fetlock Meadow's pillared entrance. I began the difficult navigation through the winding subdivision streets that included a golf course. By the time I turned onto Trotter's Ridge Drive, the unusual amount of traffic had prepared me for the sight of Will's cruiser and a line of other cars parked on the street.

The absence of a black pickup kept my heart steady. I parked and walked past several imposing stacked stone Southern Living style mini-mansions.

Before I even reached the Branson's half-circle drive, Will ambled out the front door. Wearing his tan uniform, one hand rested comfortably on his holster. He filled the front stoop with his large presence. Seemed as if Sheriff Thompson would greet me today and not Uncle Will.

"What are you doing here?" His deep voice carried across the lawn.

I froze in the drive, studying Will 's deepening frown.

"I thought you were finished with this business after our talk last night."

"I'm just here to get paid, sir," I said, hoping a half-fib would slide me back into his good graces.

"Nobody's home. Besides, I'd think a trip to the ER is enough of a lesson. You need to stay clear of the Bransons until we catch this guy. The whole town's talking about you robbing dead bodies. Don't look too good, hon."

I scrunched my mouth to the side, chewing over Will's request. I didn't want to explain that I wanted to show the Bransons the preliminary painting in hopes they would sign a contract. Any more talking and Will would most likely slap me with a restraining order.

"What's going on here?" I said. "Too many cop cars for a duty call to the bereaved parents."

"Someone broke into the Branson house early this morning. JB is livid." He ran a hand over his buzz top. "The perp ransacked his office and the first floor without the alarm engaging. Even with guests staying. This guy is bold and dangerous."

"Kind of interesting they'd search a house filled with guests. You think it was an inside job?"

"Can't say yet." He leaned against the doorframe. "I have a lot on my plate right now. Is Casey working today? If I get a minute, I might stop by the farm and grab a bite. Don't want all of Halo interrupting my lunch. You think y'all have some dinner to share?"

"Casey made chicken yesterday."

Before I could finish my thought, tires screeched on the blacktop. I turned my attention to the street. A faded aqua blue Chevy Geo skidded around the corner of Trotter's Ridge Drive.

Through the cracked windshield, I glimpsed a mop of frizzy, brown hair. A half second later, I realized the car angled for the Branson's drive where I stood gawking.

She took a tight turn into the driveway, barely missing the front bumper of Will's Crown Vic. Brakes squealed in protest as her foot pounded them to a stop.

I scrambled for cover and landed in a band of monkey grass.

A black pickup roared up the drive and jerked to a halt behind the Geo.

"Aw, hell," I muttered.

Will strode to my side, offering me a hand up before turning toward the crazed driver.

"My baby," the woman shrieked, heaving herself from the Geo. "What have they done to my Dustin?"

She slammed the door, rattling the loose license plate in back. A denim jumper draped her portly shape. Exposed flesh hung like raw biscuit dough off her beefy biceps.

Luke's low voice interrupted her heavy wail. "They aren't here, Virginia. Take the show somewhere else." He strode forward, concentrating on the grief-stricken woman.

The caterwauling ended with a practiced stop.

Will and I exchanged a glance.

Virginia planted pudgy hands on her ample hips. "How dare

you talk to me in that tone. My son is dead. I have every right to be here."

"I'm not saying you can't be at the funeral. I'm here to tell you no one's home. And to keep your scheming self away from my mother. Try the grieving routine somewhere else. You're not fooling anybody."

She pointed to the cars lined along the street. "If nobody's home, what are all these vehicles doing here? You were always a little liar. Always trying to get Dustin in trouble. You ruined his chances to go to school, you jealous hateful backstabber. I wouldn't be surprised to find out you murdered my baby."

Luke's steely eyes sliced through her, but he remained mute.

Will coughed and left my side to approach the ex-Mrs. Branson.

"Ma'am? I'm Sheriff Thompson. Luke Harper here is correct. The family is not home. But since you made such an entrance, I'd like to talk to you."

Virginia started to pivot, then saw me in the monkey grass.

I glared and brushed pine straw from my acid-washed jeans. Luckily, my striped sequined t-shirt could survive a roll in the straw without showing dirt.

Virginia swiveled back to Will. One hand flew to the lumpy denim chest and the other smoothed the brown frizz falling past her shoulders.

"That girl came out of nowhere, Officer. She was lucky I saw her at all." At my snarl, the squeaky voice rose to a plaintive squeal. "I am dis-traught with grief. My son has been mur-dered. I just arrived in town and could only think to come here first."

Will gave her a patient pause and glanced at the battered Geo filled with heaped clothing, empty fast food bags, and Diet Coke bottles. "That's Sheriff, ma'am. The first place you thought to come was your ex-husband's?"

"Of course."

"Not the funeral home?"

Her lips pursed.

"Or your son's place? Do you have any other relatives around

Halo? Those aren't Forks County plates on the Chevy, but it looks like you've been in your car a while. How long have you been in town?"

"Hmph." Virginia arched an eyebrow at Will. "That's my business. What are you doing at my husband's house? Where is JB?"

"Sorry ma'am, but I don't believe your business goes that far. You might as well follow me out of here. I need to know where you've been the last few days. We can talk at Cooper's Funeral Home if that suits you. Otherwise, there's the Sheriff's Office."

He motioned Virginia toward her car and grabbed his radio. Will hooked a thumb at me. "You two get out of here. My deputies are inside and don't need you hanging around. And I got my eye on you, Mr. Harper." He pointed a finger at Luke while raising the radio to his mouth and strolled to his car.

I glanced at Luke. The sheriff's comment didn't seem to phase him.

His grim eyes remained riveted on the Geo. "You up for another round at the Waffle Hut?"

"Not the Waffle Hut."

The guy left me in a puddle in that parking lot not even ten hours ago. Not to mention he used to stiff me for the check at a similar establishment once upon a time.

A breeze rustled the dark curls brushing the back of his neck. My eyes trailed across his shoulders and snug jeans.

Dangit.

"Maybe I am a little hungry," I said. "Meet me at the Country Kitchen on Magnolia. You can tell me where to find your mom. I've got some explaining to do about last night."

Foolish to spend time with Luke again, but I was curious about the Branson skeletons who kept popping out of their closets.

And I really was hungry.

WIRED from three cups of coffee and a half-carafe of maple syrup,

I pushed my plate to the side and drummed paint-speckled nails on the laminate tabletop.

Luke eyed my fingers, took a bite of biscuit, and chewed. I had shown him the painting and received a grunt in response. The extent of his conversation skills hadn't increased since we slid into the orange vinyl booth and ordered breakfast.

Like our middle-aged waitress whose perky ponytail did not match her blasé manner, Luke kept his focus on the clientele and not on me.

"What is up with that?" I uttered aloud.

Luke's eyebrows lifted. He didn't realize my question proceeded from an imaginary debate.

"How did you know Virginia was going to show up at your parents' this morning?"

Luke slowly chewed his bacon, then wiped his lips with a napkin. "I was waiting for her on 101, across from the BP. I wanted to get to her before she upset Mom."

"You knew she was coming?"

"She called JB's lawyer yesterday, so we knew she'd be coming to the house today. Virginia's been around for a while, though. She's holed up in Sweetgum, which is why I figured she'd be coming north on 101."

"Sweetgum?" The incorporated area couldn't even be called a town. Its population included a shanty trailer park, three farms, and a smattering of double-wides along the highway.

"Amos Fewe has a trailer in Sweetgum. He keeps bees and sells honey at farmer's markets. One of Virginia's boy toys."

"I don't get that. I saw Virginia. Where would a woman like that get all these guys?"

"No accounting for taste, I guess. Virginia was better looking when she was young but let herself go. She thinks she's crafty. She runs with those who are looking for easy scores." Luke grinned and stabbed the gravy coated biscuit with his fork. "In more ways than one, I guess."

I wrinkled my nose. "Enough said. So you think Virginia was hanging around with this Amos Fewe before Dustin was killed?"

"But I don't know why." Luke sighed and dropped his fork. "Amos sells more than honey. One of those trailers that burned down last week was a meth lab. Sheriff Thompson and his boys were all over Sweetgum. Jake Fells said they were ready to raid the lab when someone tipped them off. Arsoned the place before the deputies could get in. Jake's the one who told me he saw Virginia lurking around Sweetgum."

I swirled the dregs of my coffee and thought about another cup. The excitement of my brush with the burglar and restarting Dustin's project kept fatigue away last night, but lack of sleep began taking its toll. My hand jerked the cup, splattering drops of brown liquid on the table.

"You don't think Virginia hit me on the head last night, do you?"

"That's a pretty big leap."

"It's suspicious she's been here since Dustin died but didn't bother showing up until the day of the visitation. Isn't it?"

He nodded warily.

"Maybe she snuck in to view his body in private or something. She wouldn't know your mom hired me to paint him. I probably surprised her. Or maybe she thought I was doing something to Dustin. I was leaning over his body at the time. Her maternal instincts caused her to crack me in the skull."

Maybe that's what my mother would do.

With that thought, my excitement extinguished with a fizzle. Express her guilt for leaving us at the farm by popping someone on the head? I was blessed with a strong imagination, but sometimes it stepped sideways from logic.

"That's a good one," said Luke. "I don't think Virginia's conscience has ever been guilty, if she even has one. And she'd want an audience for grieving for Dustin. If she conked you on the head, it's because she didn't want you in the way of a robbery."

Luke pushed his plate away. "Did you forget Dustin's place

and my mom's house got hit, too? I think you need to get out of Halo. Boredom is playing games with your imagination. You're too talented for this town, anyway."

"Stop ripping on Halo. I chose to live here. I'm not bored. Besides, I have gallery space on the internet. I don't need to live in a big city."

I thought about the struggle for commissions that landed me Dustin's portrait. There weren't a lot of options for another job in Halo to supplement an artist's life.

Sighing, I slunk in my seat. "At least I don't have to pay rent. I'd probably be working at a Waffle Hut if I moved to Atlanta."

"You're surly enough for it. And you'd look pretty cute in the uniform." Luke grinned. "If they make them in a kid's size."

"I'd shoot myself if I had to wear the same color every day." I curled my lip in distaste. "I don't know how Uncle Will does it."

"You get used to it. Not all of us are that concerned with our clothes."

"Right. Guess you wore a uniform every day in the service." I looked at his hands lying on the table and thought of Dustin's hands in my portrait. "When did you get in town, anyway?"

"I—" Luke cut off his statement with the chime of the bell hanging at the entrance. His eyes drifted to the open door and stayed.

I glanced over my shoulder, recognized the bushy goatee and whipped back around. Scrunching my nose, I slid further into the booth.

"Creepy Pete," I muttered. "Todd's roommate. Don't let him see me. He's overly friendly and not in a good way."

"Introduce me." Luke kept his eyes riveted on Pete, who spoke to a local near the register.

Pete's baggy jeans brushed the floor, hiding dirty work boots. A thick metal chain linked a belt loop to an oversized wallet stuffed in his back pocket. His dirty t-shirt with cutoff sleeves completed the ensemble. Better to show off a multitude of tattoos covering shoulders to wrists.

More tattoos covered other parts of his body that I had been unfortunate to see on a trip to Todd's apartment.

Creepy Pete was unfamiliar with modesty.

"Did you not hear me say I don't want him to see me? That's the opposite of 'introduce me.'" I arched an eyebrow that Luke neglected to notice. "Why do you want to meet Creepy Pete anyway? You didn't like your step-brother. You aren't going to like Pete. I can guarantee you that."

"I'm not looking for a new friend. I'm looking for information."

With my lips set into a thin line, I turned my head from the approaching Pete, refusing Luke's insistence on an introduction. Unfortunately, Pete had already zeroed in on me and stopped at our table anyway.

"If it ain't a Cherry. Sweet and juicy, just like I like 'em." Pete chuckled at his long-running joke and tipped his mesh trucker's cap, flapping a curtain of greasy brown hair. Dull olive eyes ran over my t-shirt and back to my face.

"More like tart and tangy," Luke murmured, flashing his dimples.

"Jerk," I mouthed and turned to the bastion of white trash culture. "Pete."

"Haven't seen you in a while. Where you been hiding?" Pete searched my face then gave his eyes free reign to wander over my chest again.

"In a cave," I replied in my flattest tone.

Pete laughed. "You were always a funny one. Too bad Todd left you at the altar. I take that back. Leaves you on the market. Pickings are slim in Halo."

"What?" I straightened in my seat and swung around to face him. "Listen skeez, I don't know where you're getting your information, but I was not left at any altar."

"Don't get your panties in a wad, girl. Can't blame Todd for not wanting to settle so young. Did he leave you with one in the oven?"

The hairs on the back of my neck rose in a rush of anger and my lips pulled back into a snarl.

Before I could shoot a caustic remark, Luke pulled me back into my seat. "Easy now."

Pete blinked at Luke in slow-witted realization that I wasn't alone. "Who're you?"

"Friend of Cherry's. You're Pete? Still working for Mr. Max?" Luke's voice dropped lower. Keeping his eyes on Creepy Pete, he released my arm and rested his hand near mine.

Pete studied Luke with suspicious contempt. "Why you want to know?"

"Heard you were a pretty decent poker player."

"More than pretty decent, according to Mr. Max. I'll probably go pro one of these days."

I snorted.

Luke's hand clasped over mine.

I tried to pull away, but he tightened his grip. Staring at his long fingers curling around my small hand, I drew my foot up his leg.

Feeling my toe against his calf, a lazy smile stretched across Luke's face.

I swung my leg back and smacked him in the shin.

"Pro, huh?" Luke's voice wobbled with surprised pain. Tightening his grasp on my hand, he yanked.

Half my body shot across the table, dragging the hem of my t-shirt across a plate of syrup.

"I guess Mr. Max would know with the money he puts up for games," continued Luke.

Pete nodded noncommittally and watched me press my boots against the back of the booth to regain my balance.

"Todd said he couldn't understand Mr. Max," said Luke. "What kind of accent is it?"

"You got plans for that hand? Because I plan on leaving with it," I hissed.

Pete slid in next to me. "I can understand him. Better than

Dustin did, too. Mr. Max's from one of them Russian type coun-tries. Ain't a Commie though. I made sure of that before I started working for him."

"How patriotic of you," I said.

"Sure am. Max liked to play some dumbass game called Baccarat." Pete leaned back in his seat. "He said it was a little like poker. I said, 'if it's a little like poker, play poker, man.'"

"You can pronounce his last name?" said Luke. "Todd said it was impossible."

"Ain't impossible if you're not an idiot."

"Todd's not an idiot," I spat.

Luke squeezed my hand, making me gasp. He shot me a warning glance, but I burned Pete with my glower anyway.

"Listen, Todd's my boy, but he ain't likely to become a rocket scientist, now is he?" Pete continued, oblivious to our tussle. "Some people call Mr. Max the Bear or just Bear. People in the know."

Luke nodded and relaxed his grip. I wiggled my fingers.

Pete glanced at our hands and my body dangling over the table. "Does Todd know you're seeing this guy?"

His eyes took another trip over my rear swaying over bent legs. They zeroed in on the skin between my raised t-shirt and jeans. "You could really use a tramp stamp. It would enhance your backside in such a way so your ass wouldn't appear so scrawny."

My eyebrows shot to my hairline. "That's it!" I thrust my arms forward and smashed into Luke's chin.

His head jerked back and our hands parted.

I fell forward on the table, knocking over our coffee cups, and landing my chest in the plate of syrup. Pushing up, I grabbed napkins from their metal box holster and shoved Pete with my boot.

"Get out," I commanded.

He scooted off the seat, rubbing his thigh. "You don't have to be so bitchy."

"Perverts bring out my best side." I turned to Luke. "And you can pay the bill for once. You owe me eight years with interest."

"Come on, sugar. That was fun until you punched me."

I dabbed napkins over my sticky shirt until I noticed Pete's interest and flung the wadded paper on the table.

Luke's eyelids lowered. He flashed me a look hot enough to curdle the spilled half-n-half pooling on the table. "You keep showing me a good time, and I'll make it worth your while."

"Never mind, I don't want you paying for me." I dug into my pocket, pulled out a five, and threw it on the table. "I don't know what I'm doing here anyway. I have work to do."

I spun around, bumped into Creepy Pete, and forced myself to walk out the door with my last shred of dignity.

I yanked the door open of my rusty truck and threw myself onto the bench. The wrapped canvas waited beside me.

Priorities, Cherry. I needed to find the Bransons. And change out of my maple infused t-shirt.

Taking a deep breath, I studied the black truck parked next to me. Luke had been in town before the murder, and I hadn't known about it. Virginia had also been nearby, as well as this Mr. Max.

How had methamphetamine labs and underground gambling rings gone without my notice in our tiny town?

And why couldn't I figure Luke?

I grabbed a tissue and took another swipe at my dirty shirt.

More importantly, why couldn't I get through a Luke encounter without wanting to take a baseball bat to his pretty new truck?

SEVEN

REFRESHED and redressed in a fuchsia and lime green camo-print tank top, I pushed a row of multi-hued rubber bangles up my forearm and grasped the corners of Dustin's canvas. I finally found Wanda camped out at JB's dealership office, taking a much-needed hiatus from family and cops.

I started to slide the canvas off the Datsun's bench when I felt someone behind me. Peering over my shoulder, I expected Luke's smirk and almost smacked my elbow on the metal door in surprise.

Ronny Price hung behind me, running his hands over his glossy hair. "Need some help, hon?"

I pivoted forty-five degrees, my left hand still grasping the painting.

Ronny wore a persimmon shirt and a rust colored tie. I had to admire Ronny for his choice in colors that would normally be too flamboyant for Halo. He liked a little bling, and as a car salesman, his panache was practically expected.

"Like the tie, Mr. Price."

He beamed.

"I appreciate your offer," I said. "But the paint is still tacky. I don't want it to stick to the wrapping."

"I'll be careful." He reached across me to grab the edge. "Looks too big for a little girl like you."

The consummate salesman, one who wouldn't take no for an answer.

I don't usually trust my work in other people's hands, but I also didn't want to wrestle him for it in the dealership parking lot. With my luck, I'd end up with paint globs in my hair, the canvas ripped down the middle, and both Bransons as witnesses.

"All right then, if you're careful how you hold it. Can you brace it between your hands without touching the front?"

"Of course." He gave me a salesman smile, better than the one I pulled out for customers. We slid the wrapped canvas out of the truck.

"Oops," I muttered.

Wanda's crumpled bag, smashed under the large painting, threatened to dump off the floor and onto the asphalt. I caught it with my knee, pushed it back on the floor, and slammed the door shut.

Ronny strode across the blacktop toward the dealership entrance.

Grasping the folder with the contract, I scurried after him and opened the door, so he could pass through sideways. We cut through the showroom where new cars rested in sexy poses.

My longing bounced off the tinted windows of a gleaming Mustang. I ran my hand over the robust frame. Stealing a deep whiff of new car smell, I ogled the beauty. A battle between lust and envy broke within me, but the price on the manufacturer's sticker cut the seduction faster than a cold shower.

I gave the trunk a booty smack of admiration and jogged toward the back door.

We traipsed down a friendly apricot colored hallway, passing several tiny sales offices, then a long window with a view into the garage. I squinted into it, trying to catch sight of Cody, but lost him in the sea of coveralls bent over and under vehicles.

Ronny stopped at the end of the hall, waiting for me to catch up. I hurried to open the door, and we stepped into a waiting room.

"Hey Barb," called Ronny.

JB's trusted office manager looked up from her desk and patted her hot-rolled curls.

"Are JB and Wanda inside?" Ronny nodded toward the door she guarded. "Cherry Tucker's here to see them."

Barb smiled. "Hey there, Cherry. Let me just see." She shoved her rolling chair back from a desktop littered with stacked papers and cat statues.

Along with the dealership, JB owned four quick lube shops, a catfish restaurant, and an unknown quantity of silent partnerships in Central-West Georgia. As his personal assistant, Barb Mason piloted the businesses with efficient aplomb from her perch at the dealership. She and twenty porcelain cats.

"Hey, Miss Barb. Nice to see you again."

Barb heaved her round figure from the chair.

My smile disappeared as Ronny thunked the painting on the floor. I darted forward to rescue the canvas from leaning against an armchair. "Thanks for your help, Mr. Price."

"No problemo. Enough with the Mr. Price. I think you're old enough to call me Ronny." He winked and smoothed his hands over his hair before settling into an armchair.

The door to JB's office swung open. Barb leaned her wide posterior against it, waving me in.

I bent forward to palm the large frame's sides.

She pointed toward the painting. "Do you need help with that?"

"No, ma'am." After Ronny's manhandling, I didn't want anyone touching this painting.

Upon entering JB's office, I murmured admiration for the

numerous white tail trophies adorning the walls. Halo grapevine reported the Branson home held even more exotic prizes from hunting trips to Montana and South Africa. I had never seen them, but my relationship with Luke wasn't exactly the take-home-to-Momma kind. Luke didn't share his private home life, and at the time, I didn't care.

After two minutes of carefully unwrapping Dustin's portrait, a stunned silence filled the room. Wanda clutched her sides with tears running rivulets down her face.

"It's amazing," she said. "It's like a work of art."

JB tossed the contract folder on his desk, tipped back in his office chair, and steepled his fingers under his chin.

"Lookee here, Cherry. I admire your gumption, but we can't have you painting our son."

"I don't understand, sir. You said if I finished it for the funeral, you'd consider buying it."

"That was before you tried to rob Dustin."

I clenched the painting before me. "I didn't try to rob Dustin, sir. I did trespass. I admit to that. But only to get a jump start on painting. Cooper's not pressing charges."

"Cooper's not pressing charges, yet," said JB.

Wanda wandered to the window and feigned interest in the parking lot.

"There's talk in town you pulled that crazy stunt to drum up your art business. Playing on folks' sympathy. Get yourself in the newspaper."

"What? Who's saying that? It's a lie. I have the bump on my head to prove it."

"If your story about getting attacked by a burglar is true, why was nothing stolen?"

"But," I stumbled through my words, "how could I hit myself in the head?"

"Shawna said your studio is going under." Wanda spoke to the window, dabbing at her eyes with a tissue. "JB, maybe you're too hard on Cherry. Poverty can make you desperate."

"Shawna said my studio is failing?"

I felt my blood pressure skyrocket and set the painting aside before I inadvertently snapped it in half. Shawna worked fast. I sailed under her radar too long, and the vixen was making up for lost time.

"I've known you practically your whole life, Cherry." Wanda turned her back on the window. "'I'm sure you didn't mean to hurt us."

"You really believe I would tear up a funeral home and desecrate a body for advertisement?" I sucked in my breath. "How could you think such a thing? I went without sleep to work on this painting."

"Unless someone else steps forward, I don't know what to think," said JB. "To be honest, I'm pretty tired of thinking about the whole rigamarole."

He rubbed his temples with his fists and dropped forward in the chair.

I felt a pang of pity for his haggard features and Wanda's puffy eyes. Even if Dustin had fallen to the sins of drugs, their son was dead. Some prank-playing lunatic wasn't allowing them a proper bereavement.

"I will prove that I'm not trying to scam you, sir. And I'm going to finish this painting. Signed, sealed, and delivered by the funeral. You think it's impressive now? Wait until you see it finished."

"Honey," Wanda said. "That's not necessary."

"Oh, it's necessary all right." I jerked my shoulders back and pulled up my chin. "Someone's out to ruin my reputation, and I'm not about to let them. I don't know if the same person broke into your house and Dustin's apartment, but I assure you, it was not me."

"I've got a meeting." JB rose behind his desk. "This painting was your idea, Wanda. You know my feelings." He stalked out of the office.

With a sickened heart, I carefully re-wrapped Dustin.

"It would be a beautiful painting," Wanda said with a teary sigh.

"It will be a beautiful painting. I guarantee it." I swiped the unsigned contract off the desk and stuck the folder under my arm.

"I'm counting on you buying this painting, Miss Wanda. For our agreed price. I won't let you down." With my fingers splayed away from the front, I grasped the sides of the painting.

"We'll see, hon. I want to help you. But if it's true what people are saying about you, JB won't let me pay for that painting."

"Don't you worry about that. I'll figure out what's going on. I can't have folks thinking I'm a grave robber."

Wanda opened the door to the waiting room. I sidled through.

Barb looked up from her computer. Her hand toyed with a cat balanced on top the monitor. "Bye now, Cherry. Please tell your granddaddy I said hello." Barb twirled a finger around a fat brown curl with a disturbing amount of coyness.

I stopped for a double take. "Ma'am?"

"Ed. Please tell him I said hello."

"Will do."

"He doesn't play cards, does he?"

"Ma'am?"

"Cards. My last, uh, male friend played cards every weekend." She pushed a cat to the far end of the monitor. "I heard your Grandpa doesn't play."

"No, Grandpa was never one for games. He spends most his time with goats and fishing, though."

"I see." Barb moved the cat back to its original position and sighed. "Tell Ed I said 'hey' anyhow."

"Yes, ma'am." I beat a hasty retreat out the office, almost trampling Wanda in the process.

In the hallway, a tall, stocky man in ironed chinos and a silk golf shirt huddled with JB and Ronny Price. The three men watched me clomp through the doorway holding the painting. I avoided eye contact with JB as I began the trek back to the showroom.

"Wait a minute, Cherry."

I heard Wanda's sing-song and stopped to pivot back, clasping the frame's awkward size against my chest.

"About the items I gave you."

For a moment, my face must have projected the blank interlude in my thoughts.

"Dustin's special things. For the memory box. I guess you could still do that. It won't have your name on it or anything, will it?"

"No ma'am, I don't sign shadowboxes." I sighed. "I've got Dustin's things in my truck. I was fixing to go through them today. I won't let you down."

I fired off a rapid smile and turned back toward the men blocking the hallway.

Their attention drifted from Wanda to me. The third man raised a magnificent brown eyebrow and studied me with interest. With his massive frame and square jaw, he looked like an offensive lineman dressed for a meeting with the NFL Commissioner. Before I maneuvered through the small crowd, he brushed past me to walk down the hall.

"Come with me, Mr. Price," he growled in a thick accent.

"Mr. Avtaikin?" Ronny called, pushing past me to hurry after the large man.

I took two steps backward, trying to recover from Mr. Avtaikin's jostle. The folder under my arm commenced a slow slide. A stout squeeze pressed the folder into my side but caused my palms to slip from the painting. I jerked a knee underneath to steady the canvas.

A quick glance behind me revealed JB and Wanda hadn't noticed. They had already returned to his office. I hopped toward the wall to recover my hold on the awkward frame while squishing the folder against my side.

I sidled down the hallway with my back against the wall and the painting pushed against my chest like a crab carrying a giant clam. My shoulder blades struck air. I had reached the recessed window for the garage.

Through the window, I glimpsed Cody leaning against a wall, drinking a soda. He faced the garage doors with blank absorption, oblivious to my hard stare. Most likely dreaming of Dustin's Malibu.

I continued my scoot along the wall until a doorknob poked my spine. Bumping my hip against the lever, the door swung open quicker than I expected. I spun to the side and caught the door frame against my shoulder.

The folder dropped from my armpit and the contract splayed across the floor. My knee jerked up and saved the painting from falling, but the other foot landed on a piece of paper that scrunched and ripped beneath my boot.

As I hopped and cursed, I realized I'd interrupted the end of a heated conversation in the small office. Ronny and Mr. Avtaikin gawked without taking the time to wipe the snarls off their faces.

"Sorry," I stuttered. "I lost my grip on the painting."

They stood motionless for a beat before relaxing. Their furious stares had been meant for each other and not for me.

"Perhaps a cart next time is better," the large man said in his heavy accent.

He grabbed my elbow, jerked me to standing, and bent to pick up my ripped contract. Slapping the papers into the fallen folder, he jammed the lot into the back waistband of my jeans.

"Plenty of room in there, I think," he said, giving the folder a pat.

Did he just shove that contract in my panties like it was a twenty at a nudie bar?

"We'll talk later, Price." Mr. Avtaikin lumbered to the showroom door. His large frame and bulky upper body pushed his shoulders forward, making him stoop. He swung open the showroom door without a backward glance.

Ronny ran his hands over his pompadour like he was putting out a fire.

"Tough negotiator." Ronny bleated a short laugh before collapsing in the chair behind the desk.

"What kind of vehicle is he buying?"

"Vehicle?" Ronny studied me as if he'd forgotten I stood in the doorway with a folder stuffed in my back end and a large painting centered on my front.

"I can't imagine it's a Fiesta."

Ronny gave me another deer-in-the-headlights look.

"He's the guy with all the fancy vehicles, right? Cody told me."

"Cody," Ronny pulled the syllables into a long, thoughtful phrase. He popped up from his chair. "I don't know a Cody, but he's right. Mr. Avtaikin is a collector of cars."

"Collector of other things, too." I fished. "Civil War stuff?"

"Have you seen his collection?"

"No, sir. Cody said you talked about his Civil War collection and there was a cannon in his front yard."

"Sure is. I don't think it works, though. Does it make you nervous thinking someone in Halo has a cannon in their yard?"

"Why would that make me nervous?"

"Some women don't like guns. And it's a pretty large piece of artillery."

My eyes twitched, longing to roll in their sockets. Was this a come-on line? What a tool.

"Speaking of that, little lady, you look like you need help." He jumped up to take the painting from me. "I'll get you to your truck."

Remembering his previous mauling of the portrait, I kept my grip on the painting. "I'm fine. I can handle myself."

"Really?" Ronny's fingers stroked his gleaming hair. "I don't mind. I could follow you. Just in case."

"No, thank you." I stepped out of the office and shuffled down the hallway. I didn't need the folder shoved in my pants to keep my back ramrod straight, but it certainly helped.

At the door of the showroom, I leaned against the wall with my knee propped up to hold the painting in place. I managed enough clearance to wedge a shoulder between the door and frame.

Ronny watched with a wrinkled brow.

"See? I can manage just fine."

I grunted and pushed the rest of my body through the door, careful to not let the painting scrape the doorjamb. Trying for casual grace, I minced through the showroom with aching arms and a folder shoved down my pants. Customers gaped. I kept my chin high, my demeanor calm, and managed to avoid walking into any display models. A customer opened the giant glass front door, and I stiff-legged it through the parking lot.

When I reached the Datsun, Ronny stood with his hand on the door handle. He spun around at my approach and smiled.

I regretted my earlier ogling of the shiny Mustang. Slick as a whistle Ronny was going to salesman me until I whipped out a down payment. I don't think he quite understood how little art paid. Especially since I was currently working for free.

"I know you didn't want help, but I thought the least I could do was open your door for you. But it's locked."

I offered him a slow, serious blink and shifted the painting to rest on top of my boots. My hand snuck in the front pocket of my jeans and pulled out my keys. "Can never be too careful."

"Right. I guess you really didn't need my help." His friendly grin sank and his hands fell to his side.

A red hot blush crept up my neck. Good Lord, was he hitting on me?

"That was nice of you anyway," I maneuvered to turn the key in the lock. Grabbing the folder from my pants, I tossed it on the seat of the truck.

"Do you want me to move that bag so you can get the painting in?"

Wanda's crushed shopping bag lay on the truck floor like a used McDonald's sack. He looked at me hopefully. I shook my head. The light dimmed in his eyes again.

"Thanks anyway." I lifted the canvas and steadied it against the bench. Slamming the door closed, I turned to face Ronny and resisted the urge to wrinkle my nose. "See you around."

That would be the last time I compliment a guy on his clothes without thinking of the consequences. He probably thought I was checking him out.

"See you soon." He waved and trudged back to the dealership.

I clambered into the truck. This day had not started well. Shawna was spreading new rumors about me. Maybe her Paintograph business wasn't doing as well as she claimed.

Come to think of it, that ring looked too tacky to be real. Shawna always did have champagne taste on a beer budget.

Maybe she played up her success to hide a giant hole in her checkbook. I wouldn't put it past her to make me look bad, although hitting me in the head pushed the envelope. However, she was a big girl, strong from her trips to the gym.

I rubbed the back of my head. I had no doubt Shawna would set me up, but would she steal from her uncle? Who else would want to make me look bad besides Shawna?

JB feared for his reputation. Luke's behavior bordered on bizarre. Wanda buried her emotions in shopping bags. Virginia wore the trappings of a con artist meth-head. Ronny Price gave me the creeps.

Or maybe I was just at the wrong place at the wrong time.

Just like I had been when I stumbled on Mr. Avtaikin and Ronny. The accent was a dead giveaway. Mr. Avtaikin had to be the infamous Mr. Max. I understood why they called him the Bear, too. He had the manners of a hairy beast.

What had he and Ronny discussed that caused them such a furor? And what was JB's relationship to the Bear?

I turned the key in the ignition. First things first, I needed to finish this painting. And the memory box.

"Cherry," hollered a voice from the parking lot.

I stared into the rearview and saw my baby brother trotting through the crowded lot, waving his hands.

"Wait." He popped the passenger door and glanced at the painting. "Hey."

"Shouldn't you be working?"

"I'm taking a break. You want to run me over to Mather's Tire Shop?"

"Why aren't you running yourself over to Mather's? For that matter, don't you have tires at the dealership?"

"I don't need tires." Cody lifted the painting and slid under it, kicking Wanda's bag into a corner. "I want to see that Malibu. I thought you could drive me. I can walk over to Shortie's BBQ after. Some of the boys are meeting there for lunch. I'll catch a ride back."

"Be careful with the painting. It's still a little wet." I puffed myself into big sister mode. "You're almost out of gas, aren't you? And what kind of mechanic gets a break from now till lunch? I didn't see you busting your butt in the shop."

"Stop your henpecking." Cody slid a worn Dewalt cap over his eyes and settled the painting on his lap, further hiding his face from view. "Is this the dead guy painting? Is that why you walked through the showroom like you worked the wrong side of a pole? Terry Reynolds saw you and told everyone."

"That's all I need. I'm sure Terry Reynolds does a lovely imitation of me walking with a folder shoved down my pants."

I glared into the sunlight. If this town remained fixated on me, I'd have to draw a few of the Branson issues into my spotlight.

Starting with the joker breaking into Dustin-related residences, who might be a murderer.

EIGHT

CURTIS MATHER'S TIRE SHOP occupied a corner of Highway 19 and Oak Leaf Road, a good location gone to waste.

Mather's is one of those shops few people seem to use but still stays in business. The only colors decorating the gray cinderblock building's lot were from various vehicles parked helter-skelter. Stacks of tires helped to hide the trash and pools of miscellaneous liquid that never seemed to evaporate on the dirty concrete.

Cody hopped from the truck, completely in his element. His nose quivered like Peter Rabbit's in McGregor's garden, and he almost ran through the open doors of the garage.

My nose seized at the noxious mixture of diesel and rubber. I readjusted the painting on the truck seat, throwing a look of regret at the now ragged lump that was Wanda's shopping bag.

However, I was as curious as Cody to enter the shop. I didn't care about the Malibu. I wanted to see the spot where Dustin had been offed. Judging by the crowded lot, other locals had a similar interest. It seemed Curtis Mather might capitalize from Dustin's notoriety.

It took a minute for my eyes to adjust to the dim interior of the shop after the blinding sunshine and I shaded my eyes in the entrance of a raised garage door.

Curtis Mather stood a few paces away in gray coveralls, wiping his hands with a dingy cloth. He ran the grubby rag over his shiny head, leaving a streak of grease behind, and stuck a hand in my direction.

I grasped the slippery fingers with hesitation but gave him a hearty shake anyway. Curtis Mather may be the local Pigpen, but he seemed friendly enough.

"Ma'am." He beamed a toothy smile.

"I'm Cherry Tucker. I thought my brother, Cody, came in here?"

A quick glance showed vehicles filled the three bays. However, Cody and the Malibu remained to be seen.

"Ah," he replied, stuffing the rag into his back pocket. "He went round to the back. Interested in the 'Bu. It's back there."

"I'm surprised it's still here. Didn't JB take it home with him?"

"Naw. Didn't want nothin' to do with it. Told me to keep it for my distress under the circumstances." He snorted. "Didn't even come down to check on it or to see where his boy was killed. Pretty cold, but then the boy gave him enough trouble, I suppose."

Wandering to a rolling metal cabinet, he opened a narrow drawer. His hands drifted over the tools and he grabbed a tiny screwdriver.

"I told your Cody I'd sell it to him if he's interested."

Curtis shot a cool look at me, assessing our capital worth under thinning eyebrows. Easing onto a stool, he began cleaning his nails with the flat end of the screwdriver.

"It's a '77. Got a 2300 Holley carburetor. Engine's not done, but Dustin put on a new gas tank. I could get a good price on the Autotrader, but I need the space. Business is picked up lately."

"I saw that." I wasn't going to do Cody's negotiating for a car he didn't need, so I changed the subject. "I guess a lot of people are interested in Dustin Branson's death."

"Mmhm." He pointed the screwdriver toward the far bay. "Happened over there on t'end. Police finally took off that damned yaller tape and let me get back to work over there. Just in time, too. Can't believe how many people need rotations and oil changes this week."

I wandered toward the pit where a blue GMC sat on the lifts. "It doesn't bother you to work where he was murdered?"

"Naw." I turned to find Curtis Mather watching me. He ducked his head and began work on his other nails. "He's just dead, is all. The good Lord deals with him now. Had to clean up some mess though. And now I'm missing a boy. 'Course that Dustin, he weren't much on working anyway."

I wished I could be as complacent about life's trials as Curtis Mather. I circled the truck but could see no evidence of a grisly murder here. It looked like any other dirty garage floor.

"Except my wrench."

"Sir?"

"I wished I could get the wrench back."

I waited for him to continue, but his dirty nails captured his attention. "What wrench?"

He looked up and fixed me with clear blue eyes. "My torque wrench that sumbitch killed the boy with. You think when they catch him, the police will get my wrench?"

"I thought they didn't know what the killer used to hit Dustin?"

"Got to be my torque wrench," Curtis Mather sputtered. "It's missing, ain't it? Don't take two and two to know that sumbitch must of hit the boy with my torque wrench, then."

I glanced around the garage with its sticky floors and grungy walls.

Curtis Mather followed my glance but pointed toward the open drawer of gleaming screwdrivers.

"I'd know if my tools was missing. That's what I told the sheriff," he added with a defensive nod. "A monkey could figure that out. Dustin were working on restoring that Malibu. Only reason he'd show up for work most days. At the time, Dustin must've been changing the oil. Found the socket wrench and the plug underneath him.

"As I figure it, Dustin's working that wrench, loosening the oil plug, when that sumbitch picked up my torque wrench and popped Dustin on his noggin. Let all that oil drain all over Dustin, too. What a mess."

He shook his head. "Couldn't even bring his own weapon."

I couldn't tell what angered Curtis Mather more, the gall of the killer to take an innocent life or stealing his wrench.

"At first, maybe they thought it was an accident. But you don't get your head split in two from changing oil. I told the sheriff that, too."

"I guess someone must have been pretty angry with Dustin."

"Well." Curtis scratched the grease spot on his head, smearing it further. "That boy had a mouth on him. Pretty sneaky, too. I probably should've fired him, but never got round to it. I figure he got himself messed in something pretty bad. I don't know nothing about it, though. Not my business."

"Yes, sir." See no evil, speak no evil, get in no trouble with the sheriff.

"Say, that brother of yours. He play poker? We have a friendly Texas Hold'em sometimes meets."

I shook my head. That's all Cody needed, another way to lose money.

"How about you? We could use some fresh blood. Just some old geezers, but you'd give us something nice to look at while we pass the cards."

I smiled my sweetest. "I lost one man to gambling and don't plan on wasting any more Saturday nights with a bunch of men who think sitting on their butts for hours on end staring at the same fifty-two pictures is the best thing since sliced bread."

Curtis' shocked look brought me up short.

"Sorry. I've got personal issues with poker. But thanks for asking."

I grabbed the doorknob of the heavy metal back door and

heaved it open. My brother leaned over the open hood of a beefy buttercream car with a white Landau top.

Cody glanced at me and whistled. "Pretty, ain't she?" He released the hood from the prop rod but held it overhead for a last look at the car's internals.

I had yet to see him gaze at a girl like that.

"How did Dustin end up with a classic like this?"

"I don't know." Cody caught the falling hood in his hands before gently dropping it in place. "Don't care. I've got to have this car. Swivel bucket seats. Love to take a date in that."

"Yeah, real romantic. One problem. You don't have the money for it. Did you tell Mr. Mather that?"

He waved his hand at unimportant considerations like money. "We'll work something out. He mentioned needing a mechanic. Maybe he'd let me take it out of my paychecks."

"You've got a good job at the dealership. This place can't keep you in cars. Soon as the gossip about Dustin's murder wears off, people aren't going to need new tires from Curtis Mather."

I pinched the bridge of my nose to keep from smacking him. "Don't make any dumb decisions."

He raised his brows and smirked. "Like going to Vegas and getting talked into a wedding?"

"I'm about done with that old joke. Hope you find out the block's cracked."

AFTERNOON SUNSHINE POURED through my living room picture window and spread over the easel where Dustin's unfinished painting rested. A palette of mixed colors, a jar of water, and an assortment of brushes waited on an elderly walnut end table draped in a paint-speckled cloth. A thin whine of electric guitar, a heavy bass, and drums thrummed through my iPod. Cold beer lingered in the avocado-green fridge in the kitchen.

I stood in bare feet surveying my domain with a smile.

"I think you need to touch up the paint on your sign outside," said Shawna, strolling through my front door with nary a knock. "Looks a little faded."

Pursing her glossed lips, Shawna swept her gaze over the living room I had converted to a studio.

The bright sunlight highlighted the cracks in the plaster walls and paint dribbles on the old varnish of the ninety-year old wooden floors. Framing samples stacked against one wall hid a scorched hole that once was an outlet. Luckily, my gallery of ten by ten canvases of friends and family covered the oozy spots on the wall backing the kitchen.

It could be worse. When I moved in, we found a family of chipmunks living in a cabinet next to the fridge.

And Casey wonders why I don't cook.

"Actually, why bother?" she said. "This house should be condemned. When you get a real job, you should get a new place."

"What do you want, Shawna?"

She wandered over to the fainting couch that sat beneath my gallery wall and toed the claw foot with a wedge slingback. "Do you really like the whole grubby bohemian chic thing or this a statement of your expense account?"

"That's an antique. I'm going to recover it. It's a classic."

"Like your truck?" She stared at the portraits adorning the wall and tapped her chin with a French-tipped nail. "I don't see Luke in this collection. I got the feeling y'all had known each other once upon a time."

"We're familiar." I stalked to my easel.

While she eyeballed the paintings, I tossed a wet cloth over the paints and a sheet over Dustin's portrait. Crossing my arms, I stood wide legged with a foot pointing toward the door and waited for Shawna to get to the point.

"He spends a lot of time driving around Halo," she said and wandered to my battered roll-top desk. She flicked imaginary dust off the edge and leaned against it, crossing her long legs at the ankles. The dark cropped pants and billowy, sheer top suited her. I tightened my arms across the paint-splattered wife-beater I wore for painting.

"Does he? Maybe he's trying to wear in the tires on that new truck."

"I think he's looking for somebody."

"What do you want me to tell you, Shawna? I don't keep tabs on Luke."

"It's almost time for the visitation. You'd think he'd want to hang out with the family. Dustin's mother showed up today and made a whole big ruckus."

"Can you tell me what's on your mind? I'm kind of busy. I'm sure you didn't come over to shoot the breeze."

"You got any tea? I'm dry as a bone."

My curiosity kept me from overthrowing Grandma Jo's breeding. Cracking open the ancient fridge, I heard thumping sounds drift from the living room. I snuck back to the living room archway and glimpsed Shawna pawing through the drawers of my desk.

I thought about interrupting her search, but the roll-top only housed art supplies. Jars and bottles of paint occupied the deep bottom drawers. The desk didn't hold much interest unless she came to borrow a cup of gesso.

Scurrying back to the fridge, I fixed a glass of tea and ambled into the living room.

Shawna sat perched on the faded quilt covering the old divan.

"Thank you." She took the mason jar I offered. I had regular glasses, but I figured I'd play into the redneck theme. "Mercy, you make some good tea."

"Thank you," I replied in my sweetest drawl. "The key is making sure the sugar dissolves when you brew it."

I had no idea if I spoke the truth, but it sounded good. Casey always made the tea at Grandpa's house. This jug bore the TruBuy label.

Grabbing a stool near the easel, I plunked it before the couch. "So what brings you by, Shawna?"

I crossed a leg over my knee and studied the she-devil

disguised as a debutante. "Did you want to sabotage my painting like you did the other night at Cooper's? What'd you do while I was in the kitchen? Spray paint on my canvas?"

Sweet tea shot out her nose. "I did no such thing."

"Must of crossed your mind or the tea would've stayed down." I hopped off my stool and crossed the room to the canvas sitting on the easel. Pulling off the sheet, I studied the painting. "Guess I didn't give you enough time. Of course, you didn't knock me out today."

"I wasn't going to sabotage your painting. How could you accuse me of such a thing?"

"Then why were you looking through my desk?"

"I wasn't looking..." She stopped. "I wanted to see if the joints were dove-tailed. It looks like an antique."

"Bull hockey." My eyes narrowed. "Fess up."

"Where's Dustin stuff? I want to see what you're doing for the shadow box."

"Why?" I thought of the crumpled bag in my truck with guilt. I barely skimmed through the sack the day before. Other than a few glitzy pieces of jewelry, the collection comprised of old toys and high school treasures.

"I heard Aunt Wanda telling folks about it. Virginia Spring-houser claims she should have Dustin's effects, and she hit the roof when Aunt Wanda told her about the memory box. That was after that guy came to the house, asking if he could take a look at Dustin's room."

"Who was this other guy?" Somewhere within my central nervous system, something pinged and my nerve endings stood on high alert.

"I don't know. Big guy with an accent. Said he was Dustin's boss." She matched my surly look. "I didn't realize she gave you the shadow box job."

"It's none of your business. That's between me and Miss Wanda."

"Dustin took some stuff from me, and I want it back."

My eyebrows took a trip to the top of my forehead. "Tell me what it is and I'll let you know if I have them."

"Just some old photos," she said, finding sudden interest in her nails. "Where's Dustin's things? I'll take a quick look. I didn't mean to interrupt."

"I don't have Dustin's collection here. You talk to Miss Wanda and ask her if the photos were included."

"I can't do that." A fiery blush licked her cheeks and crept up her face, the unfortunate consequence of fair skin. The red did make her blue-green eyes pop.

"Then I guess you're out of luck."

"You're the one out of luck," she hissed. "No way will I let you have that commission. I need JB's support to get Paintographs licensed and trademarked."

"Shawna, you can do that on your own. You're just trying to ruin my studio business."

"You and your high and mighty art crap. You didn't deserve that Rotary scholarship. You didn't even go to a real school."

"What in the hell are you talking about?"

"I'm talking about you trying to one-up me since high school. I'm a Branson. You're nothing. Your momma didn't even want you. Give me Dustin's stuff. I need those photos. Now."

"You need to leave," I said, crossing to the door. "Now."

"I'll be back." She strode to the doorway. "I peeked at your stupid masterpiece. It's not so special. You didn't even make Dustin look like an angel."

"Angel view, dummy."

"And you suck at making tea." She wrinkled her nose. "It tasted funny."

I slammed the door on her back and ran through the living room to the back kitchen door leading into my carport.

Sneaking between sawhorse tables piled with junk, I waited until Shawna drove off in her yellow Mustang and eased open the truck door to grab the crumpled shopping bag. I rummaged through the items, looking for photos. I hoped to find Shawna in some compromising position, but that'd be a weird thing to include in a memorial shadow box.

Though I couldn't imagine what snapshot would necessitate her breaking into people's homes.

The phone rang and I ignored it.

A shoebox looked promising, but it mostly held random jewelry, high school medals, and two Matchbox cars.

No photos.

I tossed the shoebox back in the bag and leaned against the truck. While I'd been ignoring the memory box, both Virginia and Mr. Max had expressed interest in Dustin's possessions. And now Shawna. Could one of them have broken into the Branson house or Dustin's apartment or the funeral home? Shawna almost admitted to sabotaging my painting so she could secure the commission. She still figured high on my suspect list, especially after that drama-queen outburst.

I zipped back into the living room and studied the portrait again. Nothing seemed amiss. I scanned the area around the easel. A corner of something white poked out from under the cloth-draped table.

I lifted the paint-splattered cloth. A tube of Alizarin Crimson lay crumpled on the floor. Sucking in my breath, I yanked the paper-towel off the palette. Gobs of red paint had been mashed into my prepared mixes with a good sable brush, now ruined. And a new round brush I used for detail work was missing.

"That bitch," I said to Dustin the painting. "At least she didn't touch you. I shouldn't have turned my back on her. She worked fast."

I snorted. But so did I. Her tea tasted funny because I spiked it with ipecac syrup.

Before I could cross the room to clean my palette, my phone rang again. Stomping to the roll-top, I checked the phone. Casey. I watched the face of the phone for the voicemail sign to pop up.

No voicemail.

I glanced over my shoulder at the painting. The phone buzzed on the desktop a third time.

"I need a ride to work," said Casey when I finally answered.

"Last time I checked, that's not my problem."

"Come on, Cherry. Cody took my car, and he's not back yet."

"Cody is running your car on gas fumes? Where's Grandpa?"

"Fishing. Been gone all day."

"And Cody's car?"

"Something about flushing the radiator and he forgot to buy coolant. The hood is up and a pan sitting underneath it. He left it to finish. That was three days ago."

"He better not have left old coolant sitting out. If Tater drinks it, it could kill him."

Casey yawned. "Naw. Grandpa already yelled at him to get rid of it. Tater's just fine. Eating the blueberry bushes as we speak."

"When do you have to be at Red's?"

"Five o'clock."

I heaved a deep sigh. That was a little over an hour. I could start work on painting, but I'd spend much of that time remixing the paint Shawna ruined. "I have an idea. I need to work on the memory box anyway. I'll bring it over, and you can help me sort the stuff."

"Deal," she said. "I'll get you some wings or something at Red's to pay you back."

My stomach heard "wings" and spasmed with joy. I changed out of my painting clothes and scooted out the door with a final look at the portrait.

"Looks like I'll be painting you in the dark once again, Dustin." I thought for a minute. "Maybe Casey and I better take a hard look through your stuff while we're at it. I'd love to find some nekkid pictures of Shawna in *flagrante delicto*. That would make this day so much better."

IMPATIENCE RODE the gas pedal to the farm.

My timeliness was rewarded with Tater galloping toward me. His stiff tail wagged at the yellow truck's entrance.

With brakes pumping, the Datsun shimmied into a crawl down the long gravel lane. The large goat crisscrossed the drive before me, bleating joyously. We continued our game of chicken, creeping toward the house.

I jammed the gearshift into park and laid on the horn. Two white hooves slammed against my driver side window, and a narrow white head followed. I waited for Tater to finish licking the window and eased open the door.

Before I could get a foot on the ground, he pushed his giant head through the open door and stood on his hind legs, shoving his front end onto my lap.

"No! Stay out of the truck."

Tater answered by pushing his bent front legs against my belly to catapult his back end through the door.

I grunted, grabbing my stomach. Back hooves whizzed past my face. I slid out the door, landing on my knees in the gravel drive.

Tater pranced across the bench, his head and shoulders stooping to fit in the truck.

"Tater. Get out of there." I waved a hand through the open door.

Tater danced to the other end of the bench. Muddy hoof prints spotted the seat. I glanced down and saw muddy prints marking my tank top.

"Dangit."

I yanked open the passenger door, hauled Tater out, and grabbed Wanda's shopping bag.

Inside the house, I snagged a kitchen towel. "Casey," I called from the empty kitchen, mopping my bright camo tank with the wet towel. Two smeared prints remained just under my breasts.

"That's just great."

Trying to ignore the clammy feeling of the wet tank top, I focused on the shopping bag contents I dumped on the kitchen table. Dustin's collection — Miss Wanda's choices for Dustin's collection — didn't resemble the Dustin I knew. The private impression of Dustin could be different than the public, but I feared Wanda chose items that seemed valuable or nostalgic without knowing what they meant to him.

"What's all this?" Casey wandered in from the living room and snagged a diet soda from the fridge. "Dustin's knickknacks?"

"Looks like Dustin had some awards for wrestling."

"I don't remember him wrestling." Casey took a deep drink from the can and sank in a chair. "And I knew the wrestlers pretty well in high school. Maybe he stole it from Luke. How's Luke at wrestling, Cherry? He still pretty good?"

"I wouldn't know."

"Cody said you looked pretty hot and heavy in the Waffle Hut parking lot."

"If you call a kiss on the forehead hot and heavy," I grumbled, spreading out the loot on the table.

Casey snorted.

"There's also some Transformers with L.H. painted on the bottom, obviously Luke's. Now, this class ring has the correct graduating year. I can use that." I moved the ring to a separate pile.

"A Pink Pig piggy bank," said Casey. She grabbed the bank and shook it. "Something's in here. You remember riding the Pink Pig at Rich's Department Store in Atlanta?"

"I barely remember. We must have been pretty young."

I fingered a heavy silver belt buckle studded with turquoise. Another large silver buckle incised with filigree had a bas-relief lion's head and what looked like ruby eyes. A shabby stuffed dog lay next to the shoebox.

"I don't know how Wanda wants me to fit all this in a shadow box. That dog is too big, and there's a ton of little things. I'm going to have to build a lot of tiny shelves or look for a readymade. Maybe a printer's drawer."

I began to replace the smaller items in the shoe box. "I hate to bring it up with her, but I'm wondering if any of this stuff is really his."

"What do you mean?"

"Look at the belt buckles. I don't know much about them, but they look expensive. Do you think Dustin would have bought them?"

"Not sure. Lots of guys wear blingy buckles now." She pointed to the turquoise and silver buckle. "This one looks a little cowboyish for a guy like Dustin, but the other one is cool."

Casey picked up the large buckle with the sculpted lion's head. "Wow, it's heavy." She stuffed her t-shirt into the front of her jeans and held the buckle to her button fly. "How's it look?"

"Expensive." I plucked it from her hand and tossed it in the shoebox.

"Ooh, a Pound Puppy. I had one of these." Casey snatched the brown and tan dog and squeezed it against her chest.

"Give me that."

"Wait a minute," Casey said. "This dog has something in it. I can feel it through the stuffing."

She placed it on the table, and we kneaded the Pound Puppy with our fingertips.

"I feel it, too. Flip it over."

The loose stitching on the belly made it easy to manipulate a hole big enough to feel inside. I curved a finger into the stuffing and pulled out a thin wooden pipe with a metal bowl and Zigzag papers.

"Guess we found his stash."

"Anything else in there?" Casey picked up the pipe and smelled the bowl while I ran my fingers inside the puppy.

"No." I sat with my chin in hand and watched Casey. "You think I ought to show this to Uncle Will?"

"Maybe. But I thought Grandpa said the police went through his things already."

"These were Dustin's effects that Wanda collected after their search. I think it was in his bedroom at the Branson house, not his apartment. You think they could have missed this?"

"Dunno." Casey shoved the paraphernalia back into the toy

dog. "It's not like a pipe and papers is that big of a deal anymore. If there were weed in there, the police would have confiscated it."

"You're probably right. I'll set the dog aside, just in case. The other items, I'm not so sure about. If the police searched Dustin's belongings and Wanda chose these things, I'd think it'd be safe to put them in the shadowbox. Wouldn't you think?"

"What are you getting at?"

"If I hand over Dustin's possessions to Uncle Will, he would know I have another job for the Bransons. And I need the job. And Will won't want me to do it."

"Are you not a grown woman?"

"You don't understand. He'll probably seize the stuff as sheriff. He's pretty ticked I snuck in Cooper's to work on the portrait. I can't let him know about this. I'm going to assume the police saw these goods and passed on it."

"I need to get ready for work." Casey hopped up from her seat. "You play with the toys, and I'll be back in a minute."

I nodded and grabbed the piggy bank. Sliding my fingers under the rubber stopper on the bottom, I popped out the plug. Jewelry and coins spilled on the table.

"Good Lord," I called to the back of the house. "I think Dustin was a pirate."

I gave the pig a final shake and skimmed my fingers inside the ceramic, feeling for any stuck objects. The pig hid no photos. I grabbed the dog and searched it once again.

"Dang. I was really hoping for something. Even one of those little digital memory cards." I tossed the dog in the shopping bag.

"Wha'd you say?" Casey sauntered through the living room doorway in a tight black t-shirt with County Line Tap printed across her chest. She carried a pair of sneakers in one hand.

"I'm looking for blackmail items and I don't see any here." I gawked at my sister. "What are you wearing?"

"What do you think?" She spun in a slow circle so I could get the full effect of the litter of brown curls erupting from the top of her head. A spiked, metal cuff gathered the fountain of glossy ringlets on her crown. Spiked leather collars circled her neck and wrists, and a studded belt cinched her skimpy Daisy Duke's.

"I think fishing saved Grandpa from a heart attack." I gathered up the rest of the shopping bag memorabilia. "We're going to be late. Let's hope the effect keeps you from getting fired. At least you'll count on good tips."

"That's the idea," Casey sang, banging the screen door open with her hip as she slipped on her shoes.

"Avoid bending over if you can help it." I caught the screen door and froze at my sister's piercing shriek.

"Tater's in your truck bed," Casey screamed. "Help me haul him out. I'm late."

"I hate that goat." I pounded down the porch stairs to my truck, leaving the bag behind. "I swear I'm using him for gyros one of these days."

NINE

RED TAPPED ON HIS WATCH, shaking his head at Casey as we traipsed into the County Line Tap.

"Not my fault." Casey scooted toward the kitchen before Red could argue.

His frown deepened within his rusty beard. The sharp eyes watched Casey's hip action as she bumped through the swinging door. I slid onto a barstool before him. He turned his freckled face toward me with a moan.

"Your sister drives me crazy," he said. "Good thing the customers like her."

"I feel your pain." I studied the bright green eyes. "But she's harmless. Like you said, the customers like her."

Red and I shared a sigh born of ten years acquaintance. I started sneaking into County Line Tap when it was just an old dive bar positioned two feet off the old town line. Young Red kicked my skinny, under-aged butt right out of the bar. I had an obsession with karaoke then and didn't feel the law applied when you weren't going to drink.

He admired my persistence. I admired his patience. And I had a grand twenty-first birthday with Red tending bar.

Red ran a hand through his thick ginger hair and scratched his beard. "Anyway." The hand smacked the wooden bar. "What'll you have?"

"Since I'm here, the usual."

I turned on my stool to survey the dim room. Flat screen TVs and local sports memorabilia, including a narrow shelf of trophies for the County Line's baseball team, covered the long beige walls.

In my opinion, Red's cried out for interior resuscitation. Hopper's *Nighthawks* diner portrayed better decor. When he bought the tavern and revamped it into a sports bar, Red cashed out his interest in interior design other than adding a new trophy to his shelf each fall.

At the far end of the room, Red had erected a short black platform. On this simple stage rested amplifiers, microphone stands, and a drum kit with STICKS painted in florescent orange across the face of the sparkling bass drum.

I had almost forgotten I promised Todd I would watch Sticks' debut performance the following night. He hinted at a song or two written for me. After participating in the "what rhymes with" conversation with Todd in the past, I didn't have high expectations for his new repertoire of songs.

Red's attention fixated on Casey, as did the two-top she currently graced. She turned from taking the table's order and waggled back to the kitchen with the men's eyes glued to her shorts. I could feel Grandma Jo rolling in her grave.

"What in the hell is she wearing?" Red grabbed a glass and thrust it under a tap, tilting the mug as the golden liquid began to froth. He slid the beer toward me.

"Oh, you know Casey." My finger traced a snowflake design in the mug's layer of frost. "Anyway, what's going on with you? Looks like you're going to have Sticks in here regularly?"

Red sighed and cupped a hand under his chin to lean on the bar. He watched me take a tentative sip of beer and then a larger gulp. "We'll see. They sound pretty good, but I told Todd it depended on the customers."

"He'd better hope for women customers then."

"I saw his new tattoo." Red snorted. "Nice cherries."

"Don't start with me."

"I didn't think you could do it."

"Do what?"

"Settle down."

"With Todd?" Beer threatened to foam out my nose.

"You don't fool me." Red dropped his arm and touched my hand. "Todd's a nice guy and thinks the world of you. He's a lot smarter than he lets on. You could do a lot worse."

"It is nice to be appreciated."

"He adores you. I don't believe what everyone is saying. I think you pushed him away."

"What's everybody saying about me?"

Red patted my hand. "I understand your family problems. But you're not the only one who has a no-show for a mother. Look at this Dustin who got himself killed. I've seen his momma in here, and she's total trash. You Tucker kids do pretty well. Don't let your mother issues ruin your chance at happiness."

"What in the hell are you talking about?" I snatched my hand away. "What's everybody saying about me?"

"All I'm saying is you should have given Todd a chance. I heard how he jilted you and that whole business of you tearing up Las Vegas in your wedding dress to find him, begging him to come back. But I know you. You must have pushed him away. I saw this show about self-sabotage—"

"WHAT?"

"Self-sabotage." Red grabbed his bar rag and mopped up my spilled beer. "It's when a person does something subconsciously to ruin their chance at—"

"I know what self-sabotage is," I said through gritted teeth. "Did you say you heard I tore up Las Vegas in a wedding dress to beg Todd to marry me?"

Red shrugged. "That's what's going round."

I pushed off the stool-rest with both feet and jumped to the ground. "I'm going to kill Todd."

"Don't blame Todd. Don't be a victim to yourself."

"Stick to watching the Braves. I don't think those celebrity rehab shows are doing you any favors." I aimed for the door and spun back, grabbing the bar to keep myself upright. "Wait a minute. Did you say Dustin's mother was in here? Virginia?"

"Yeah," said Red, shaking off my abrupt change with a slow eye blink. "She used to meet Dustin here occasionally. I thought they might be dealing in the parking lot, though, so I had to run them off."

"Wow. I had no idea."

"That's good. I don't want County Line to get a bad reputation. I count on families coming in for the hot wings as much as I do the drinkers."

"Do you think Dustin got killed because of dealing drugs? Grandpa thinks so."

"Wouldn't put it past him."

"Thanks for the beer." I polished off the mug and slid it to Red. "I've got to go home and paint." I turned toward the exit.

Casey grabbed my arm. "I've got those wings for you." She guided me to a table. "Just wait here. If you stay long enough, you can give me a ride home."

"Come on, Case. That means I'll be here all night."

She placed another mug before me. "This'll keep you quiet for a little bit."

"I can't sit here and drink beer until closing. I've got to get home and finish a painting."

"Whatever. I can hear your stomach pitching a fit. Just wait for the wings."

I did want the wings. Leaning back in my chair, I kicked my feet up on the rungs of the chair opposite.

My table offered a complete view of the narrow room. I watched the families eating dinner for a moment. Kids climbed over their chairs and chattered while their mothers picked at abandoned french fries. The fathers' eyes zeroed in on the Braves game.

Near the little stage, a party of seven women worked on margaritas and wine, ignoring their nachos and wings. They wore the pastel scrubs of nurses or assistants at local doctor offices. I enjoyed watching their camaraderie for a moment and wondered what it would be like to go out for Thursday night drinks after work.

I nursed the beer. A lonely feeling knocked at my door. I recognized that feeling and told myself to cut it out.

That was the feeling that almost got me married to Todd.

At the bar, Red resumed his friendly bartender persona, snapping his towel while he told a joke to a burly man in camouflage pants and a Bass Pro t-shirt. My eyes trailed past him to two guys at the far end of the bar huddled around a video game. Creepy Pete's had removed his trucker cap, but the bushy goatee and long hair were easy to spot.

I recognized the other guy as Jackson, Todd and Pete's other roommate. Jackson worked a regular nine-to-five for a local exterminator company. He had a nice personality and wasn't bad looking — clean cut, medium build, wire glasses — but he faded into the background around the lusty likeability of Todd and disturbing nature of Pete. Maybe Jackson hung around them to soak in the weird limelight that accompanied guys like Todd and Pete.

Maybe Jackson couldn't find other roommates.

Now, why would Mr. Max hire guys like Dustin and Pete? It wasn't like they were reliable or smart. Or even personable, for that matter.

But guys like Pete and Dustin sought respect and money the easiest way possible. Mr. Max probably found them easy recruits for his questionable business activities. My concern centered on Todd and the other good people in Halo who could get pulled into Mr. Max's orbit. Men like him would chew up and spit out a sweet bonehead like Todd. Dustin's murder had already tainted our little town.

I swigged my beer, feeling a surge of outrage at this foreign interloper. Shoving away from the table, I wandered to the bar.

Red washed glasses with his eyes on the Braves game.

"Hey," I said and leaned on the bar between Mr. Bass Pro Shop and Todd's roommates.

Mr. Bass Pro Shop glanced at me, extending a smile over his ruddy cheeks. His eyes took a short trip over my fuchsia tank top and jeans and back to my face.

"What're you drinking, hon?"

I raised an eyebrow and considered the round belly perched against the counter for lack of room and the scuffed work boots that dripped dried mud under his stool. He'd probably keep someone happy in deer sausage, but I wasn't interested. I shifted a quarter-turn to face the other side of the bar.

Red hopped forward in a protective quickstep. "What do you need, Cherry?"

"Cherry? I like that name."

I eyed the hairy man over my shoulder. "No thanks, but glad you like Cherry. My daddy named me after his favorite gun."

Bass Pro's attention fell back to his beer.

I turned back to Red and leaned closer, pointing my mug toward the far end of the bar. "When'd you get that? Is it poker?"

Red glanced at the guys and back to me. He grabbed another wet glass. "That video game? Got it about a week ago. Local guy sells them. It's got poker, trivia, and some other games on it."

"Does it pay out?"

"Are you crazy? I'd get busted for that. If they're doing that on their own, I don't know anything about it."

"Some of them pay out."

"Sure, I think the Quik Stop may, but I'm not that stupid. The laws are tricky about the amount, and I'm not losing my business over a game. What's with all the questions?"

"It's nothing. I'm just curious."

"You know what they say about curiosity and the cat."

I studied Pete and Jackson for a long moment and wrinkled my nose at the idea of talking to Creepy Pete. But I wanted to know more about Mr. Max, the Bear, or whatever he was called.

If it meant putting up with Creepy Pete, so be it. Luke wasn't the only one that could ask a few questions.

I carried my beer to the end of the bar. Slipping past Jackson, I placed myself before the video game. "Now what's going on here?"

"You're blocking our view," Pete groused.

"Hey, Cherry," Jackson said. "What're you doing here?"

"I drove Casey to work. I'm just waiting on some food." I studied the video monitor. Five playing cards blinked above a table of numbers. I puckered my mouth at the unimpressive screen. "This is what you guys are doing? How about a game where you can shoot something? At least there's skill in that."

Jackson chuckled. "Haven't seen you in a while. Sorry to hear about you and Todd."

"Don't worry about me and Todd. We're still friends."

Jackson nodded with a nervous glance toward Pete.

Tonight he wore a black concert t-shirt and faded jeans that engulfed his legs. A large rope of fake gold circled his neck and another hung off his right wrist.

"Move it, Cherry," said Pete.

"What's the rush? You were pretty chatty this morning. Run out of words?"

Pete licked his lips and flipped his hair behind his shoulders. "You didn't seem so friendly then. My leg's still sore where you kicked me."

"I was having a private conversation when you walked up and started insulting me. Is that a nice way to start my day?"

"Where's the guy you were with?" Pete's scowl lifted into a sly smile. "You socked him a good one. Got him whipped pretty good, huh?"

"You kicked Pete and hit a guy?" said Jackson.

"Pete exaggerates." I tipped a shoulder up. "I met your Mr. Max today. What's his deal?"

"Why are you so interested?"

I stepped closer to Pete, skimming my back against the bar. "Had a little run-in with the Bear at JB's dealership. He's missing some manners."

Pete shrugged.

"I heard he collects a lot of antique stuff. And runs games for bigwigs with a huge pot."

Pete glanced around and started nudging me toward the wall.

"Dustin was his right-hand man, not you?"

"Keep it down, woman." Pete grasped my elbow.

I whipped my arm away. "Don't call me that."

We cornered ourselves in a niche between the end of the bar and front door, out of earshot from Jackson. He watched us for a moment, thought better of joining, and turned back to the video game.

"You don't like being called woman? You're so picky. No wonder Todd gave you the boot. Probably likes his cherries sweeter." His eyes skimmed over my body. "Hope my boy got some good mileage out of you before he turned you in."

"Watch your mouth."

"Why are you so interested in my boss?"

"Because I'm painting your dead friend and it makes me wonder who split his skull, that's why. Don't you want justice?" I placed one hand on my hip and positioned my beer mug between us.

"I don't know nothing about it. I already told the cops that."

"But you know something about Mr. Max," I persisted.

"Mr. Max has a lot of different businesses. Some of it's import and export. Some gaming equipment like this one here in the bar."

"Gaming equipment? What about drugs?"

"Drugs?"

"I thought I heard Dustin's murder was related to drugs. Isn't Dustin's mom mixed in with that crowd?"

"She hustles. Maybe she sells a little smoke, but she mostly scams. But I don't know nothing about that neither. I only know about poker." He quickly looked away, realizing his mistake. "You're nosier than a biddy tonight."

"Like I said, I'm interested because of Dustin." I crossed my fingers behind my back. "And I kind of have a thing for guys that play poker."

He appraised me with a long, disturbing look. "Well now, Miss Cherry. Guess we finally found something to talk about. Maybe you're looking for an invitation to see some real action, not like the bitty games Todd plays?" He chuckled. "And I ain't talking about poker."

"Let's stick with Mr. Max's games. They must be high dollar."

"Now I'm not saying he has a card room, but if he did it's nice and fancy. Not like the usual back porch stuff in Halo."

"So he's got a big house. What's he need with you?"

"Mr. Max is a smart man." Pete lifted his chin. "He didn't want just anyone getting into his kind of place. He has a guest list."

"Then you were bouncers. Why couldn't he put a lock on the door like normal people?"

"We were more than that. And he has a slick alarm system. He just doesn't like turning it on so people can be free to look at his old junk."

"You were guard dogs?"

"Not me. Dustin was more of the guard dog," he said with a sniff. "Kept hoping somebody would try something so he could intimidate them, you know. He was my boy, but he could be meaner than shit."

He shook his head. "Dustin was always trying to impress the boss like that. Like when Max needed us to collect on a fish who borrowed from the house, Dustin always took those jobs. Such a show-off."

"Thought he was special because he was a Branson?" I thought of Shawna.

"He hated the Bransons. Could have had an easy job at one of his dad's places and wouldn't do it."

"What do you mean he'd collect on a fish?"

Pete's eyes shifted to the side. "There's a lot of money at Mr. Max's. Like you said, the pot was big and it ain't a cap game. Ten grand to get in the door, he keeps ten percent. Most of the guests were good for it. It's supposed to be classy. But every once in a while, you'd get a goober in there who'd put up the front money but would lose his shirt and couldn't pay out. So Mr. Max would loan him money to play and send Dustin out later to collect."

I whistled low. "Was Dustin collecting on someone when he was murdered?"

"I thought he was changing his oil." Pete squinted one eye and scratched the grizzled beard. "But now that I think of it, Dustin said he was hunting for Mr. Max a day or two before he was killed."

"Hunting people, animals, what?"

Pete shrugged. "Dunno."

"Did you tell that to the police?"

"What for?"

I sighed. "Do you think Mr. Max could have killed Dustin?"

"What for? Dustin worked for him."

"Maybe Dustin saw or heard something he shouldn't have. Maybe Dustin was hustling him. Use your imagination. Don't you watch TV?"

"You sure are interested in Dustin. Did you have a thing for him, too?"

"That'd be a big no." I finished my beer in one gulp and gained some confidence from the amber liquid.

"You know what I think?" Pete pushed a greasy lock behind his ear before dropping his hand to the wall behind my head. "I think it was the step-brother."

I sputtered a fine spray of foam back into the mug and wiped my mouth on my arm. "What?"

"Just a minute." Creepy Pete broke off, grabbed the empty mug from my hand, and returned with two beers.

I took the mug, shocked at Pete's generosity.

"You owe me three bucks," he said. "Unless you'd like to pay me back another way."

A disturbing smile played across his face, and the dull olive eyes warmed. "You know, I've been telling you a lot of stuff I shouldn't. Why don't you make it worth my while? I'm not particular."

My stomach turned a somersault. I fished three dollars from my pocket and smacked the money in his palm. "Just go on with your story about Dustin's family."

Pete stole a few steps closer. His breath smelled of beer and menthol cigarettes.

I sucked on my beer, hiding my disgust and building courage.

Pete leaned into the wall next to me. "Dustin had a step-brother. They hated each other."

"Yeah, I know. Luke Harper. So what?"

"He got out of the Army a couple of weeks ago. Shows up here, gets in a big fight with Dustin, and then disappears. Comes back after the murder."

"That doesn't mean Luke killed him."

"Dustin told me lots of stuff about that Luke. Said he was psycho. Liked to fight him for no reason."

"He's not psycho. You never met Luke before today?"

"What do you mean before today? I've never met him period. He'd been in the Army the whole time I knew Dustin."

"Just as well if he's psycho," said a voice behind me. A hand slipped around my waist. "Cherry means you must have met him at the visitation today."

I pivoted to my left.

Luke shook his head and tightened the grip around my waist, pulling me into his side. "Hey, hon. Thanks for waiting on me. What're you guys talking about?"

Pete slammed his beer on the bar. "I didn't go to the visitation. I

don't like funerals. Cherry didn't say she was waiting on anyone."
He swung his accusation back to me. "I thought you said you're
here to drop your sister off."

"I must've forgotten about him." I elbowed Luke in the ribs. He
was scaring away the fish right when I had him on my line. And it
took a lot of disgusting work to get him this far.

Pete thrust his chin and turned toward Luke. "What'd you say
your name is?"

"I'd rather not say," I said.

Pete's eyes narrowed.

"Wouldn't want Todd to hear about this."

My cheeks grew hot. That had to be one of the dumber things
I'd ever said. I rubbed my face, wondering when the beer had
caught up with my brain. Or maybe it wasn't the beer. Maybe it
was Luke.

"You screwing around on Todd?" Pete's face lightened in
excitement at the gossip and dropped to a glower. "Wait a minute.
He dumped you. What're you saying?"

What was I saying? I couldn't lie worth a damn.

"I was not dumped at any altar and quit spreading gossip like
an old lady at a church bazaar." I chugged the rest of my beer and
shoved the mug into Pete's chest. "I'm done explaining myself
to you."

Luke followed me as I marched out of the bar.

Three seconds later we stood in Red's foyer between a rack of
real estate ads and a gumball machine.

"I was doing just fine until you showed up."

"Really? Didn't look like it." Luke rocked back on his heels.

"Creepy Pete was telling me all sorts of stuff about Dustin."

"Like what?"

He took a step closer, his eyes steady on mine. His hand
brushed against me, and a shock of electricity ran down my arms.
Without breaking eye contact, his fingers captured one of my
wayward hands.

"What did you hear?" he repeated.

I took a deep breath, concentrating on playing hard ball. "None of your business."

"Not going to share?" Luke's long fingers stroked the back of my hand. "Maybe we should work together. We used to be good together."

"That was a long time ago," I said, but allowed Luke to swing our hands up to his chest.

Speaking of a long time ago, it had been a long time since a man held my hand to his chest.

I stifled a sigh. "I need to get my wings. Drunk or not, I'm still starving."

"Let me. I owe you dinner. We'll take them back to your place and eat there."

"You owe me a hell of a lot more than a platter full of hot wings. I'll bet my dinner and walk it home. I'm leaving Casey my keys."

I pulled my hand from his and fished my keys from my pocket, triumphant in winning the battle of logic over loins.

Without missing a beat, Luke leaned over and caught me full on the lips.

He tasted warm and sweet and delicious. My arms found their way around his shoulders. One hand dangled keys. The other hand snuck fingers through the dark locks curling across the back of his neck. My feet pushed up onto my toes, stretching to meet his stoop. I almost swooned with the flashbacks to our nights of fogging up the windows of his black four-by-four.

I might have moaned, but I heard Luke sigh before sliding our faces apart. We wobbled under the Coors Light sign for half a minute before Luke yanked the keys out of my hand.

"I'll give these to Casey and take you home."

And, somehow, I just couldn't find the words to argue.

TEN

THE KITCHEN DOOR slammed against the wall, shaking the yellowing linoleum beneath our feet. The smell of hot wings wafted through the night air as a Styrofoam container flew onto the countertop and skidded to a stop. Wings and sauce splattered against the backsplash.

Luke's hand, freed from carrying takeout, returned to my body pinned between the open kitchen door and his lean physique.

My right hand smacked the wall in search of the light switch. The left clung to Luke while he nibbled a trail of kisses down my neck.

With my eyes closed the lights no longer mattered. My right hand forewent its search of the light switch and joined the left in the more enjoyable pursuit of reacquainting myself to Luke's delectable body.

This was probably a bad idea. My inner voice — the one that sounded a lot like Grandma Jo — continued a litany of complaints starting with Luke's old deeds and ending with the possibility of his involvement in Dustin's death.

But between the hormones and beer, there wasn't room for

Grandma Jo. In fact, at the moment, you couldn't slip more than a piece of paper between Luke and me.

"Hush Grandma," I thought, running a hand over the washboard under Luke's shirt.

"Did you say something?"

My eyelids fluttered open to a thick mop of ruffled, dark curls rising before my face. Luke's lazy eyes peeked from my neck.

"Out loud? I don't think so." My hands found the bottom of his t-shirt and tugged. "Just trying to get rid of this."

"Only if this can go, too." Luke yanked at the camouflage tank top. His hand crawled under the top, inching its way up my belly.

I wriggled underneath his touch and bent forward, pulling air through my nose like a frightened rabbit.

"Still ticklish." Luke kissed my shoulder. "Do you think we should shut this door or what?"

Before I could answer, he tipped his head up and found my mouth. I clung to his shoulders, not trusting my legs to stand on their own. My blood's circulation had been diverted. My feet worked no better than a ragdoll's.

We spent the better part of a minute glued to each other with my right leg hiked around his left thigh, rattling the open door behind my back. I ignored the draft blowing around us, but my nostrils picked up the aroma of hot wings. My stomach protested with an audible roar.

Luke's lips rested on my forehead. "I think we need to feed the beast."

He unpeeled my body from his, and the door swung shut. After a half second, I heard the lock turn.

"I'm taking no chances on someone showing up uninvited."

"Then you better leave the lights off. The minute the lights come on, folks stumble over here from the County Line."

"Even with your truck gone?"

"How many times a week do you think I lend it to one of my siblings or park it at Red's to walk home? Besides, there are bets laid out to see when the Datsun finally heaves its last rattle. Ronny Price is probably rubbing his hands together just waiting for me to pony up for a gleaming F-150."

"So lights off." Two hands planted on my hips and dragged me a step closer. "Can you eat in the dark, too? Maybe quiet that noise coming from your stomach while I'm kissing you."

"You need to concentrate?"

"It's not about concentrating. It's disconcerting to hear your body sound like a wild boar in death throes."

"It's not that bad." I slipped from his grasp and moved to the counter. Picking up a drummie, I licked off the sauce. "They just smell so good."

"Tell me about your day." Luke leaned against the counter and grabbed a wing.

"What? Like running a Tucker taxi service for people who have their own vehicles but don't want to drive them?"

"I don't mean your whole day. You know what I mean." He nudged my leg with his. "What did Pete say?"

His curiosity niggled at my common sense, but I recounted my interview with Creepy Pete and meeting Mr. Max. My gut told me if Luke was involved in Dustin's death, he was protecting someone else. And I doubted Luke protected Creepy Pete or Max Avtaikin.

"Now that's interesting," Luke said. "I saw Mr. Avtaikin at the visitation today. I wonder how JB knows him?"

I gnawed on a wing tip and licked my fingers. "Sold him a car? Sounds like he gets his vehicles serviced through the dealership."

"Maybe. JB was involved in some shady stuff back when he was married to Virginia."

"But you said JB straightened up when his daddy offered him a spot in the family business. Would he risk his little empire now?"

"I don't know."

My mouth full of chicken, I jumped at the smack of a hand against the counter.

"Damn. I know there's got to be some connection there."

"Are you trying to pin Dustin's murder on family?" The accusation slipped off my tongue, and I held my breath.

He remained silent for a moment. "I can't prove it was a Branson."

I let the air escape my lungs. My relief led to babbling. "Some of the Bransons are suspicious, especially Virginia. Creepy Pete is edgy and jealous of Dustin. Dustin had something on Shawna. Then there's this Mr. Max. We know he's involved in illegal activities and Dustin worked for him."

"Really, you've got nothing there, too. You need more than relationships. You need real motives."

The earlier mood had popped along with my beer buzz. The thought of the murder brought about the realization of tomorrow's funeral and deadline for the painting.

I also had another problem. I squinted at the warm body standing next to me. Luke heated my kitchen better than a roasting turkey on Thanksgiving Day. My swollen lips had nothing to do with hot sauce.

Sighing, I reached for another wing. My fingers clamped onto it just as Luke's fingers began pulling the drumstick away.

"Hey, that one's mine." I gripped the meaty end of the leg and yanked.

"How many have you had? I only had two. That's the last one." He tugged.

The drumstick slid out of my fingers.

"Give me that wing. I'm the one that's starving!"

Two quick bites and the wing was gone.

"Now I'm not hungry for chicken anymore." He grabbed my waist. Sticky fingers slid behind my neck.

"But I am."

I watched his lids lower to half-mast and lips relax as the hand behind my neck guided my face forward.

Oh boy, we were going for round two. My toes curled inside my boots. I scooted forward on the counter.

Wait a minute.

My Grandma Jo's voice reminded me about kicking him out before I did something I'd regret.

"Now Luke," I moved my hands to his chest and forced some distance between us. "As much as I am enjoying this, I am not the girl you once knew.

"Funny, you look like the girl I once knew." His hands slipped down my back. "You feel like the girl I once knew."

He leaned forward to suckle my neck.

An electric current rippled from his lips down my torso.

"You taste like that girl, too. Just dipped in hot sauce."

I tore my head back, dislodging my neck from his lips. "But now I'm a businesswoman."

"Businesswomen still get it on." Luke's lips grazed my throat. He moved my hands to his shoulders and pulled me closer. "Remember how I used to drive to Savannah, back when I was still at Statesboro?"

Savannah could be one of the most romantic cities in the country. All that moss dripping from trees and quaint squares set within interlocking cobblestone streets. Cemeteries with centuries old gravestones set amongst beautifully carved statues.

Plus, there are more bars than you can shake a stick at. All swimming in beer and oysters, in case you needed more aphrodisiacs.

His hand dropped from my neck and my top inched up my back.

I pushed the heel of one boot against the other, trying to shake off the boots without uncurling my legs.

Oh boy, oh boy, oh boy— My mantra halted with a crash from the carport.

Luke's mouth pulled away.

I thought about the crash for half a second and decided to surge on. I gave my boot another push and my foot caught in the folds of the ankle.

"What was that?"

"Nothing." My fingers fumbled with my boot.

His hands dropped from my waist and fell to my thighs.

I grabbed his face.

"Just a minute," he said. "I hear something."

"It's nothing. Probably just a cat or Todd. Don't worry about it. They'll go away."

"Speaking of Todd."

"It's annulled. I fell victim to a stupid moment of weakness—" I stopped at the sound of a sharp pop.

The room dropped into full darkness.

"Where's your gun?" he whispered. Luke slid out from my legs and dropped to a squat against the metal cabinets.

"You're not going to shoot Todd, are you?" I remained on the counter, straining to hear in the dark.

"Cherry," Luke's voice sounded strangled. "Would Todd break your security light?"

"On purpose or accident?"

"We're dealing with someone who was desperate enough to murder Dustin." The faint words floated below me. "Someone who keeps breaking and entering around town."

Luke's dark form slipped toward the kitchen door. He remained flattened against the wall while he peered through the muntin bars on the window.

"My gun is underneath my bed. I'll get it." Hopping from the counter, I slipped in my socks and zipped across the linoleum. Grabbing a chair, I regained my balance.

Luke's voice glided through the dark from the kitchen door. "Slow down. I'm going to sneak out the front door and try to see who's in your driveway." He grabbed my elbow. "Stay in the bedroom."

"It's my house," I whispered. "If someone breaks in, I'm going to greet them with my Remington."

"Don't be stupid. Just do what you're told for once."

The words wafted past me. Luke crept around me toward the archway for the living room.

I ran for the bedroom. The friction and speed of socks on linoleum worked against me. My run became a skid. I threw a hand toward my bedroom door frame to slow my progress. My arms windmilled. I shot past the door and smacked into the linen closet.

The thud and my resonating "umph" received a furious "shhh-hhh" from the living room.

Rubbing my nose, I scowled. I grabbed the door frame and swung into the bedroom. On my bed, I yanked off my socks off and crawled across the quilt. Dropping my right hand to the floor, I felt for the shotgun. My fingers closed around a metal box and swung it onto the bed. I fumbled over the combinations, but the lock popped.

A moment later I held the gun on my lap, waiting for my heart to stop pounding and my eyes to adjust to the dim streetlight shining through the window.

Three buckshot shells lay in my bedside table drawer. Flipping the gun over, I fed the shells into the tube and racked the pump. Gun in hand, I slid off the bed and stalked to the hallway to listen.

A faint snick sounded from the living room.

Just stay calm, I thought. Think of what is in your hands. Keep your head and proceed slowly. You've had plenty of experience with Uncle Will and the boys. Just pretend you're in the woods.

And the deer were possibly armed and dangerous.

My heart leaped from my stomach to my mouth. I crept down the hallway toward the kitchen. Goosebumps prickled my skin. I never had a problem with intruders before. Other than relatives, friends, and ex-boyfriends looking for an after-party. I tightened my grip on the walnut stock and my resolve.

I felt my way through the dark to the kitchen door. Peering through the glass, I tried to pick out movement in the cramped carport from the faint shine of the streetlight.

A metallic creak and click broke the silence. A vehicle door had opened and shut.

With the deadbolt gripped in my left hand, I hesitated, then flipped the lock and yanked open the door. My bare feet touched the cold concrete, and my thoughts ran clear by instinct.

I swung the old Wingmaster in a smooth arc. The shotgun fitted snugly into my shoulder, the wood stock like velvet against my cheek. Lights flashed on, flooding the darkness. I blinked into their glare.

"Cherry, it's me. Drop your weapon." Hostility sharpened Luke's voice.

"Luke?"

"Dammit, I told you to stay in the bedroom. What in the hell are you doing?"

I glowered at the lights of Luke's Ford Raptor. "I told you, this is my house. I've got every right to defend myself. I know what I'm doing. I've been hunting since I was nine."

"Yeah, and I know you can't stay still long enough to mark anything. You just like to hang out in the deer stand and drink beer."

"You've never been hunting with me. How would you know?"

"I know you well enough. They should revoke your permit for being crazy."

"I am not crazy," I shouted.

"This from the woman who comes charging out her house with a gun. Stop arguing with me. The guy's gone. Must've parked on another street."

I stepped out of the headlights to circle toward his door. Luke hung out the open window, his flexed arm hugging the door. "You don't use the sense God gave you. Don't you know vigilantes usually get themselves killed?"

I straightened into my fullest five foot and a half inch. "I wasn't planning on getting myself killed. That's why I'm carrying a loaded gun, dummy."

"I'll let that pass." He stared into the rearview mirror, ignoring my look that would kill lesser mortals. After a long moment, he jerked his head back to fix me with a chilly expression. "Go back in the house. Turn on all the lights. Lock the doors."

"And what are you planning on doing?"

"Listen, we had some fun, but this isn't a good idea. You're sticking in Halo, and I'm not."

"Not a good idea? This was your idea. You seduced me with chicken in my kitchen, and now you're blowing me off in the carport ten minutes later? Whatever." I tossed my head so dramatically, my hair whipped my shoulders. "Hey, I've got a life. And I don't need you in it."

"You don't need to be like that." He turned to the windshield and smacked the door with his hand. His eyes flew to the rear view mirror and narrowed in a disgusted squint. "And here's your boyfriend. He knew Dustin. Did you ask where he was the night you got your head knocked in?"

A red hatchback with ground effects and die-cast alloy wheels pulled up to the curb.

"He's not my—"

The eight-cylinder truck engine revved, drowning my protest. The gleaming black beast reversed down the drive, bumped into the street, and tore off into the night.

"By the way, you never told me where you were that night either. Jackass."

I waited in the dark carport, grasping the shotgun with one hand. Todd unfolded himself from the car and loped up the driveway. The perfect symmetry in his face fell out of balance as he squinted at me.

"Hey, baby. What's going on?"

"Nothing." Paranoia made me spit the word. Todd's timing was a little too impeccable. Where was he ten minutes earlier?

"What's with the gun? Have you been in a fight? Who was that?" Todd studied my appearance with growing concern. I pinched the bridge of my nose. "Are you bleeding? Babe!"

My eyes dropped to my clothes. My tank top remained rolled

halfway up, revealing the pale skin of my stomach streaked with wing sauce. Saucy fingerprints danced across my jeans and felt sticky on my back. I patted my face and static-zinged hair.

"It's just hot sauce. I'm fine. It's probably all over my kitchen, too." I moaned, thinking of the mess, and collapsed against a sawhorse workbench stacked with cans of paint and stain. A light breeze blew through the carport, adding goosebumps to my dirty skin.

"You're eating wings in the dark? With Luke Harper? Looks like you kept missing your mouth."

"Never you mind. What are you doing here?"

"I ran into the guys at Red's. They said you were there tonight."

"The guys? Jackson. Creepy Pete?"

"Jackson. And Red, of course. Didn't see Pete. Let me think of who else." His fingers strummed his chin.

"I'm not asking for a rundown of Red's patrons," I narrowed my eyes. "Not Pete, huh?"

"No."

"Speaking of Pete, what did you tell him about us?"

He flicked another glance at the shotgun. "What do you mean?"

"What did you tell him about Vegas?"

His fingers played across the drumsticks poking out of his back pocket. "I didn't tell him we got married."

"We didn't get married, Todd. Not hardly. And his story includes a little more information."

"I told him when we got to Vegas, getting married seemed like a good idea. He called me a few names I wouldn't want to say in front of you." Todd's hands whipped the drumsticks out of his pocket and beat a cadence against his hips. "And then I might have explained how we weren't married."

"Pete's telling everybody that you left me at the altar. That you broke up with me." My voice sizzled. "And I ran around Vegas in a wedding dress to BEG you to marry me."

Todd picked the wrong night to wander up my drive. How the hell could he sit motionless through an entire poker game but couldn't go three seconds without drumming around me?

"He said I said what?" Todd's forehead crinkled in confusion. The sticks rattled a drum roll against his thighs.

"Are you telling people that you jilted me?"

"You said you didn't want anybody to know what really happened." His eyes dropped to the Remington in my arms. "Can you put your gun down?"

"I didn't mean for you to say that I got dumped!"

"You didn't tell me that."

"Why would I want you to say that?"

Todd eyed the gun. The tempo against his thighs grew. "I couldn't think of anything else to say."

"Stop the drumming," I shouted.

Todd jumped. The drumsticks flew through the air.

"Sorry. Baby. Can you put the gun down? Please?" Todd backed down the driveway with his hands held before him.

"Oh, for heaven's sake." I waved a hand at him. "I'm not going to shoot you."

"Why do you have a gun? What's going on? You're freaking me out."

"Somebody was sneaking around here. And it may or may not have something to do with Dustin getting killed."

"Does it have to do with your break-in at Cooper's?"

"I wasn't involved in the break-in. I was in Cooper's when somebody broke in and whacked me a good one."

"Because you're hanging out with this Luke and asking questions?"

"That's a good point."

"Thanks."

"I've got to work." I turned to drag myself into the house. "You better stop these rumors about Vegas. I'm about up to here with it." My hand flicked the top of my head.

"You scare me, baby."

I looked over my shoulder at Todd.

The wide, blue eyes gazed back at me. "I worry about you living alone. Now you got people hitting you on the head and sneaking around your house."

"You're sweet, but you know I can take care of myself." I paused before turning back to the house. "Wait, is that why you're here all the time?"

"I know you're tough. Sometimes too tough. And a little mean. But, I admire you." A blush heated Todd's cheeks, making him more endearing. "You're tough and smart and you make cool stuff. And you're pretty sexy even though you're kind of…you know… puny. Cherry—"

"Don't, Todd. I'm in no mood for this."

"Let's go back to Vegas." His grin broke wide across his cheeks, framed by two pairs of long, flawless dimples. He beat a happy rhythm against the sides of his pants.

I gazed at the beautiful dimples with fear and trepidation. I needed to have my libido removed before I got into any more of these messes. Was this what happened to my mother? Did dimples sidetrack her from raising kids?

"You have the worst timing. Do you know that?"

"Naw." He strode forward and slipped an arm over my shoulder. "I have great timing. That's what makes me a kick-ass drummer and an awesome poker player."

"Don't start making intelligent statements like that. You deserve someone much nicer than me. Keep up the sweet talk, and I'll be all over you like white on rice. And that won't do either of us any good. Vegas was a huge mistake. I need to be grounded."

"Come on. Let me in the house. I can tell you're feeling lonely."

"I have to get a painting finished tonight." I shook my head. "And my kitchen's a mess. Hell, I'm a mess."

"How about I come in and just sit while you paint." The cerulean blue eyes lifted in appeal. He threw a long, commanding arm against the kitchen door, reminding me of Ancient Rome's regal *Caesar Augustus* statue. "Like we used to when I modeled for you. We'll order us some pizza and play some music. It'll make you feel better."

He had a point. I could use some cheering. I thought about using Todd as a model. He and Dustin shared similar coloring. Other than random perverts, Todd was the only person in Halo who would pose nude for my life drawings. I had some beautiful images of Todd. Of course, I also sketched some imbecilic drawings from Todd's self-created poses that showed off his "abs of steel" and "power guns."

I grinned and stood on my toes to peck his cheek. "Okay, you've got a deal. But that's the only kiss you're getting tonight."

"That's okay," he said, hugging me.

I relaxed into his embrace and tested for any lustful feelings, but my mind wouldn't stop buzzing over Luke's accusations. Todd couldn't be dangerous. He wasn't smart enough to plan murders and burglaries and not get caught.

Or was he? The male bimbo act fooled his poker buddies, so he didn't get the crap beat out of him when he won. Dumb luck, people thought. The dumb blond front also lowered the defenses of women like me, those naturally wary of shrewd men.

What was I thinking? This was good ol' Todd cuddling me, albeit a little too warmly for a recent breakup. I allowed that sly Luke to wreak havoc on my life. He was the one acting suspiciously. I needed to rethink the relevance of tall, dark, and vinegary. Why couldn't tall, blond, and sweet trip my trigger?

Stumbling out of Todd's embrace, I cut the light switch on. "You want to pose like you're dead?"

"Sounds kinky. Wait, do I get to close my eyes?"

I pulled him into the living room to show him Dustin's portrait.

"Dustin sorta looks like he's sleeping. He's got some nice hands there." Todd stood back, cocking his head with a critic's gaze. "Good job, baby. I'll help you get it done."

"Thanks, Todd."

"Baby?"

"Yeah?"

"You going to keep that gun with you?"

I glanced from the blued steel in my hand to the front window. Someone still snuck around Halo, invading homes and hitting innocent artists on the head. And I wanted to know who it was.

"You better believe it." I laid the shotgun on the floor beside the easel and picked up a brush.

ELEVEN

CARS FILLED Cooper's Funeral Home parking lot like it was a Friday night tailgate. After waiting half the morning for Cody to deliver the Datsun, I finally snuck out with the finished portrait while Todd snored on the divan where he had fallen asleep, pretending to be dead. I arrived at Cooper's without many minutes to spare.

The Datsun jerked to a stop at the far edge of the lot. Carrying the large covered canvas, I waded through the vehicles. My heart battered my ribcage. I didn't know if my jitters came from the forthcoming reaction to the painting of a dead guy in his coffin on full display next to said coffin, or from the pot of coffee that got me through the night.

A Branson held open Cooper's glass door. I slid through and maneuvered my way into the crowded front room toward the chapel. Cooper stood just inside the empty chapel door clad in his ubiquitous dark suit, looking all the part of an undertaker.

"Miss Cherry?" He raised brows in desperate need of a trim. "I thought Sheriff said you were, ah, quit of the job."

"I got what I needed before I had the unfortunate incident here, so I thought I might as well finish." I lowered the painting to rest on my boots. "I'm sorry about taking your key. I was just anxious to do a good job with this painting."

"I've known you to be impetuous." He sniffed. "But not criminal. That's the only reason I didn't press charges. You'll get my cleaning bill, though."

"Yes, sir. But when I figure out who actually broke in, you can be sure I'll pass that bill to them."

"I hate to say it, hon, but all this talk of proving your innocence just makes you look kind of childish. Your Grandpa Ed must be real disappointed."

"Sir—" I stopped my thought, realizing my protests needed proof. Now that the painting was finished, I had a new project: finding the offender who trashed my name. I lowered my voice. "Have you heard any more about Dustin's killer? Police say anything to you? They got any suspects?"

Cooper shook his head and pointed toward the door.

"You can ask Sheriff Will."

Will leaned against a wall, his body relaxed but eyes in constant motion over the crowd. His sensitivity to my glance bordered on psychic. His head swiveled toward me, and the brown eyes sharpened. He crooked a finger.

I sucked in a deep breath. "Listen, Mr. Cooper. Whatever you think of me, the Bransons need this painting."

"Mr. and Mrs. Branson are with family in my office at the moment, waiting for me to bring them in. I'll have Abe take it to them. We've got the other paintings in back."

Other paintings? Did Shawna make more than one?

"Thanks, sir. Be careful with this one. Paint's still tacky." I handed the painting to Cooper in time to meet Will 's approach.

"What are you doing here?" he asked.

"Just delivering the painting, Uncle Will."

"I told you to drop that gig. You deliberately disobeyed me."

I planted hands on my hips. "This painting brings comfort to Miss Wanda. Even though it seems weird and a little icky, I'm helping her. And I need to show JB I follow through on my word."

"Don't give me your sass. I am the law. I think you and your brother and sister tend to forget that. I'm investigating a murder. That's a little more important than drawing a picture, no matter how much they're paying you. You keep getting in my way, and I'll serve you with obstruction."

"You're being a little ridiculous, dontcha think?"

"Really? How's that goose egg? Heard you treated it to a few at Red's last night. Messed around with the victim's friend, then left with the victim's brother?"

"Step-brother. And I would never mess around with Creepy Pete. I just talked to him for a minute. Can't anybody mind their own business in this town?"

"Do you see what I'm saying? I'm investigating a murder, and I keep hearing about you. You know what the town's saying about Cherry Tucker? I never took you for stupid, Cherrilyn."

We stared each other down with a hostility brewed from a long familiarity.

Will broke the look with a sigh filled with patience worthy of Job. "You're like a daughter to me, hon. You, Casey, and Cody feel like my kids. And when y'all do something dumb, it gets under my skin like nobody's business."

"I didn't do anything wrong. Except for trespassing, but I had good intentions. Everyone seems to forget that I'm the one who fell victim to an intruder."

"Believe me, that's in the forefront of my mind."

"Then why don't you spend more time investigating the scum that's moving in, instead of people who care about Halo?" I spun around and shoved into the crowd, marching through the clusters of people waiting to enter the chapel.

"Cherry." A husky voice strung out my name into three syllables.

I recognized the rich resonance of my friend, Leah Daniels. Men parted to let her pass, sneaking covert glances at the plush body artists like Rubens would have given an eyetooth to paint.

She crossed the room, her hair swinging in long, dark ringlets and her body swaying to an internal rhythm. Unfortunately, her wardrobe choices bordered on cataclysmic. For today's funeral, she wore a lilac print dress that my grandma would have worn to church. If Leah would stop dressing like her mother, she could do some serious man-damage.

"Looking good, Leah. Like the heels," I said, "but where did you get that dress? The Blue Hair Boutique? Honey, the only things that'd match that dress are bunions and a pair of Depends."

Leah pressed down the polyester ruffles hiding her generous bosom. "It's my funeral dress. Momma picked it out."

"God Almighty, Leah. Stop letting your mother dress you. You're twenty-six. If you've got it, flaunt it. If I had any money, I'd purchase a pair of appendages like yours. At least then I'd appear three-dimensional."

"You're just slow to blossom."

"I'm not fifteen. Grandpa is a stick, too. I'm destined to shop in the junior section forever."

"Girl, from what I hear, that skinny butt of yours is attracting plenty of attention."

"I think it has more to do with my loud mouth." I grimaced. "Anyway, Uncle Will 's not too happy with any part of me right now. I can't stay."

Leah threaded my arm through hers and pulled me toward the chapel. "Sheriff Thompson loves you. Now Miss Wanda asked me to sing some hymns. Since you're here, you can help me."

I jerked to a stop. "Leah, look at me, I'm not dressed for a funeral."

She glanced at my denim miniskirt trimmed with brass studs and tie-dyed Panama Beach t-shirt with a handmade puka shell collar. "And you're insulting *my* wardrobe? The boots are a little much, but I think it's okay. I just want you to turn pages for me while I play."

"Please find somebody else."

"Which is it? Are you avoiding your Uncle Will or hiding from Luke Harper? Or are you slinking out with your tail between your legs because the last time you appeared at Cooper's you robbed the departed?"

Leah doesn't miss much. "If you put it that way."

"That's what I thought. Let's go." Leah strutted into the chapel, and I stole in behind her.

We slid onto padded folding chairs beside the piano in the back of the room. The rest of the crowd poured through the wooden double doors in their Sunday best. Their hushed chatter floated past us. The large Branson clan filled the front rows. Townsfolk, JB's business acquaintances, and funeral groupies settled in back.

After most of the seats had filled, Cooper led Wanda and JB through a side door. With rigid formality, Luke strode after them in a blue dress suit. Shawna, in all her flame-haired-femme-fatale glory, stuck next to Luke with a matched stride. I compared her black sundress and pumps with my attire.

Four-inch heels. As if she needed the added height. And wasn't a plunging neckline a little trashy for a funeral?

On the other hand, Luke in a suit looked hotter than a Georgia tin roof in August. His steely eyes swept the room while he waited for his mother and Shawna to sit.

Leah nudged me. "Wow, Luke looks good enough to eat. Who is he staring at?"

I glanced back to Luke and followed his line of sight.

Four rows behind the assorted Branson mob, the hulking Bear reclined with relaxed ambivalence. An arm over the back of the adjacent chair, his head bent toward the man next to him. With that distinctive height of gleaming hair, Mr. Max's funeral seat mate had to be Ronny Price.

Ronny scooted forward on the chair, as far from Mr. Max's bulky body as he could without appearing rude. Whatever the Bear whispered, Ronny didn't like it.

Slipping behind those two to get a whiff of their conversation seemed like a good starting point to my investigation. I rose from my chair.

A hand pressed on my shoulder, easing me back in the chair.

I half-turned.

Will towered over me, a massive frown on his face. "Trouble finding the door?"

"I'm helping Leah."

He waited for further explanation.

"You know, turning the pages for her while she sings hymns."

Leah waved at Will. "Hey there, Sheriff Thompson. Thanks for letting Cherry help."

"Leah. How are you, girl? Very nice of you to sing for the funeral."

"Thank you, sir. Miss Wanda was my Sunday School teacher."

"You still running the choir at New Order?"

"The SonShine Choir. I'm also the organist at First Baptist. And Cherry got me into a band that plays at Red's. We may even go out on the road."

Will blinked at me. "Did she now?"

I bit my lip, feeling a little guilty about introducing Leah to Sticks. But a gig's a gig. Artists have to stick together.

"Do you want my seat so you two can catch up?" I eyed the row behind Mr. Max and Ronny Price.

"Only if you plan on leaving," said Will.

"Oh, no. I'm here to help." I gave him my most obliging customer service smile.

"Seems like you've been a little too helpful lately." Will shot me a warning glance and circled us to take a seat in the back row.

While we spoke to Will, Cooper had shuffled to the back of the room, eager to shut the chapel doors and begin the funeral service. A conversation buzzed on the other side of the door, pulling Cooper out of his well-practiced funeral track and into the foyer.

"What's going on?" I leaned forward so Will could catch my whisper.

He shrugged and turned in his seat.

Leah and I craned our necks. As the conversation escalated, other people turned around.

The heavy wooden door flew open to bump against the wall.

Virginia sashayed into the chapel, flanked by two men. She tossed her lank hair and stood with doughy arms planted on hips that would make an Angus steer look small.

Cooper hurried back into the hall.

"What are you waiting for?" Virginia screeched at Cooper. "Go get us some chairs. I'm shocked at your service. We've been waiting half a Sunday for you to come get us."

"I'm sorry, ma'am." Cooper dropped his voice. "I didn't know you were in that room."

"Doesn't matter where I was. Now get."

Cooper teetered to a closet and retrieved three folding chairs.

Luke half-stood. His mother and Shawna gripped his arms, yanking him back to his chair. JB folded his arms and glared at the coffin, not acknowledging Virginia's presence.

"Casey's going to be mad she missed this," I said.

Leah nodded. She swiveled in her chair, watching the proceedings.

Cooper's assistant, Abe, — so short and round we dubbed him Butterbean in grade school — saw Cooper's struggle with the chairs and trotted down the aisle in rescue. He passed by with the chairs tucked inside his sweat-stained armpits. "Hey, girls."

"Someone forget to invite Virginia?" I asked.

"She told us yesterday she wouldn't sit in a room full of Bransons unless somebody paid her. Was fixing to go straight to the cemetery. Guess she and JB had some words after the visitation."

"Abe," Leah asked. "Should I do something to help?"

"Maybe you could go ahead and play something. Best get these down front. See you, girls."

"I wonder who paid Virginia to show up? "

"Seriously." Leah rose from her seat and I followed her to the piano. With a graceful sweep of her skirt, Leah scooted out the bench and lowered her body.

I stood on the far side of the piano to hide my clothing from the crowd.

"I don't need help with this. I'm just going to play some classical music until they get started." She pulled a book of music from her large purse and stood it on the music stand.

Leah's fingers worked the keys while I leaned against the piano and watched Butterbean set up three chairs in the front row, separating Virginia's group from JB with as much tact as possible.

Virginia continued to pace before the doors, waiting for an official escort to the front.

Her two companions slouched against the wall. The older man had thinning hair and a rumpled suit three sizes too big. He stared at his dusty brown shoes with a vagueness bordering on apathy.

Next to him stood a teen with dirty blond hair. His jaw thrust forward as he scanned the crowd, defiant in his stare. Jeans, work boots, and a cheap button-down fit his definition of funeral wear.

I glanced at my swirly violet and safety-orange t-shirt and felt chastised by my clothes snobbery.

Cooper approached Virginia with slow concentration, thrown off his game by the bizarre events connected with the funeral.

"Well?" she said. She turned toward the men behind her. "Amos. Darren. Come on then."

Amos Fewe jerked as if surprised to find himself in a funeral chapel. He scuffled his worn shoes to the front of the room without taking an interest in the gawking crowd.

The younger man pushed himself off the wall and approached Virginia. "Momma Virginia." He took her arm. His eyes circled the heads of the assembly and narrowed in on Luke like a buzzard sighting a fresh kill.

Luke blanched and fell back in his seat to stare at the ceiling.

Shawna patted his shoulder in comfort, causing a disgusted snort to rip from my mouth.

"Did he just say 'Momma?'" Leah asked. Her fingers continued to run over the piano keys. Music to soothe the savages as the war parties threatened to form.

"That's what it sounded like. I'm having trouble keeping up with all these family additions."

"No kidding. This is getting good. You better have the play-by-play ready for Casey."

Leah reached the end of the song and let her hands fall to her lap. She turned toward Cooper, waiting for a cue to continue, while he stood before the assembly, dabbing his forehead with a handkerchief, lost in thought.

Wanda Branson canted forward in her seat.

Cooper stooped to hear her whisper. He nodded and motioned to Butterbean, who retreated out the side door and returned carrying two paintings. Cooper struggled with a third painting that outsized the first two by at least a square foot.

"Uh, oh." I slid down the piano to hunker next to Leah on the bench.

"What's going on?"

"An unveiling. I didn't think Miss Wanda would make such a production. I thought she'd pick one and just set the painting off to the side or something."

"You'll be famous now."

I pinched the bridge of my nose to quell an oncoming headache before sneaking a look.

Cooper grimaced as he fiddled with one of the three easels placed on one side of the closed casket. Butterbean handed a painting to Cooper. Together they positioned the paintings while the crowd watched with growing anticipation.

JB had buried his head in his hands. Luke's focus stuck to the ceiling. Wanda shook with tears while Shawna leaned across Luke to comfort her. Their poses created an interesting tableau, making me wish I had a sketch pad on hand.

Finished with their fussing, Butterbean and Cooper stepped to the side, revealing the paintings. With fleetness never before seen, Butterbean scuttled toward the side door, while Cooper hoofed it toward the back.

A gasp rose from the crowd, and the entire congregation slid forward in their seats.

"Oh, Lord," I mumbled and clenched my stomach.

"Oh, mercy." Leah patted my arm without taking her eyes off the paintings.

On the coffin's right sat a large painting of a tow-headed boy squeezing a flop-eared bunny. The child stared at the crowd with a terrifying grin and enormous eyes better suited on a Jack O' Lantern. The pupils appeared engorged — most likely from the artist trying to render a whimsical look — the effect seemed almost demonic.

"You think that bunny lived through the sitting?" I whispered to Leah.

"What's wrong with that child?"

"I bet Dustin scowled in the original picture, and the artist tried to cute him up, but couldn't quite pull it off. He mixed the iris color too dark. It blends into the pupil. He also forgot to add light reflection. That's what you call dead eyes."

Leah shivered. "He looks like he's about to take a bite out of that rabbit. Or pop its head off."

"I'm thinking Miss Wanda's got a bunch of those creepy clown paintings at home, too."

"To go with all the dead animals hanging on their walls?"

"At least mounted antelopes have shiny eyes," I said. "I'd rather see that than a clown painting any day."

The enormous second painting rose between the childhood rendering and my coffin portrait. Shawna had enlarged Dustin's high school senior picture using — what I suspected was — an overhead projector. Dustin posed in dark camos with a shotgun in one hand and a wild turkey hanging by its feet in the other. Vapor, depicted as puffy clouds lined in gold, hid the original background. Angel wings had been painted behind Dustin's orange vest with a halo above his hunting cap.

Laughter ripped through me. "I take it back. I'd rather see a clown painting than Dustin hunting in heaven."

Leah's forehead wrinkled. "Is there hunting in heaven? Doesn't sound biblical."

"Shawna's color mixing is murky. She outlined the image in

heavy pencil that shows through the thin tempura. And the turkey feathers have the same fluorescent orange as the hunting vest." I nudged Leah. "Look at mine next to that. You tell me, which one is going to get the commission?"

The forever-sleeping Dustin lay in his coffin bed. The focal point drew the viewer's gaze away from the closed face and toward the centered hands clasped over his jacket. He appeared peaceful, but next to the demonic child and heavenly hunting portrait, my painting looked downright eerie.

A shudder ran through the congregation. No one could look away from the odd display.

"My baby," Virginia bellowed.

"Here we go," I whispered to Leah. "Show's starting."

A middle-aged man in a gray suit scooted off a chair and walked behind the podium. He glanced at the paintings, then turned back to the congregation, paled. With his eyes on Virginia, he picked up his worn Bible and pressed it against his chest.

"Good morning, folks. I'm Pastor Earlie from New Order Church and Fellowship. We are gathered here today to mourn the death of Dustin Bartles Branson."

The preacher shot another look at Dustin's childhood portrait. His eyes remained riveted for a long beat, mesmerized by its disturbing imagery. They flickered over the new portraits, and a trembling shook him. If he had his wits about him, he could have claimed the spirit moved him.

"I'd like to start the service with a passage from Second Corinthians, ah..." Flustered, Pastor Earlie peeled his eyes from the paintings to stare at the ceiling.

The congregation sucked in their breath. It was an exceptional day when a reverend could not recite verbatim an appropriate passage from scripture.

"Dustin Bartles? I thought Virginia was a Springhouser?" I said.

"Remember, we used to make fun of him because he was named after a wine cooler," Leah murmured.

Pastor Earlie continued to flounder with his memory. He flipped open his Bible, feeling the weight of disapproval from the townsfolk.

The Methodist Flower Guild ladies pursed their lips and whipped out the complimentary Cooper's Funeral Home fans. A heavy scent of lavender and rose beat through the air as they fanned away their discomposure.

While the attendees waited for Pastor Earlie to regain his poise, Virginia used the break in the service for a tactical move.

"What in the hell kind of picture is that?" Virginia said, pointing to my painting.

The crowd shifted in their seats.

Wanda, dabbing her eyes with a tissue, turned to look at Virginia in stunned disbelief.

"Just simmer down, Virginia," JB said through clenched teeth. "We're paying for this funeral. We decide what gets put up front."

The congregation quieted to listen. The fans beat slowly, pulling heat from the brewing argument.

"He is my son." Virginia planted a hand on her drooping chest. "You are making a mockery of him."

"Oh no," Wanda sniffled. "We are immortalizing him in art."

"You're what?" Darren snickered.

"I can't stand to look at him like this," Virginia howled. "Take those ugly pictures away."

"Hey." I straightened in my chair. "Just look at the lighting in my painting. That's a Flemish Renaissance technique done with acrylics. Come on now. I didn't paint Son of Sam there or Saint Turkey Stalker, but there's no way you can claim my painting as ugly."

Shawna turned in her chair. "An angel is inoffensive. You painted a dead body."

"Because that's what they wanted," I said. "A true work of art. You want to get paid for something a six-year-old could have made with macaroni and glitter. You tried to sabotage my painting because you knew you weren't good enough."

"Now, now," said Wanda. "Shawna did a nice job. She didn't have all the art classes Cherry did."

"Then why is she claiming she's an artist?" I muttered.

"Okay, folks." Pastor Earlie waved his hands above the podium. "Feelings run high when we're about to say goodbye to a loved one. That's understandable. Let's be civil toward one another."

Butterbean edged toward the coffin. Art made Butterbean nervous. He told me that once over a beer.

"We're leaving those paintings where they are." JB turned to face his ex-wife.

Butterbean skipped backward in retreat.

"The hell you are." Virginia shook a finger toward the paintings. "You are offending me. I've a mind to sue you."

JB stared at Butterbean. "Don't you touch those paintings, Abe. My wife wants them there. They stay put. She tried to raise that good-for-nothing. Wanda's got every right to have what comforts her here."

"And what were you doing while she was raising our son?"

"Paying off his court costs. He obviously got that from you."

"You insulting my mother and my dead brother?" Darren launched out of his chair.

"Who are you anyway?" Luke swiveled his gaze from the ceiling to Darren. "Dustin doesn't have a brother."

Wanda hid her face in her hands. "Y'all! This is a funeral! Have some respect!"

"You need to take this outside, Darren," said Luke.

"I'll mess you up and take you down." Darren slapped his chest. "Dustin was more of a brother to me than he ever was to you."

"That's not saying much."

"Stop it," Wanda wailed.

"Get that piece of shit art out of this room," Virginia roared. "I'm suing this funeral home, John Branson, and the artists."

The entire congregation held their breath in anticipation of what may become the greatest funeral story ever seen in Forks County. Any Halo citizen who missed Dustin Branson's funeral might as well prune themselves off the small town grapevine for shame.

That included Grandpa, Casey, and Cody. For once I'd be the one with a firsthand report.

Wait a minute. Did Virginia say she was going to sue me?

"You can't sue me, you old cow," I said.

"Shush." Will spun in his seat and waved a hand.

"You going to do something about this scene, Sheriff?" I asked.

"Are you kidding? This is getting good. I'm interested to see what shakes out of this mess." He checked himself with a quick glance to his neighbors. "Of course, nobody's breaking any laws. If Cooper needs me, I'll step in."

Pastor Earlie pounded a hand on the podium. "Please. Have some respect for the dead and the grieving. Young man, sit down. Now the passage I had in mind..."

Unfortunately for the preacher, his words fell short on the instincts of family pride. The non-nuclear Bransons began to circle their wagons. Women slipped forward to surround Wanda. Shawna bawled with affected hysterics. A few young men shoved out of their chairs in reaction to Darren.

Luke remained seated, arms crossed, with the fury of an aggrieved stepchild slapped across his face.

JB and Virginia faced each other, hurtling snarling comments back and forth.

Amos Fewe, oblivious to the building riot around him, pulled out a cigarette and took a long drag.

"Sir, you cannot smoke in here." Cooper's voice rose to a warbling shriek from the back of the room.

The congregation gasped. It might have been the first time they had heard Cooper emit such passion. Several elderly ladies rose from their seats to only drop back again, caught between propriety and desire for gossip.

Mr. Max didn't pretend any political correctness in enjoying the show. His booming laugh echoed across the room.

"Oh no." Leah grabbed my arm.

A young well-muscled Branson kin stomped to the front row. I recognized him as Charlie Turnbuckle, star defensive tackle for Halo High's Fighting Angels. He thrust out a trunk-like arm to grab Darren.

Darren, most likely trained from youth in the art of dirt yard fighting, stepped away from the flying hand. He swung a knuckled fist toward Charlie's head and smacked him in the side of the neck.

Charlie grunted, lowered his head, and charged. Darren jumped to the side and grabbed Charlie's shoulders. He wrapped an arm around Charlie's neck, moving in for a headlock.

It was like watching a badger wrestle an elephant.

"Get 'em, boy," Virginia yelled.

"The paintings," Wanda cried. "They're going to wreck my tribute."

"Like hell." I jumped up from the piano bench. Scurrying down the aisle, I focused on nabbing my painting and moving it to safety.

Pastor Earlie passed me on his way back to Cooper, ready to hand over the situation.

I flew to the front row, ignoring the shouting around me.

Darren clung to Charlie's bent neck, attempting to pull him to the ground. Charlie's hands swung at Darren's legs.

I slipped behind the grappling pair, just as Darren kicked his foot out. I bumped against the coffin.

"Watch it, you idiots," I yelled and tried to shove around them. "Take it outside already."

"Cherry, you damn fool. Get out of there." Luke's reproach burned my ears.

"She's always trying to steal the spotlight," screeched Shawna and rushed to the front. "If her painting is so dang important, so is mine."

Darren pressed his shoulder into Charlie's neck and tightened his headlock. Charlie grunted again, jerked his body to standing, and whipped Darren's wiry body to the side.

I hopped back and felt the metal bar of the coffin dig into my backside.

Shawna circled them, intent on grabbing her painting first. Trapped between the casket and the wrestlers, I watched Shawna move her painting to safety.

"Shawna," I said. "Move mine, too."

Like a Bronco bucking his rider, Charlie shook Darren.

Shawna glanced at the wrestlers and darted to Dustin's childhood portrait.

Darren's feet lifted off the ground and scrambled for a foothold in mid-air. Knobby knees threatened to jab me. Steel-toed boots kicked near my shins as Charlie reached overhead to pry Darren off.

I cast a look sideways and saw Shawna wiping her hands as she took her time examining the childhood painting in its new position.

She ambled toward my painting and halted. "Mercy," she said, fluttering a hand before her face. "It's too risky to get near your painting. So sorry."

My focus snapped back to the fight before me. I bent backward over the coffin to get away from the flying limbs.

Charlie pitched back, tumbling Darren toward me. We careened into the coffin, and it rumbled over with a massive thud. A tangle of arms, legs, and oak paneling dumped to the ground.

"Holy crap," I shouted. I felt body parts on top and under me. *Dear God,* I prayed, *please don't let any of these limbs be Dustin's.*

People scrambled around us as another thought crossed my mind: I wore a skirt. I tried to feel for the position of my clothing without touching any other person's body.

"Cherry," Leah cried. "Are you all right?"

"Get up, Charlie. I think you've squashed Cherry." Luke's voice carried from a few feet away.

A heavy weight eased off my legs. I took a cautious peek and almost choked.

Mr. Max's face loomed over mine. He cast me a toothy smile. "The fight is too quick for helping you. You are not broken? You've no padding, I think." His accent smothered his English.

"Say what?"

"He's asking if you're hurt, hon."

I rolled my head to the side. Will stood next to Mr. Max.

"I don't think so."

Mr. Max's large paw grasped my upper arm, and my body flew off the ground. He held me until my legs straightened and drew balance from my feet.

"Hey now, watch it." I smoothed out my skirt and felt to find where my hair had landed.

Behind me, Butterbean, Cooper, Luke, and Pastor Earlie busied themselves with righting the still closed casket back onto the table.

My painting remained on its easel untouched.

A gaggle of women encircled Shawna, patting her with exclamations for her heroism.

"You saved the paintings," said Wanda, pulling Shawna into a tight hug. "Thank you for risking your neck. Those silly boys could have hurt you."

"Huh," I said.

"Cherry, are you sure you're okay? You're looking kind of puny." Leah fluttered over me, her hands clasped over her throat.

"I'm fine." I flexed my arms. "Just shook up. I missed the coffin and bounced on the carpet."

"Do you need me? They want me to drive to the cemetery and set up a portable keyboard." Leah glanced toward the side door.

Cooper ushered the coffin out of the room. Now that the riot had passed, he resumed presiding over the dead and grieving with sober authority.

"Go on. I'll see you tonight at Red's."

Leah leaned over for a quick hug and peck on the cheek. "You're going to love Todd's songs," she whispered.

Men turned to watch her careful progress after the coffin. You couldn't hide booty like that, even with hips swaddled in purple polyester.

I turned back to find Mr. Max's glance slip from Leah back to me. "I know you."

"What do you mean?" I threw a glance toward Will, but seeing me unhurt, he had moved on to haul Darren out of the chapel. "How do you know me?"

News traveled fast in Halo, but I doubted someone like Mr. Max would be interested in local gossip. Unless he hinted at an attempted late night funeral home mugging.

"You carried a painting in the Branson car shop. This painting is very good. Very fine brushstrokes, good color, nice lighting. Where did you study?"

"Savannah College of Art and Design." I narrowed my eyes. I wasn't used to locals singing my accolades so specifically. "Why are you so interested?"

"My mother, she also painted. She was excellent artist. The state paid for her school. Top university. But she married my father. No more painting. Too many kids. And she was working." He folded his large hands behind his back and nodded with solemnity. "We were poor."

"Oh, that's too bad," I said.

"Yes, too bad." A wry smile struck Max's mouth. "Your country is rich. You are lucky."

"Well," I said, wondering where this conversation headed. "The country may be rich, but not all of the people in it are."

"Surely you don't refer to yourself. You are very talented. You must command a high demand for your work."

"You would think."

"It's not true?"

"People appreciate the arts in Halo. I believe they are proud to have a local artist. However, that pride doesn't always extend to their wallets."

"I see," he said. "It's a matter of economics."

"Speaking of economics." I began with a terrible segue, but I had nothing else and I needed information. "What are you doing here?"

"At the funeral? I know Mr. Branson for business, and his son, Dustin. I am here showing my respect, of course. Why else would I be here?" He folded his arms and glanced about the room. "Although now I'm not certain the funeral is to continue?"

"This doesn't usually happen. They'll still expect everyone at the cemetery, I guess. But I meant, what are you doing in Halo?"

"Ah, I see. I am here for business and pleasure. I became interested in your American Civil War when I lived in my own country. Later, I came to this area to examine the historic site. I like this town. It's cheap land. Very quiet."

"Very quiet in terms of the law?"

"The law?" Max narrowed his eyes. "I don't know what you imply."

"I imply that I've heard a thing or two about you."

"I hope what you learned was pleasurable." He grunted and lifted a thick eyebrow, returning my scrutiny. "I imply that it should be."

"Touché," I said, thrilled with the chance to use movie French.

"Maybe you'd like to see my collection. It's quite extensive."

I thought about Dustin's effects and Mr. Max's request to see Dustin's room. "Do you collect belt buckles?"

"I collect all manner of items related to your war between the American states. Did you know it's considered the first modern war?"

"I don't know much about that. But I do know Manet's exhibition about the same time is considered the first modern painting."

"*Le Déjeuner Sur L'Herbe.*" A smile creased the long lines in his broad face. "You know art history well."

"From school. But here's how I remembered the painting: 'a naked chick picnicking with two dudes in suits.'" I laughed and broke out in goosebumps. I was trash talking Manet with a murder suspect running an illegal gambling establishment in his basement.

"Now what could you two be chatting about?" Luke strolled from the side door. "Cherry, shouldn't you be running along now? Painting's done and delivered. I'll make sure you are paid."

"I'm having a private conversation."

Luke moved around me to stand next to Max. "Mr. Avtaikin, we're going to finish the service at the cemetery. If you'd like to join us, you can ride with me."

"Don't you need to ride in the limo with your parents?" I glanced toward the Branson clan convening by the doorway. "Besides, Shawna'll be disappointed."

"So she said."

"Caught up on all the Eagles news, then?"

"I'd rather drive myself." Luke glanced at Max.

Likely hoping the Bear would take his offer for a ride, so Luke could scoop me on information.

"It is very hospitable of you to offer to drive, but no thank you. Artist, I did not receive your name." He held out his hand. "Maksim Avtaikin. Some call me Max."

Luke threw me an irritated look.

I tossed one back. "My name is Cherrilyn Tucker."

Max's hand swallowed mine. "I hope to know more about you," I paused to emphasize the next word, "Bear."

"Cherry." Luke rolled his eyes.

Max ignored Luke, focusing his piercing blue eyes on me. "You know my name means bear. It is my, what you call, nickname. I look like a bear, no?" He pawed the air and tossed his large head back with a laugh. "So I can call you by your nickname, too? Cherry?"

I bit my lip. "I guess so."

"Time to go." Luke nudged me with his foot.

"*Au revoir, mon* Cherry?" Max chuckled and lifted my hand to his mouth.

"Come on, man," Luke sighed. "Really?"

Max dropped my hand with a laugh. "Just a joke, friend. Her name makes a good use of words."

"Bear," I said. "I'm wondering about your relationship with Dustin. Just how well did you know him?"

"Enough, Cherry." Luke grabbed my arm and yanked me to the door. "Goodbye, Mr. Avtaikin. Very nice to meet you."

"He didn't get to answer the question." I called over my shoulder, "We'll continue this another time."

"You may count on it," said Max. "I'll ask around after you. I want to know more about you, artist."

"Me, too."

"Why are you provoking Mr. Avtaikin?" Luke muttered, frog-marching me to the parking lot. "You're dumber than Todd McIntosh. You two deserve each other."

"What are you talking about?" I shook my arm from Luke's hold. "I was just trying to get information."

"You weren't getting squat." He gripped my shoulders. "Stop this. I know you suspect Mr. Avtaikin and Pete, but this is not how you go about getting intelligence. He was just flirting with you anyway."

"It wasn't flirting. You should have heard our banter. It was like something from a 007 movie. I got to say touché."

"Oh my God." Luke dropped my arms to smack his forehead. "You are certifiable. Please, just go home. I've got to go to the cemetery and hold my mother together. This day just continues to be one long nightmare."

"Where's Virginia?"

"Hopefully she hightailed it back to Sweetgum with Darren. More than likely she's waiting at the cemetery. Why?"

"She left Amos behind. Not that he noticed. He's higher than a kite." I squinted in thought. "Butterbean said Virginia wouldn't come to the funeral unless she was paid. Do you think someone paid her, knowing she'd disrupt everything?"

"I don't know about that. But leave it alone. I'll worry about Virginia. Stay away from her and Mr. Avtaikin. And Creepy Pete. No more questioning. You don't know how to do it anyway."

I watched him retreat into the circle of Bransons standing in the foyer. Luke couldn't order me to not ask questions. I had a name to clear. No one would commission portraits from an artist who constantly had dead bodies dumped on her.

All of Halo probably thought I was into performance art.

"Why don't you ride with me, Mr. Avtaikin?" I mimicked in a nasty drawl. "You'll tell me everything I want to know because I'm Luke Harper and I'm just so good at everything I do."

Luke said he'd make sure I'd get paid, but I didn't count on it. The only person who appreciated my painting today was a man named after a bear. That thought depressed me.

Reaching the sidewalk, I realized I had passed the Datsun. I jumped on the sidewalk as a mass exodus of cars poured from the parking lot intent on following the hearse through stoplights. I watched the cars depart as I fumed.

Who did Luke think he was, calling me ineffective? I found out Dustin worked as a heavy for the Bear. Everyone else thought it was a drug deal, but poker connected Dustin to Mr. Max.

I sucked in my breath. Grandpa said they believed the murder resulted from drug deals in the tire shop. Could Max be the distributor, Virginia the maker, and Dustin, the middleman? I needed to talk Cody out of working for Curtis Mather.

But Creepy Pete didn't connect Mr. Max to drugs.

Then who killed Dustin? Creepy Pete? He seemed jealous of the relationship between Max and Dustin. I could picture Dustin mouthing off and Pete clocking him. Or maybe Luke was right about his stepdad. Would JB be so embarrassed by Dustin that he'd kill his own son?

Or did sweet Miss Wanda turn on her stepson, causing Luke to protect her by fixing the murder on JB? Luke certainly didn't like me asking questions. He made that plenty clear.

However, Miss Wanda taught Sunday School. She knew the Ten Commandments. I remembered Thou Shall Not Kill in there somewhere.

I wanted Shawna involved so I could shove it back in JB's face. Although maybe that was wishful, not logical, thinking.

And what was the killer searching for? The same thing Dustin had been hunting? Something like Shawna's photos?

Maybe Dustin caught her trading spit with someone important. A blackmail deal would be motive for murder.

I watched the last car bump over the sidewalk and onto the road. The blacktop looked lonely in the late morning sun.

No cars, no funeral, just a peaceful lot on an ordinary day. I flicked a glance right and left, closed my eyes, opened them, and looked again.

"Aw, hell. Somebody took my truck."

TWELVE

"I DON'T KNOW what you're complaining about, Casey," I said. "I give you rides all the time."

"Grandma Jo's show is on," Casey said, peering out her driver's side window. She swept a hand over her head, and her fake Ray Bans fell off her crown to land on her nose.

Squinting at a white minivan in the DriveIn & Eat parking lot, she shook her ponytail. "That's Brandi. That girl needs some help. Like she needs cheese tots on those hips."

Casey rolled her window down and called to a girl reaching for a drink on the loaded tray in her window. "They got salads there now, Brandi. The grilled chicken is pretty good."

I ignored her dubious nutritional Samaritanism and led her back to her own failings. "Grandma Jo is dead. She's been missing her shows near about ten years now."

"I watch them for her."

"Don't blame your TV addiction on a spiritual communion with your dead grandma." My stomach uttered a protest as Casey turned onto Highway 19.

"Why does your body make that God-awful sound whenever

we hit the blacktop?" Slanting a look toward me, she gunned the motor of her Firebird.

My head slammed against the fabric seat. I wrestled the seatbelt off my neck and pushed it over my shoulder.

"My stomach knows where I'm going. What did Cody do to your engine?" I eyed her black t-shirt and skinny jeans for signs of midday cooking. "Speaking of tater tots, if you're making me come to the farm, are you going to feed me?"

"Mac-n-cheese?"

"Homemade or box?"

The sunglasses barely hid her kohl-lined eye roll. "Like Grandpa would allow box. Homemade. Leftover from dinner. With ham and pimento."

"Now that sounds nice. I didn't get to eat all my wings last night."

Casey flashed me a wicked grin. "Eat anything else?"

"Don't be trashy. I'm a perfect example of clean living."

"It's not trashy to make out with Luke Harper in front of God and the world in the County Line doorway?"

"Shut up."

I folded my arms over my chest and stared out the front window. We flashed by a thick stretch of Loblolly pines. Their wispy trunks waving at the sky calmed me. Sun dappled fields half grazed by horses filled the open spaces between the spindly pine forests.

I had a sudden urge toward the contemplative life of a landscape painter. I could see myself sitting quietly in a pasture with my easel, more Courbet's Realism than Monet's Impressionism

"What I want to know is what happened after Todd showed up at your place," Casey continued.

"How did you know Todd showed?"

"He wandered into Red's after work as usual. He saw your truck in the parking lot and ran in like a dog after a bone. Felt so sorry for him, we thought we'd help him out. Todd perked right up. Finished his beer faster than usual to see if you made it home all right. He reckoned you must have walked."

"You didn't tell him that I got a ride with Luke?"

Or what Luke and I had been doing in Red's vestibule?

"Hell, no. What would be the fun in that? We laid bets to see which one might show back at the County Line. Red bet on Todd. Jackson on Luke. I said it'd be you. Said you'd probably kick both of 'em out for making you frazzled, and you'd hike back to Red's pitching a fit and wanting more food. But nobody showed up."

She pursed her lips. "Two men in one night? I want details!"

I grasped the armrest as the Firebird skidded in a tight turn onto the gravel lane leading to the farm. We bumped along the long drive, churning dust. The dopey-eyed horses lining the fenced lane watched our progress. Alerted to our arrival, Tater bounced up from a nap under the oak and waited.

Of course, he never played chicken with Casey.

"Get your mind out of the gutter. I had a painting to finish, which I did with Todd's help as a model. Luke brought me home and ate some wings. That kiss was a singular moment of passion that quickly fizzled when we remembered that he's a dog and I'm no ..."

"Angel?"

"That'd be you. No, I'm no teenager looking for his kind of thrill."

I didn't need the town hearing I got rejected by Luke when they already thought Todd dumped me on our wedding day.

"That's true. You're certainly not a teenager." Casey grinned and jammed the gearshift into park. "Is that why you're still letting Todd McIntosh hang around? Maybe you should think about settling down before the gray hairs accumulate."

Shooting her a look, I popped the car door.

Tater caught me half bent and managed to shove his nose into my shirt sleeve.

I pushed him off. "Give me a break. You're older than me. I don't see you settling down."

"Ah." She slammed the door shut. "Got to have someone to settle down with, right?"

I followed her into the kitchen, where the radio blasted the farm report. Grandpa sat ramrod straight with his bony arms crossed and a can of tobacco on the table next to him.

He squinted at me as I walked in. "What're you doing here? Is it dinner time already?"

I leaned over the counter to turn down the radio. "Grandpa, you need to get your hearing checked."

"What for? And hear about you pillaging cemeteries?"

"I didn't pillage a cemetery. I got caught in a funeral home. Don't worry. I'm going to figure out who really tried to rob Dustin and clear our name."

"You should have thought about that before you broke into Cooper's." Grandpa picked up his can of tobacco and tapped it on the table. "Casey, are you going to make me dinner?"

"For goodness sake." Casey flipped around from her trek to the living room and stalked to the refrigerator. "Why can't you two get your own food?"

"Tell me, little Miss Britches, whose house are you living in?"

"I'll get the food," I grumbled. "Doesn't anybody care my truck is gone?"

"That piece of crap finally die?" The screen door slammed into the wall. Cody tramped in and kicked Wanda's shopping bag on the floor. "What happened? I just dropped it off this morning."

"It's not dead, just missing. So you didn't take it either? Maybe I better call the police."

"The police?" Cody grunted. "They're not going to find your truck. Who'd want to spend time looking for that piece of junk? Just call your insurance and maybe you'll get some money for a new one."

My eyes glimmered at that thought and then considered the Datsun's worth. "I couldn't even put together a down payment with what they'd give me. No, I'll call Uncle Will and ask him to keep an eye out for it."

"Why would somebody steal that truck?" Casey slung several plates on the counter. "It's old and falling apart. Besides, everybody in town knows it's yours. You've been driving it since high school."

"Exactly." I plopped on a chair next to Grandpa.

He spun the tobacco can on the table and glanced at me. "Somebody stole your truck? Where'd you have it parked? That's what happens when you hang out at bars. You kids play too wild."

"It was parked at Cooper's. Can't get safer than that, I would think."

"Cooper's?" Cody slid into the seat across from me. "You were at Cooper's today? For the Branson funeral? I heard it got pretty interesting."

Casey pivoted from the counter. "Interesting how?"

I leaned back in my chair and folded my arms, readying myself for telling the story of the year. "Oh, let's see. Y'all know JB's first wife, Virginia Springhouser? Doesn't live in Halo, but hangs out in Sweetgum some. I guess she planned on avoiding the funeral service because of some altercation at the visitation. But she showed up anyway with Amos Fewe and a kid claiming to be Dustin's brother."

"Amos Fewe?" Grandpa leaned back in his chair and scratched his cheek. "Don't know him."

"Lives in Sweetgum, keeps bees, and sells wacky tobacky on the side," Cody explained.

"I thought it was meth," I said.

"Naw, I think someone else was mixing meth there. Burned their trailer down."

"Anyway." I stared at Cody for a beat, wondering where he got his information. "Amos was three sheets to the wind. Virginia stomped in like a bull ready for a red flag, hollering at Cooper because he didn't usher her in when he didn't know she was there. Then, she gets into an argument with JB. And her son, or whoever he is, gets in a fight with Charlie Turnbuckle. All this before Pastor Earlie can spout any scripture."

"No way," Casey stared at me. "Two fights at a funeral? I thought the Bransons were rich."

"Rich doesn't buy you class," said Grandpa.

"Poor doesn't buy class either," I said.

"From what I heard, you were part of that altercation." Cody raised his eyebrows at Grandpa.

"Cherrilyn. First I heard you were breaking and entering and robbing the dead, now this? Did I raise you to fight at funerals?"

"No, sir." I glowered at Cody. "I was not involved in a fight. I accidentally got in the way of this Darren and Charlie Turnbuckle when they were wrestling."

"I heard one of them knocked you out. You fell right into the coffin. Shawna Branson tried to save you but was too late."

"That's not what happened. Shawna Branson did nothing to help me."

"Cherrilyn B. Tucker. Your grandmother is rolling in her grave." Grandpa swiped the can off the table and shoved it in his pocket. Laying an arm on the laminate table top, he leaned into our conversation and riveted his focus on me.

"Tell them what started the fight." Cody snickered.

I narrowed my eyes. "Where're you going with this, Cody?"

"Turns out the fight started because the Bransons set up some paintings of Dustin. One picture was so God-awful creepy; people started pitching fits. Virginia went insane with shock. Old women were fainting. Kids screaming. Young guys started fighting. And Cherry's right there in the middle of it, trying so hard to defend her painting, she gets knocked in a coffin."

"Good Lord in heaven." Grandpa ran his hands over his face. "What are you doing to us, Cherry? This is what happens when you get above your raising. I didn't like you traipsing off to Savannah to hang out with all those fruitcakes. Everyone said, 'Let her go. She's got some talent, let her do something with it.' I said, 'Why not go to a school with some football then?'"

He shook his head in disgust. "But no, you never listen to me or anyone. Had to go off to that crazy school and become 'an artist.'" He moaned. "Look what it's done to you. Ruining folks' funerals. I've a mind to jerk you out of Gam's house and bring you back here where I can keep an eye on you."

"Cody." I thumped the table. "Will you tell him that is not what happened? Grandpa, you know Cody exaggerates."

Cody shrugged his shoulders and folded his arms behind his head. "That's just what I heard."

"That's not what happened. And it wasn't my portrait that freaked everybody out."

"So it really was a painting that caused them to go crazy?" Casey leaned forward on her arms. "I think there was something about like that on TV. A cartoon made all these kids have a seizure. Is that what happened with your painting?"

"No, that's not what happened with my painting. My portrait is beautiful. A gorgeous deep purple underpainting, which was a perfect tone. Very moody but still somber. And when I overpainted the cool with warm flesh tones and some pearly highlights, the hands popped from the blue suit. Dustin had wonderful hands. He could have been an artist with those long fingers. The hands almost glow in that coffin."

"Glowing hands?" Casey wrinkled her nose. "No wonder people had seizures."

Grandpa shook his head in shame, while Cody barked with laughter. He leaned back in the rattan chair until the hoop resting on the floor began to tip. Tears ran down his face as he snorted and choked on the glowing hands image.

"It was Dustin's childhood portrait that caused fits."

"I heard Shawna Branson had a nice drawing of Dustin as an angel," said Cody.

"An angel in camo gear holding a dead turkey. Has everyone gone insane?" I stomped away from the table toward the door, bumping Cody's chair on my way. "Y'all are just mad because you didn't see that funeral in person. And no one had a seizure."

"Someone might have had a seizure." Casey nodded. "I'll ask around."

"I was there," I shouted and kicked the bag sitting next to the door. "Dangit, this is Dustin's collection. I hope I didn't break anything."

I squatted to check the contents. "I need to finish this thing."

"Call me when dinner is ready. You best watch yourself, young lady. That house in town belongs to the family, and I can take it back, taxes and all." Grandpa drew his wiry frame out of his chair. His shrunken body straightened with dignity and voice shook with righteous indignation. "You know the Tucker reputation falls on you three kids now. It may not be fair, but that's the way it is."

The screen door slammed against the wall.

I jumped up and turned to face Cody, but he had slipped through the living room doorway.

"You better run, Cody," I called after him and flashed a look at Casey. "Why do you two love to get me into trouble?"

"If you'd look around, we've got nothing better to do."

"Then you're going to help me figure out how to fix my reputation while I make the memory box."

"Yes, ma'am."

"And you can heat me some mac-n-cheese."

FUELED BY SCRUMPTIOUS CHEESY NOODLES, I puttered with the memory box collection in the sunny kitchen. Casey sat across from me, eager to discuss the various possibilities leading to Dustin's death. True to her nature, Casey quickly poked holes in my favorite theory: Shawna battering Dustin to death in outrage over the humiliation of a sex scandal.

"Can you see Shawna risking breaking a nail?" Casey asked. "She's into mind games. If Shawna killed someone, she'd hire a hit man and not dirty her hands. You just want to get back at her for spreading rumors about you robbing Dustin's corpse."

"Was she behind that?" I pounded the table, causing the toy cars to roll. "I knew it. She knew my painting would outclass hers.

Which it did, glowing hands or not. Why does she want to ruin me?"

"It's not just you. You're an easy target. I heard in high school, she bullied a cheerleader into dropping out of school. Cheerleaders don't usually lack self-confidence."

"Neither do I. Or at least I don't let anyone know when I do."

"No kidding. Why do you think Cody and I have such fun with you?"

"Anyway," I shot Casey a hard look, "you don't think it was Shawna."

"I don't think you could pay her to go in a dirty garage. She's just a bitch, not a killer."

"Luke said Dustin was hit from behind. Which means Dustin knew and trusted whoever killed him. He was looking up, getting ready to drain oil, when pow."

"If it was the torque wrench," Casey said. "You're going on Curtis Mather's assumption."

"He seemed pretty certain. Whoever it was knew Dustin would be working on his Malibu in that garage after hours. Alone."

"That's where he dealed. Everyone knows that." Casey picked up a jeweled watch and tried it on her wrist. "I like this one. Do you think Miss Wanda would notice it gone?"

"Red said Dustin and Virginia tried to sell drugs in the County Line parking lot." I glanced at Casey. "Put the watch back. That's all I need, getting accused of stealing Dustin's jewelry. And why do you think Miss Wanda is letting me make this memory box if she believes I tried to steal Dustin's baby teeth?"

"Because she knows you didn't try to steal Dustin's baby teeth. It's obvious you were there to paint. Why would you make such a mess if you were going to steal something?"

"Exactly. Then why does everyone believe Shawna and not me? You know I had an appointment to do some framing for Mrs. Malleck and she called and canceled? I'm losing jobs over this thing."

"You know how it is in Halo." Casey tossed the watch on the

table. "Appearances mean more than fact. You were at the wrong place at the wrong time and therefore you are guilty of something."

A half-smile twisted the corner of her mouth. "And I think the charge of trespassing still applies."

"Trespassing I can deal with. But you're right about appearances. Maybe Dustin's death was drug related. But there are a lot of folks who didn't like Dustin. Shawna admitted he had incriminating pictures. He worked for Mr. Max who runs a poker game in his basement for highfalutin people with deep pockets. JB has some secrets. If Dustin would have incriminating pictures of his cousin, you think he would sell out his boss or his dad? Or his step-brother?"

"With Dustin, anything is possible." Casey snagged the lion's head belt buckle, tilting the face, so the light bounced a ruby glow on the tabletop. "You don't buy stuff like this by working at an old garage."

"Good point." I positioned a few old coins between the cars and the class ring. "And speaking of garages, what do you think happened to my truck?"

The clatter of Tater's hooves on the porch followed by the sound of gravel churning in the driveway caught our attention. We flicked a glance toward the window over the sink. Casey hopped up and peered through the gingham curtain.

"Why don't you ask the sheriff? That's him now."

"Help me hide this stuff. If Uncle Will knows I'm doing another job for the Bransons, he'll kill me himself."

UNCLE WILL and I contemplated one another across the kitchen table while Casey rattled dishes behind us. She plonked a steaming cup of coffee before Uncle Will and returned to the counter. Soup bubbled on the stove. Sweet, smoky bacon popped and sizzled on the griddle pan.

Will rubbed a hand over his face and let it drop next to the coffee cup. "Thank you, Casey honey, but you don't need to go to all this trouble."

"No trouble, Uncle Will."

Will sniffed and threw a glance at me. We both knew Casey used a project in the kitchen to listen to our conversation.

I wiggled in my chair. I couldn't control myself from staring at the bag holding Dustin's collection by the door.

Dragging my eyes back to the table, I tried to concentrate on Uncle Will. "So what brings you by? Rest stop on your journey? How was the burial? Hear anything about my truck yet?"

"The burial was quiet, thank the Lord." Will drummed his fingers on the table.

I shot another glance toward the bag and looked back at Will with a forced smile.

"At least that's what my deputy said. Virginia Springhouser disappeared. I had Chris Wellington take Darren and Amos Fewe to the cemetery and stick with them. Darren, by the way, is not her son. He is Amos Fewe's son."

"Why'd she pretend to be his mother?"

"That remains to be seen, but most likely to get back at JB." Will paused and sipped his coffee. "Now Cherry, I need to talk to you about something."

I crossed my arms over my chest and leaned back in the chair. My eyes wandered back to the shopping bag. "What? Is this about what happened at the funeral? That was not my fault."

"I have news about your truck."

I straightened in the chair.

Casey flipped the bacon from the pan and spun around to listen. "Did you find it?"

"We did." He held the mug between his hands and rotated it clockwise three times.

The pause seemed ominous. I glanced at Casey. She gave up the pretense of cooking and slipped behind my chair.

Will filled his chest with air and expelled it with slow delibera-tion. "Cherry. I need some details about last night and this morning. Let's start with the Datsun. You drove it to Cooper's this morning and arrived a little before ten?"

"What's this about, Uncle Will ?" Casey spoke for me. She tightened a hand on my shoulder.

Will flickered a glance to Casey and looked back at me. "Just answer the question, Cherry."

"Yes, sir. I picked up Casey yesterday and drove it to Red's last night. Left it there and got a ride home. Casey took it home, and Cody dropped it off at about nine-thirty this morning. I took him to work and got to Cooper's just before ten like you said. Is my truck okay? Did someone take it for a joyride and get in an accident?"

Will rotated the mug in the opposite direction. "Who might have seen your truck last night at Red's?"

"Uh, a table of nurses. A couple families. Red, of course. Who were those men at your table, Casey?"

"Trevor Collins and Lobby Smith."

"Anyone else?" Will pulled out a small notebook from his shirt pocket.

"Big hunter at the bar," I said.

"Merry Blake," Casey said.

"And I talked to Pete Billocks and Jackson Raydorn. They're Todd McIntosh's roommates. And Casey said Todd showed up later, after I left. But my truck was still there."

Will scratched the names on the pad and tapped the pen against the table.

Casey flopped onto a chair. "Don't forget Luke Harper."

He scribbled the name. "Anyone else?"

"Not really," Casey said. "It was pretty quiet. Oh, a big table for a Little League team and all their coaches and parents. They were from out of town, though." Casey stuck out her lip and rubbed it. "A couple came in late. I don't know them either."

"Okay." Will flipped the cover on his notebook shut and took another sip of coffee. "Cherry. Last night, you took your sister to Red's and left with?"

"Luke Harper," I said with a small cough. "And some wings."

"And he left your house at what time?"

"About an hour later. We ate some wings and then heard something out in my carport. He took off soon after that."

"Say that again?"

"We heard noises in the carport, sir. The lights were off in the house," I ignored Casey's snigger. "But the light in the carport was on. Somebody broke it. Luke went out to check. I got my gun out. That somehow ticked Luke off, and he left."

"What gun is this? Karl Tucker's Remington?"

"Yes, sir." Some fact tickled my mind. Something Casey had said earlier. "Hey Case, when did Pete leave?"

"Before Todd went to your house."

"Todd McIntosh went to your house, too?"

I sounded like the town harlot but with nothing to show for it.

"Todd came a minute after Luke left," I said. "It was Casey's idea of a joke to send him over and see what would happen."

"Peter Billlocks." Will massaged his cheeks with one hand. "Did he return to the County Line Tap, Casey?"

"No. He threw a hissy after Cherry and Luke left. Took off after that. I'm sorry, Cherry. That was another reason why I sent Todd to your place. I got the feeling that Pete might follow y'all home and make a scene."

"What did you do with the gun, Cherry?" said Will.

"Took it in the house, of course. I had to finish the painting. And Todd came in with me. I used him as a model."

"What did you do with the gun?" Will repeated.

"I, uh." My thoughts ran over the evening. "I walked in with Todd. Did I put the gun down then? I must have. On the counter? No wait, he said something to me about it in the living room. I know. I set it by my easel. I felt nervous."

"What time did Todd McIntosh leave?"

I scooted around in my chair and stuck my hands under my legs. "I don't know. He was asleep when I left. On the lounge in the living room. Somebody's always crashing at my house. You know that."

"Have you talked to Todd today?" Will pushed out of his chair and pulled the radio from his belt.

"No."

I glanced at Casey. She shrugged.

"What is going on?"

"Mrs. Leonard saw your truck driving down your street around ten-thirty this morning. After you got to Cooper's. She has shingles and didn't go to the funeral. But lucky for us, she kept an eye on the square, same as always. Someone stopped at your house and forced their way in through the back door. Then they drove your truck back to Cooper's and parked it in back. Cooper found it after the burial."

"Someone used the Datsun to break in my house and then returned it?"

"Why would they keep it? It barely runs," said Casey.

"Someone broke into my house?" I took a shaky breath. "Oh Lord, Todd. Was Todd still there?"

"Not that we're aware of. I'm going to need you to come to the house and see if anything is missing."

"Did they take my gun, Uncle Will ?"

"That's what concerns me. Someone shot Peter Billocks with a shotgun. He was found next to your truck."

"Shot? Is he dead?"

Will nodded his head with closed eyes. "Let's go see if your gun is missing."

My stomach dropped to my feet. "Oh my stars. Lord Almighty, help me. Somebody used my gun for murder." I laid my face on the cool tabletop and blinked away the black spots dancing before my eyes.

"We don't know that for sure. No weapon was found. Billocks' car was spotted across the street from the funeral home in the old pharmacy parking lot. Probably saw your truck drive into Cooper's and walked over to confront you. We found empty liquor bottles and other paraphernalia in his vehicle. I'm going to have my dispatcher put some calls out for Todd McIntosh."

Will walked around the table to stand behind my chair.

"Thanks for the coffee, Casey. Can I take one of those bacon sandwiches to go?" He cupped a hand on my head. "You'll be all right, sugar. Problem is you Tuckers attract bad luck like a magnet."

"What am I going to do?" I whispered.

"I bet Great Gam is rolling over in her grave knowing some deranged killer waltzed through 211 Loblolly and took daddy's gun like it was the door prize at a Mary Kay party," said Casey.

Casey was right. Taking a deep breath, I sat up. I found my feet and rustled up some resolve to accompany Will to my violated home.

It's amazing what you can make yourself do when someone steals your daddy's gun and sets you up for murder.

THIRTEEN

THE SIGHS RIPPING through my chest occurred at a frequency similar to a pregnant woman at a Lamaze class. My pointy, little chin rested on folded arms. And my boots dangled from a wood and pleather barstool.

Another Friday night at Red's. This time I showed for fear of being alone, and I didn't like that feeling one bit.

The County Line thrummed with people and piped in music. Folks from Halo and parts nearby poured in to get their Friday night drink-on. At the far end of the room, Todd and his band fiddled with the microphones and a soundboard. Excitement for Sticks' debut performance mounted in the smoky atmosphere, putting the wait staff in a dither over the abundance of orders. Whiskey shooters and pitchers of beer floated around the men's tables. Margaritas and nachos flowed at the women's.

Todd as front man on drums drew the females in flocks to Red's, filling the area before the stage. The male customers appeared in anticipation of the ladies' liquored-up fallout, tolerating the music during the wait. At this point, the Sticks fan base was entirely female and Todd-centered.

Red stood behind the bar with crossed arms and a clean rag flipped over his shoulder, his concerned sentinel look.

Everyone knew someone stole my gun and truck and Pete's life. Halo folks viewed me with a mixture of pity and scorn, something akin to finding a fox caught in a rabbit trap.

Because the Tucker kids were a hair short of a "from across the tracks" identity and because I had further sullied our name by tussling with Dustin's dead body (twice), this rare tragedy meant I had somehow brought it on myself.

Casey, Cody, and I may not resemble a loving family in good times, but our familial loyalty kicks in for a crisis. Casey whizzed in and out of view, dressed in a vampish version of her uniform, to check if I ate or talked. Cody scoped me from three stools away where he could check on me yet remain open to romantic liaisons without a sister cramping his style.

Any unknown man close to my stool received a custom Cody snarl. His attempt at brotherly protection was sweet, although I doubted a killer would approach me in a bar to thank me for my truck and gun.

"My life is in the toilet, Red. We're talking a serious septic tank situation."

Red propped a thick arm on the bar. "Come on now, hon. The sheriff will catch this guy. You're going to be okay. You've got plenty of people looking out for you."

"I know. But what if Todd had been home when the killer broke into my house? And poor Creepy Pete. He was nasty, but he was somebody's son. Gunshot to the abdomen. With my daddy's gun."

"Did they find your gun yet?"

My head rocked on my arms for a hearty no. "Didn't think I'd ever feel this way about Creepy Pete. It's like Jack the Ripper is knocking off white trash mouth-breathers instead of prostitutes. A very conflicting feeling."

"I know what you mean. Hate to see anyone taken like that, but those boys were troublemakers. That Dustin had his fingers in a lot of different pies. I heard he was at the arson in Sweetgum."

I shot up in my seat. "Where'd you hear that?"

"Here, obviously. I'm privy to all kinds of things. Can't remember from who. Most of what I hear, I take with a grain of salt."

"No wonder Uncle Will's having trouble sorting it out. The more I know, the more confused I get." I fingered a wing and reached for the beer.

Red grunted and pushed the wings closer.

"I just feel like the answer is staring me in the face and I can't see it."

Red flicked his gaze to the vestibule door as another group strode into the crowded tavern. I recognized several younger assorted Bransons in the group and held my breath.

I expelled it with a huff.

In blue jeans, denim shirt, and boots, Luke sauntered behind the group, looking like a cowboy in a Levi's ad. Shawna trolled in beside him, swapping out her little black dress for blue jeans and a tight pink cheetah-print top. But kept the four-inch heels, of course.

My eyes narrowed, and a scowl burned my mouth. I sucked on a wing and swigged my beer. Using the mirror behind the bar, I kept an eye on the group as they shoved some tables together.

"Isn't that the kicker? My life was just fine a week ago. Luke Harper walks in, and now I'm a mess all over again. And I told myself never again. He runs hot and cold. And still manages to pull me in every time."

I took another swig of beer. "Luke played me like a cheap fiddle. I'm telling you if I was Sampson, he's my Delilah. At least with Todd, I knew who was in charge. That's another kind of exasperation, though. I don't want to be lead dog all the time."

"There's always more fish in the sea. We grow 'em good looking enough around here. You'll find someone else to make you a mess. Besides, you've got bigger things to worry about. Like this homicidal maniac running around."

"Thanks for reminding me."

"You know what your problem is, Cherry? You're like a Jack Russell with ADD. You need to figure out what you want instead of just hopping around, wasting a lot of energy."

"That's just Cherry's way, Red. The only time she's focused is when she's drawing or making something." Leah scooted in next to me. "She thinks with her hands."

"Sure doesn't think with her mouth. That's another problem. What can I get you, Leah?" Red whipped out a napkin and placed it in front of her.

"Dr. Pepper. Thank you, Red."

"Hey." I gave her a quick hug. "You make out okay at the burial?"

"I heard the news."

"I'm alright. Just a little down in the dumps. Red's right, though. I need to figure this out."

"Figure this out?" Leah questioned.

Red hopped back with the Dr. Pepper and placed it on the napkin.

"I aim to get my gun back. I'll be damned if I let this bastard get away with shooting people with my gun."

"Don't we have a sheriff for that?"

"Don't worry, Leah. I'm not going to go after him myself. I'm not that crazy. But I've talked to a few people in town, including Creepy Pete before his murder. I've got a few thoughts about who took it."

"Like who?" The Dr. Pepper fizzed and popped in Leah's hand. She paused to consider me before taking a sip.

"Virginia left the funeral early. She could have easily taken it. Creepy Pete could have stolen my truck, broke into my house and taken the gun, and when he returned to Cooper's, someone wrestled him for it and shot him."

Red draped his arms on the bar, leaning in to listen.

"Uncle Will thinks whoever took the truck used it to park at my house and break-in unnoticed. The killer could also have an accomplice. Shawna probably wouldn't dirty her hands on Dustin, but she might hire somebody to kill him. But that's true of any of the Bransons. Makes me look pretty bad, too."

I glanced at the Branson table. "My feelings for Creepy Pete were well known, and he was shot with my gun. Maybe I'm unlucky, or maybe I'm being set up.

"I got a couple of other people on my list, too. I need to start eliminating suspects. Uncle Will says he knows all about the gambling at Mr. Max's, but it's too circumstantial to tie to the killing. He pretty much rolled his eyes when I told him about my conversation with Max at the funeral."

Red and Leah exchanged glances.

As my mind wandered from the suspects, I stole a look at Leah's outfit. Pressed jeans, red pumps, and camisole peeking behind a jacket? Miss Melanie struck again. Leah needed to move out of her mother's house or start collecting cats for her future occupation as town spinster.

"This is what you're wearing tonight?"

Leah nodded and smoothed her black twill suit jacket, checking the buttons held everything in place.

"You didn't iron those jeans, did you?"

"Lay off, Cherry," Red said. "I think you look real nice."

"Thank you." Leah flashed him a gorgeous smile from Maybelline Royal Red lips.

Red's freckles faded into the glow of his blushing skin.

"Leah knows I don't mean anything. But look here, sister, you're rocking out tonight. You can't wear that."

"Momma and I thought the jeans with heels was kind of rockish."

Spying Casey behind the bar, I flagged her. "Case, you need to help Leah. She's planning on taking the stage looking like a forty-five-year-old soccer mom."

Casey studied Leah for a moment. "To start with, you've got on too many clothes."

Leah fiddled with the hem of her jacket and darted a look at the amount of skin Casey revealed to Red's customers.

Maybe pulling Casey in wasn't such a good idea. Still, our options were limited, and Casey did have a flair for this.

"You're performing a role. Tonight you're not the choir director or the piano teacher. Tonight you're a rock star."

"Amen," Casey said. "You just come with me, and I'll fix you up."

"Now Casey, I appreciate your—"

"Casey doesn't share her secrets with just anybody," I said. "You're going to look fantastic. Y'all get moving. The band is starting soon."

I grabbed Casey's arm before she skipped off with my friend. "Shoot for rock star, not porn star. This is Leah we're talking about. She's still gotta hold her head high in church on Sunday."

"I know. Besides, I don't want her to steal all the men tonight." She winked and fluttered her fingers at Red.

"And what about your customers?" he bellowed.

She maneuvered Leah toward the kitchen, swaying her hips in a skirt hiked high enough to charge admission.

Red shook his head. "I hope you know what you're doing. If Leah's mother gets wind of her looking anything like Casey..." he stopped in terror of the thought.

I grabbed another wing and waved it at Red. "Don't worry about Miss Melanie. Anybody who'd tattle on Leah is not the type to show up at the County Line."

Red groaned and moved down the bar to take an order.

Leah made a great point earlier. Grabbing some napkins and a stray pen, I began doodling ideas. The first drawing ripped the thin paper. With a lighter touch, the second try gave me a fair sketch of a bear, a hand of cards, and dead Dustin. On the third napkin a heifer, a smoking trailer, and Dustin appeared.

However, the last napkin paired Dustin with a sketch of a rakish man with dark curly hair and dimples. I hesitated and then drew a question mark between them.

"You doing those funny sketches of people? Like they sell at Six Flags?"

I shuddered at the memories. Ronny Price hovered over my shoulder, examining the drawings with interest. With blue jeans, a braided belt, and avocado dress shirt, he showed a fondness for the preppy line from Bell's Department Store.

I bit my lip to prevent my admiration of his color choice, remembering his misinterpretation of my earlier interest.

"Hey Ronny, I'm just doodling."

"I'm teasing." A half smile played across his lips. He smoothed the gelled pompadour with both hands.

Cody raised his chin to observe my admirer. Seeing his boss's boss, he curled his lip and turned a blind eye to my situation.

I laid my arm across the napkins and shifted to face Ronny.

"The painting you did of Dustin was very good." Ronny eased himself into the empty stool next to mine.

"Thank you. I feel satisfied with the portrait. Especially considering the difficulty I encountered trying to finish it."

"Difficulty?"

"Let's just say it's been a rough couple of days." I slipped another napkin between us and let my pen drift across it.

"That's what they make tequila for, right?" He gave me that salesman chuckle that sounded like a self-provided laugh track and turned on his stool to study the busy bar.

I glanced over my shoulder and locked eyes with Luke.

After a couple of seconds of the no-blink game, I slid my gaze to Shawna. She waggled her fingers and dropped her hand on Luke's arm.

"I'm surprised the Bransons would come here after the funeral," said Ronny. "Although I guess the young ones wouldn't be interested in hanging around the house."

"They lack maturity. Particularly certain Bransons." I eyed Ronny, realizing maturity might have its benefits. His age came with advantages, like dressing well and money. He probably didn't stiff dates at the Waffle Hut.

He probably took his dates to somewhere nicer than the Waffle Hut.

Not that I wanted to date Ronny Price, but I counted on him being good for a drink or two.

"What did you think of Shawna Branson's painting?"

"Her painting?" He blinked and turned in his seat to face me. After a quick assessment of my solitary situation, he eased into a comfortable angle. "I'd say Shawna Branson's painting was not as good as yours. You're very talented."

"Thank you," I said, feeling vindication roll through me and break on the shores of self-righteousness. "Mine wasn't perfect — maybe the hand color was a little too strong — but I spent a lot of time on that work. It's not like I colored in a blow-up photo with tempura paints. How could she charge portrait fees for that? There wasn't even a sitting. Not that Dustin could sit for anyone."

I straightened on my stool and peeked over my shoulder at Luke. Finishing a remark to a cousin across the table, he swigged his beer and glanced at the bar. I scooted on my stool closer to Ronny and felt the tingle of satisfaction at Luke's eyebrow quiver.

Swinging my attention back to the bar, I glanced at my empty bottle. If I could keep Ronny's attention, I might gain some helpful information. And it didn't hurt to keep Luke guessing. Maybe it would prevent him from dancing with Shawna when the band started because if that happened I might do something stupid. Like, go home with Todd.

"I could use another drink," I said. "This week has been so stressful, and I feel like letting my hair down."

"Hey, Red," called Ronny. "How about a couple of drinks over here?"

The simplicity of men sometimes made life easy.

"Thanks."

"My pleasure," he said and leaned closer to be heard over the noise of the crowded bar. "So what are you working on now? Art wise?"

"I lost a framing job today and got a call from the art league in Stillwater. They're putting off the local artist show where I was supposed to exhibit. This funeral gig hurt my career."

I lobbed an angry glance in the bar mirror at Shawna. Her attention riveted on the stage where clusters of women were trying to catch Todd's attention. I added a pin-up figure with horns and a pitchfork to the circles on the napkin. My pen sketched in a tiny mustache and beard on the girl's face.

"Too bad you can't do more for the Bransons. Those folks have plenty of money."

"Oh, I have another little job. A memory box. You probably heard about it." I grabbed another napkin and drew a gridded box. Tiny cars filled in the holes.

Ronny leaned closer to listen. "What's a memory box?"

"A deep frame partitioned to show objects. It can be for anything. Baby or wedding mementos, usually." I gnawed the pen cap, thinking of Dustin's treasures. I hadn't encased the items yet, wanting to discuss their validity with Miss Wanda. I added a belt buckle to the little box on the napkin.

Ronny pulled out his wallet and threw some bills on the bar as Red approached. I eyed the drink set before me with suspicion. Ronny picked up his rocks glass. The ice tinkled in amber liquid, and he tipped it toward me. "Cheers."

"Sure," I replied. My brow furrowed at the long stemmed martini glass filled with magenta liquid.

We clinked our glasses together. Ronny took a strong sip of his drink while I hesitated. "What is this?"

"I got you a Cosmo," Ronny said. "Do you like them?"

"I don't know. Never had one. I mostly stick with beer. What are you drinking?"

"Scotch on the rocks." Smiling, he took another sip. He slid closer. "I think we may be some of the few sophisticates in Halo. I admire you for being an artist and going away to school. I like living in Halo, too, but sometimes the people here don't understand quality. Not like me. Or the Bransons."

Ronny turned in his seat and lifted his glass to the table behind us. I stole a glance in the mirror at Luke who nodded toward Ronny and half-heartedly lifted his beer.

Sophisticated? That's not a word I'd ever used to describe myself. I glanced at my bedazzled tomato-red Henley. I had replaced the tiny buttons with orange and pink rhinestones and decorated the back in a kind of Pointillist beach scene. My denim cutoffs had purple and blue rhinestones along the pockets and seams. I drew the line at bejeweling my boots.

"Speaking of the Bransons, how do you like working at the dealership?"

"Truthfully, some days are better than others. Been hit hard by the economy. But when it's good, the money is great. A couple of years ago I bought a condo on the Gulf. Padre Island. Incredible beach and close enough to slip over to Mexico whenever I feel the call for fresh tequila."

"What's JB like?" I fished carefully. "Seems like he'd be a difficult boss."

"I don't think of him as a boss. We're more like equals. I'm head of sales, you know."

Ronny slurped the rest of his scotch and shoved it on the bar. "But if you really want to know, he can be a pain in the ass. Especially with this Dustin business. Not that I don't feel bad for the family."

"How do you mean? He hasn't appeared like the grieving father to me."

"Exactly. He's trying to work all these deals in between the visitation and funeral. At least, I think that's what's going on. He's always in meetings or on the phone, and I haven't had a chance to talk to him. He even blew me off the other day to meet with that jackass."

"Which jackass would that be?" I waved at Red and pointed toward Ronny's glass. Liquor seemed to be loosening the greased slickster, and I had a feeling where the conversation headed.

"You met him the other day at the dealership. I think you experienced his so-called European sophistication and first-class personality."

"Max Avtaikin? He did lack a bedside manner. I've also heard that Mr. Max runs a little poker game in his fancy basement."

"Really?" Ronny pointed at my empty glass as Red turned. "Make it two, Red."

I glanced at the refill Red poured into Ronny's glass. The Cosmo tasted like candy, and Ronny's admissions spurred me to something stronger.

"Let me try one of those instead." I fluttered my eyelashes. "If you're buying, Ronny."

"Sure, sure," he said. His hands drifted to his hair.

Red stared at me as if I had grown horns. "You want a scotch? How about a beer?"

"Single malt for the lady," Ronny said. "Spare no expense, barkeep." He shook his glass to make the ice cubes swirl and took a large swallow. "Like butter down your throat. Warm butter."

I grasped the glass Red offered and socked back a strong slurp. Tears sprang into my eyes and a shuddering cough shook my lungs. "Kind of burns. All the way through my sinuses." My nose hairs felt singed.

"You're funny."

Noise swelled from the far side of the bar. I twisted in my seat. Before the stage, a table of women hooted in ecstatic revelry. Todd had reappeared on the stage. He smiled and waved at their enthusiasm. Grabbing a notebook off the floor, he strode toward the kitchen.

I watched him exit the room in a stiff-legged swagger. He had changed his cargo shorts for tight, black faux-leather pants.

Shawna swooped in between Cody and Ronny, running a hand over her smooth updo. "Excuse me," she called to Red. "Your wait staff is dawdling like we're willing to wait all night. We need menus and a better waitress."

Red handed her menus and scuttled to the far end of the bar to lecture Casey.

Shawna arched an eyebrow in my direction. "I'm surprised you'd show your face in here tonight, Cherry."

Cody whistled low and tipped his cap back.

Ronny's head snapped to the right. He gave Shawna a once-over followed by a hair smooth.

"I can't think why," I said. "I usually pay my tab."

The laughter trilling from her glossy peach lips reminded me of a jay squawking.

She fanned her bosom, directing the men's eyes toward her bounty. "Always joking. But humor is a coping mechanism. If my life were as unfortunate as yours, I'd guess I paint on a happy face, too."

"I suppose you would, considering how much paint you use on your face anyway."

"Didn't your mother teach you not to talk so ugly?" She snatched the menus and slid away from the bar. "Oh, I'm sorry. I guess she couldn't, considering she wasn't around."

"Ouch," said Ronny.

"That's nothing," I said, taking a strong pull from the scotch. "You should have heard what she said about me in high school. You might have if you were at my senior homecoming football game when we played Line Creek. That was before they started locking the broadcaster's booth."

"Everything okay over here?" Casey asked from behind me.

I nodded. "You remember Ronny Price?"

"Sure, from Branson's dealership?"

"Casey Tucker." Ronny slid off his stool and held out his hand. "Nice to see you again."

Casey allowed him to pump her arm. Her grip had the obvious consistency of overcooked noodles. "Y'all need anything? Cody's taking off."

"Beer," I mouthed. I could feel the scotch desensitizing the end of my nose. And my feet felt farther away than usual.

"I could use another scotch. Dewar's is fine, Casey." Ronny climbed back on the stool and slid an arm along the bar, making a private space for us to talk.

I scooted closer to keep the conversation between us.

"So you don't like Mr. Max so much?

"I find him ill bred." Ronny slurped his drink in expectation of the next round. "And a social climber. Although I did sell him his Escalade."

"He does have humble beginnings," I conceded, thinking about my conversation with Max at the funeral. "And he knows his art. And history. But what about the gambling? I'm worried about his influence in Halo."

A beer appeared on the counter before me. I picked it up grate-fully, leaving the hard stuff to Ronny. The scotch had numbed my lips. I smacked them, trying to regain feeling.

"Influence? I guess Avtaikin is making himself known in certain circles." Ronny watched my mouth, fascinated with my lip exercises.

I noticed his interest and stopped. "You ever see Dustin Branson with Mr. Max?"

"Dustin? I heard he worked for Mr. Avtaikin. JB didn't like that at all."

"Dustin got in a lot of trouble, didn't he?"

"Unfortunately, Dustin couldn't stay out of trouble. He lied and stole." Ronny leaned closer. "I think Mr. Avtaikin turned a blind eye to certain things Dustin did, but maybe he didn't know about it either."

"What? Dustin stealing?"

"Yes. Pity, really. Dustin was a mess."

I nodded and squinted one eye in concentration. "Do you know exactly what he stole?"

My stool jostled as someone slid into the seat next to me. I spun to the left and locked on eyes the color of slate after a recent rain. Watercolor would capture that darkened expression of mixed irri-tation and exasperation Luke wore so well.

"What are you doing up here?" I said. "Slumming it?"

I didn't give him a chance to answer and whipped back around, spilling beer en route.

Ronny's hand found my shoulder to keep me from tumbling off the stool.

"Hold on there, little lady." He pushed another martini glass toward me. "I ordered you another drink." He slid it closer. "Enjoy."

"You're hitting on Ronny Price?" A low voice breathed in my ear. "You're not fooling anybody, especially me. I told you to stop interrogating folks."

Portraying lazy indifference, Luke swiveled on his stool and leaned into our circle, pushing a glass of water toward me. "Evenin', Ronny."

Luke glanced at my stack of sketches. "You doing bar napkin portraits now, Cherry?" Luke flipped through the stack. A crease marred his forehead and tugged down his dark brows.

"Leave those alone." I swiped at the inky napkins and snatched one. Tearing, it stuck to my fingers. Ink bled through the thin paper and tattooed my fingertips. I drug my fingers across the bar, making little paper pills on the sticky surface.

"How are you, Luke?" Ronny asked, trying to get back to the higher ground of sophisticated conversation. "How's Miss Wanda holding up?"

"She's doing as well as can be expected, sir. Thanks for asking. It's been a strange day, to say the least. Strange week."

"So it has. Looks like your gal is missing you." Ronny gestured to the Branson table with his glass.

I looked over my shoulder. Shawna's face held the diligent smile of the seasoned debutante. Fresh lipstick and the correct amount of eyeliner maintained a mask of pleasant affability. Her eyes, however, appealed to Luke for relief from impending boredom and revealed the irritation at his choice of location.

"Maybe she'd like my Cosmo." I pictured flinging the Cosmo in her face as payback for my ruined palette. Petty is as petty does.

"Good idea. Why don't you bring her back a Cosmo, Luke?" Ronny held up his hand for Red. "Don't want to keep the little lady waiting."

"You trying to get rid of me, Ronny? Better view of the band from here. Y'all go on with your conversation."

"Cherry, you want to get out of here?" Ronny pushed his glass away.

Luke extended an arm across the bar, his hand settling near my elbow.

I shook off the interfering hand and smiled cooly at Ronny. "Let's not get ahead of ourselves." I had gained some information and enough alcohol to numb my worries. Mission accomplished as far as I was concerned. I felt a little sorry for Ronny, but I wasn't that cheap of a date. It had also occurred to me Ronny held some grudges worth exploring. "Sticks is getting ready to play."

The recorded music stopped and a lull settled over the crowd. A young man trudged onto the stage in black Pumas with an electric guitar slung over his back, bandito style. He wore a t-shirt reading "Beer Advocate," although his lack of gut indicated more muscle than love handle.

The bassist, tall and thin as a Georgia pine, planted himself on the edge of the short stage. His ash blonde hair waved past his shoulders, and a mustache ran into his beard. Brown eyes blinked at the crowd in either fear or crazed belligerence.

"Now where did Todd dig up this bunch?" I called to Red. "A college boy and a reject from Lynyrd Skynyrd?"

After a moment's delay, Todd swaggered onto the stage in the tight pleather. Crimson colored drumsticks twirled through his fingers. Like steak and gravy, he appeared all sizzle and smooth. A sigh rolled through the women's section.

Todd's ripped t-shirt and tight pants left little to the imagination. I fanned my cheeks, warmed by alcohol and a sudden shot of adrenaline.

"Good Lord," said Luke. He swigged his beer in contempt.

"Oh my," I said and straightened on my stool. That strange magic cast by musicians washed over me. Me and every other women in the audience. I suddenly remembered what had enticed me to Vegas.

Ronny fidgeted on his stool and ordered another drink.

"Put your tongue back in your mouth, Cherry." Luke folded his arms over his chest, unimpressed with Todd's transformation into rock god.

"Would you like another drink?" Ronny asked me.

Luke shot Ronny a glance that would have withered grapes into raisins.

I shook my head, not to give Luke the satisfaction, but to stop my world from spinning. "Ronny, I did want to talk more. But just now I'm having trouble remembering about what."

Todd maneuvered into the tight spot behind the drums with a final spin of his drumsticks. He wore the rocker persona with the right combination of confidence and hunky male deliciousness. The other men on the stage faded in my sight, as did the two on either side of me.

While I salivated over Todd, a shrill whistle blew from the audience followed by a hoot. Someone else had appeared on stage. I shook my head, took in the newcomer, and blinked in surprise.

"Wow," said Luke. His arms unwrapped from his chest and slid to his knees as he peered at the stage.

A woman in tight jeans and a tiny black cami stood before the lead mike. One hand twitched at her side. The toe of her red pump rubbed a small track in the stage floor. Her hair towered high above her head in a backcombed beehive. Metallic rods stuck out of the upsweep in different directions. Her body undulated in majestic curves, the camisole and jeans straining to hold everything in place.

"Holy shit."

I glanced over my shoulder. Red stood slack jawed with one hand clasping the bar rag on his shoulder.

"Leah?"

Red nodded. "No wonder her mother tries to cover her up."

Taking advantage of the silence that had fallen over the crowd, Todd grabbed his microphone. "Hey y'all. I'm Todd. That's Sid and Llewellyn. She's Leah. We're Sticks because we rock."

Todd raised his drumsticks overhead and struck them together three times. The guitarist licked into a smooth chord set before the rest of the band joined him. Leah's voice faltered over the first few notes, grew in strength, and deepened into her full, sensuous tone.

The audience sat spellbound through the first half of the song before returning to their drinks. By the chorus, Leah let go of her fear, grabbed the microphone and belted the lyrics. The song evoked a vampire theme, but Todd always did have a fascination with the undead.

"Your love's sucking the life right out of me. You think it tastes so sweet just to watch me bleed."

The lyrics faltered in meaning, but I hadn't high expectations for Todd's writing. However, his drumming had the frenetic elegance of a Jackson Pollack painting.

My focus slipped between Leah and Todd. Casey's ingenious creation of Leah's clothes and beehive befuddled and excited me. Todd's ripped arms flying over the drum set befuddled and excited me in an altogether different way.

Casey sidled in between Luke and I. "Hey, they're not half bad," she yelled in our ears.

"What did you do to Leah?"

"Do you like it?"

"You're a genius." I dipped toward her.

Casey threw out a hand to push me back in place.

"Where'd you get the clothes?"

"I took off that ugly jacket and pinned the jeans and top to tighten them up. Easy peasy." She smiled, feeling proud of her work in trashing up the untrashy.

"Wow. You're good."

"The forks in her hair were Todd's idea."

"Forks?" I leaned forward, slipping on the pleather, and squinted at Leah's hair. "Are those the metal bars in the bird's nest? Her head's gonna hurt in the morning."

"So is yours. Are you drunk?"

"Yes," said Luke, his eyes on the stage.

"No," I said, glaring at Luke.

"Maybe," I corrected. "It's all those drinks Ronny bought me." I swung my head to my left. "Where'd he go?"

"Oh, probably the rooster's room. I haven't seen you this tight in ages," Casey laughed. "Did you have fun?"

"Not really," I yelled. "I was with Ronny Price."

"At least he was buying," she nodded with economic astuteness.

I pointed my cup at Casey before taking another slurp of water. "I think he might know more about Dustin."

"You have no business asking about Dustin," said Luke.

"My reputation is ruined. And I gotta find out who has my gun."

"She's got a point." Casey nodded. "Can't have some stranger walking around shooting people with Daddy's gun."

"Exactly."

"I think you have more to do with ruining your reputation than you give yourself credit," said Luke. "Let the police do their job."

"Oh, they've got plenty to do." Casey leaned back against the bar with her eyes on the stage. "Look, Leah's fixing to sing another song. Besides, Cherry's doing pretty good with her list of suspects."

I shook my head at Casey, but she took no notice.

"And Cherry did notice something strange about Dustin's collection."

"What collection?"

"You know, the stuff your momma got for the wall box. Cherry thinks half the items are not even Dustin's. Miss Wanda probably didn't notice because she was so upset and all. Some of it looks expensive. Some of it's drug related." Casey flicked a knowing side-glance toward Luke. "And some of it's yours."

"Where is this stuff?"

"At Gam's house, I think." Casey shook my arm. "Honey, is your little project still at the farm?"

"I hid it." I crossed my arms and couldn't help grinning at my brilliance. "Until I talk to Miss Wanda."

"Hid what?"

They were drowned out by Todd's voice, this time crooning a ballad about a runaway bride: "By the time she bailed me out, she'd bailed on me."

"Wait a minute." The lyrics took weight, and their significance floated to the top of my liquor-addled brain. "That's about me."

I threw up my hands to stop Casey and Luke from talking and listened to a few more bars.

"That's me. Isn't it Todd?" I yelled across the room. The music drowned out my bellowing. "Is this song about Vegas?"

I launched off the stool, my hands clenched at my side. I stood immersed in the lyrics and caught "bets off the table" and "white, fringed boots."

A shriek of laughter ripped from Shawna.

Leah harmonized with her eyes closed, head tipped up, and hands rising and falling with the rhythm.

As he sang, Todd's wistful look matched the slowed tempo. I watched him drawing out the story into a bluesy tale of heartache, with me as the evil wench from hell. Lyrics about *my* failure to become a wife.

With all of Halo to hear.

Of course, he left out his gambling habit that left me a poker widow on our wedding night. My sight blurred to crimson edged with a throbbing magenta.

"Grab her," Casey said. "She's heading for the stage. No telling what she'll do. But if she ruins Leah's big night, she'll hate herself in the morning."

An arm flung around my middle yanked me off my feet. Two seconds later I stood in Red's vestibule, puffing with exertion and the desire not to get sick.

I glowered at Luke, not trusting my voice to the queasy feeling in my stomach. I expected him to turn back through the door, but instead, he ushered me into the cool night air. I set my lips together and gave him one of my fierce looks, even though it made my temples pound.

However, Luke wasn't looking at me. His thoughts were turned inward as he ushered me toward his truck. Finally, he laughed.

"That song was about you?"

"Yes.

"I have to give Todd credit. He may not be as dumb as I thought. But he sure is an idiot."

FOURTEEN

I WOKE to a fierce ache in my temples, throbbing with each breath I took. A whiff of brewing coffee floated under my bedroom door, jump-starting my motor with the promise of a life-saving caffeine injection.

Took me ten minutes before I finally stumbled to the bathroom to face the grim necessity of working through the results of last night's bender. Midway through brushing my teeth, my mind started a recap of the night's fuzzy events. I had a gaping hole in time that began at Red's and ended with me now standing in my Pepto-colored bathroom clenching a neon green toothbrush between my teeth. Something happened because that coffee wasn't making itself.

"Hello?"

I slowly inhaled the rich caffeine before poking my head into the dim spare room. Nobody lay in the tangerine cast-iron bed. But someone had tucked the matching patchwork quilt into neat hospital corners. No clothes were scattered across the floor. The tipsy, three-legged bedside table was bare of anything but a lamp and clock. I shut the door.

"Casey?"

I pattered down the hallway in my blinged-up Henley and panties. It appeared I hadn't the energy to change into PJs the night before, my boots and shorts kicked off somewhere unknown.

The kitchen also stood empty. Tiptoeing past the kitchen table and chairs, I peered around the corner of the archway to the living room. My eyes slid over the person rifling through my desk. Darting back in the kitchen, I flattened against the wall and squeezed my eyes shut.

I was such a moron. That's what I got for drinking something other than beer. Luke Harper in my living room.

For all my cleverness, I could be really stupid.

"Good morning, sunshine." Luke strolled into the room with a mug in hand. "You want coffee?" His eyes roamed my hair standing on end down to my chipped emerald-green toenails.

"What are you doing here?"

"Ever the gentleman, I took you home, tossed you in bed, and decided someone better keep an eye on you. If Todd showed up, I'd feel awfully sorry to hear you blew a hole through his leather pants."

"What would I shoot him with?"

"I heard about your truck and the missing shotgun." He sipped his coffee and leaned in the archway, crossing his legs.

Sunlight trickled from the living room into the darker kitchen, reddening the tips of his dark waves. With his face cast in shadow, his gray eyes appeared pewter. He pursed his lips and blew on his coffee, casually dropping his gaze down my bare legs.

"Speaking of that, you want to show me Dustin's things?"

"Is that what you were looking for in my desk? Gentleman, my ass. You took me home to snoop around. Something's been fishy with you all along."

I poked a finger in his chest. His coffee cup dipped, threatening to spill.

"What are you up to?" I said.

"Relax. Your sister said you have Dustin's stuff. I think it's best if you turn over his things to me."

"Why?"

"Listen, I know what you're up to. I saw your little pictures on the napkins last night. And you're questioning everyone in Halo. Very poorly, I might add."

"So?"

"Sugar, let the police do their job. You can't make detective work into an art project. Why don't you just show me Dustin's things?" He eyes flashed. "Maybe you should put some pants on, though. It's hard to resist a girl who's missing her britches, especially with legs like yours."

I caught myself before one of those foolish smiles — the kind held by slow-witted women in the presence of sweet-talking men — slid across my face.

"If I'm going to show Dustin's treasures to anyone, that person would be Uncle Will."

He peeled his eyes off my legs to scan the room again.

I had hidden the items well.

My triumphant smirk irritated him, but instead of arguing, Luke hooked a finger in the neck of my shirt and dragged me a step closer.

His sudden change of tactics caused my smirk to falter. "Stop trying to seduce me. I'm on to you. You get what you want and then leave."

"I'm not going anywhere," Luke murmured, lowering his lids to bedroom level. His long digits strolled down my spine with the nonchalance of a Sunday walk on Main Street.

I scowled at the lazy grin creeping closer to my face. It looked eager to do some damage to my lips.

"The other night your little Calamity Jane act ticked me off. I'm feeling differently now." His fingers danced around my waist and found the bottom of my shirt. He darted a look at his coffee cup, wishing he had an extra empty hand. "A lot differently. I've been thinking about that all morning."

"Luke Harper, you told me in my carport just two nights ago that we would never work out. And that was directly after you were all over me like butter on a hot skillet. I am tired of your games, and I am suspicious of your intentions. I've a mind to tell your Momma what you've been up to. Or Sheriff Will."

I've a mind? Good Lord, I was channeling Scarlett O'Hara.

"Come on. Don't be mad. Is it Shawna? I know you get jealous, but honestly, I can't help she won't leave me alone."

He squeezed my shoulder. A plaintive appeal darkened his eyes further. However, his evil dimples threatened to emerge, and I knew he thought he could use those dimples to trick me into handing over Dustin's belongings.

"To be jealous has not occurred to me."

"You know how cute you are when you get mad?"

My glare lengthened to what my grandma called slitty-eyed. "That cute stuff doesn't come close to working for me. You always get me all riled up and then take off. But not this time."

"We get each other riled up. That's why I take off." Luke's hand retreated from my shoulder, and he dropped the teasing tone. "Yes, I want Dustin's stuff. I'm not trying to seduce it out of you. I can't help myself. You're standing there in your undies."

His hand sliced the air near my legs, sloshing coffee on my floor.

"Dammit." Luke wiped the mug on his jeans. With a grunt, he kicked his heel against the archway. "I'm usually more in control. Do you think I like feeling this way? You're like malaria or something. I think I'm over you and suddenly you've worked your way into my system again. I'm trying to stay away from you, but you keep showing up and getting into trouble. This town is too small for the two of us."

Malaria? Was that supposed to be a compliment?

"You don't want to give me Dustin's junk," he continued. "Yet someone else has stolen your gun and truck and has murdered two people. What's wrong with you?"

"Nothing's wrong with me. Stop worrying. I hid everything so well even you couldn't find it."

Luke strode into the living room, his eyes roving the cracked plaster walls and stained wood floors. He shook his head in disgust. "Man, your house needs a lot of work. Why are you living here?"

"It's free except for the taxes and upkeep?" I followed him into the room and leaned against my roll-top desk. "Couldn't you come up with something better than malaria? Do people still get that?"

"I meant why do you insist on staying in Halo?"

"Duh, my family is here. Now I'm worried that Casey is going to leave and someone will need to take care of Grandpa. Besides, I like it here."

"Eight years ago you told me you wanted to move back to this P.O.S. town. For eight years I've tried to figure out why a town could be more important than me." He sipped his coffee and took a deep breath before continuing. "You know what I came up with? I think you're waiting for your mom to come back."

My jaw dropped. "What?"

"You heard me." He dropped the coffee cup on my paint table and approached me with tentative steps.

"Oh no, you don't. You can't say something like that and expect me to crumple into your arms like some pathetic loser." I straightened my spine and swallowed the sting from his words. "And you know what I think?"

The hiss of my words halted his steps.

"This isn't about me. You think you're too good for this town, always have. But it's not Halo's fault our fathers died, and neither of us got a normal childhood. At least you had a mother that didn't flake out on you."

"She might not have left, but she flaked out plenty. She was so busy trying to make Dustin love her and placate her new husband that she forgot about me."

He shook his head as if to clear his thoughts. "Just forget about all that. I don't know where that came from. Just give me Dustin's stuff, and I'll go."

"That's a huge revelation." I pushed off the desk to sidle closer to him. His confession took the edge off my anger, his vulnerability softening my approach. "You probably needed to get that off your chest for a long time now."

"Cherry." Luke exhaled my name with a bitterness that made me wince. "I'm only interested in two things. One is Dustin's effects. The other is your currently pantsless state. You got an opinion on either one?"

"You can go to hell on both subjects." I thrust my chin up and tightened my lips.

"That's what I thought." He grabbed his keys off the desk and swung open the door. With his hand on the knob, he looked over his shoulder. "Leave Dustin's murder alone."

"Back at you. You're as suspicious as anyone." Whipping around, I skipped out of the room, listening to the thump of the closing door behind me.

I wasn't sure if I should laugh or cry. I finally broke Luke Harper's spell over me.

Even worse, I think I broke the spell I had over him.

Unfortunately, like everything good in my life, that power was gone before I knew it existed.

I STOOD on my front porch dressed in jeans and a stretch lace t-shirt. Paired with a Victoria's Secrets bra and hunched shoulders, I almost looked like a B-cup.

And it was a B-cup kind of day.

I started with Luke and planned to work my way through a list that ended with the villain who helped Shawna wreck my career and murder two men who may not have been beloved, but belonged to this town.

And as my truck had been shot up, my siblings weren't answering their phones, and the sheriff forbade me to do what I needed, I demanded number two on my list to get his faux-leather butt over to my house. He needed to apologize for his insulting song lyrics.

I also needed his car.

The object of my desire, Todd's functioning vehicle, jerked to a stop at the curb while the object of my ire bounded up the slope to my porch. I fussed with a fern and waited for his apology. I had a feeling Todd McIntosh had been holding out on me, stringing me along on some joke I didn't get.

"Don't get ugly about this." Todd folded his arms over his chest and leaned against one of my porch columns. "But I've thought about it and decided not to apologize."

"What?"

Why were these men failing me? My lucky bra wasn't working.

"You can't write songs casting me in a negative light," I shouted.

"I'm an artist. I write what comes to me."

"You are a drummer who puts rhyming words together. If they string into a story, you got lucky."

"That's not fair."

"And it's not fair to write songs about life's fruit salad that's full of sour Cherry's. Or lyrics like 'flat bottomed girls may not bounce, but it's not the size of their butt that counts.'"

"That's actually a compliment."

"On what planet is that a compliment? How about runaway bridezillas in white, fringed boots that stomp all over your heart and make you lose at cards? You named it 'The Ballad of Cherrilann!'"

"See, I didn't even use your name."

"You think nobody is going to know you meant Cherrilyn? What if I paint you with a tiny penis, slap a mustache on the face, and hang it up in Red's? You think nobody will guess it's you?"

Todd's fingers halted. He drew in his breath. "You wouldn't."

"Try me. You've been embarrassing me over this Vegas thing ever since we broke up. Which was mostly your fault. I didn't tell anybody about what happened to you. And what's with the vampire song? Is that supposed to be me, too?"

"No, I just like the undead. Sid and I are writing a zombie song now."

I rolled my eyes. "No more songs about how I ruin your life or the size of my derriere."

"I promise. I didn't mean anything by it."

"You have a funny way of showing it." Yanking open my screen door, I marched inside with Todd trailing behind me. The door creaked and banged. "Why do you want to be around me when I'm always ticked at you?"

"You're just feisty. You don't mean it."

"No. I mean it.

Todd grinned at my scowl.

"Why don't you believe me?"

He continued to grin.

"Never mind. I need a favor."

"I knew you wanted me."

"I want your car." His eyebrow waggling did nothing to improve my mood. "That's not a double entendre. My truck's stuck at the dealership garage. I have a list of people I'm checking into."

"Am I on your list?"

"Considering you were with my brother at Red's when I was assaulted at Cooper's, and you have no motive for killing Dustin or your roommate—"

"I have a reason for finding his killer. I'll help you."

"I am sorry about you losing your roommate." Guilt washed over me. In my personal struggle, I had neglected Todd's grief. Pulling him toward me, I hugged him, whispering words of sorrow.

As his hand snuck past my waistline toward my flat bottom, I ripped from our tender embrace and rethought his words. "Just a minute, how did you know I was looking for the killer?"

He shrugged, an impish smile fleeing his face.

"I've been considering several suspects. But last night, Ronny Price said some interesting things about Mr. Max. I talked to Max at the funeral, so he knows me now. I figure if we go to his house together, we'd be safe enough. Especially if we drop enough hints that people know our location."

"That sounds smart."

I studied Todd for sarcasm. "I think there's a tie-in between his poker games and what Dustin stole. I want to know more about these secret games. We're going to tell him you're interested in playing in the next big poker game."

"That sounds real good."

"You're not really going to play, Todd. It's just an excuse to question him." I cocked my head. "You told me you stopped playing poker after Vegas."

"I did," he discharged the words with the momentum of a split-finger fastball.

I raised an eyebrow in disbelief, but Todd's vices were no longer my concern. I strolled to the rolltop desk. After Luke left, I pulled Dustin's collection from their various hiding places for closer examination.

"The Bear will expect money for the pot. We'll ask about collateral. I'll show him the sketch I made of this." I picked up the lion's head belt buckle from the top of my desk. "And maybe sketches of the other stuff and see what he says. I looked up this buckle on the Internet. If it's real sterling silver and rubies, it's got to be worth around a thousand dollars. Maybe more. The other buckle is fourteen karat gold and turquoise."

"That's pretty nice."

"Exactly. I should've gone into jewelry design. Wouldn't a high relief rhino head emerging from a buckle look cool?"

Todd's brows puckered.

"Anyway, there's no way something this expensive belonged to Dustin. You ever seen Dustin wear this buckle?"

"No, can't say that I have. Maybe a giant 'D' buckle at one point."

"Max might recognize this jewelry. We'll play it cool. Ronny said Max could have known Dustin was a thief. Maybe the Bear will tip us off."

I grinned with excitement. We could work our way through the list of suspects with a sketchpad. I'd give my results to Uncle Will and allow him to do the dirty work. I'd go home, make a shadow box for a Pound Puppy, and call it a day. All including a fat paycheck. Commissions would start rolling back in. Who wouldn't want a personal portrait created by an artist who solved the murder of her last subject?

"Cherry?"

I shook myself out of my Cherry-absorbed musings.

"Are you going to tell me this is stupid and dangerous and I should let the police work it out without my help?"

"No. It sounds fine to me."

"Really?" I laid the silver buckle next to the other items of value I collected from Dustin's stash. The Pink Pig bank held quite a few pieces of jewelry and odd coins. "You're very agreeable to this. Are you sure you don't see any problems with my plan?"

"I think I saw something like this on a TV show once. It turned out okay." Todd shrugged. "What could go wrong?"

I sucked on my lip. The weight of Todd's trust in my schemes felt mighty heavy. However, better not to worry Todd needlessly. His ability to live in the present made him adaptable to a sudden change of plans. "Can you handle this or not?"

"Baby, I married you. I can handle anything you deliver."

That was a scary thought. Todd's safety was now my responsibility.

And I didn't know if I could handle what I planned to deliver.

FIFTEEN

TOUCHED by that vague discomfort that occurs from sharp disparities in socioeconomic straits, Todd and I shuffled our feet on the deep porch of Max's antebellum style house.

Although it impersonated a plantation home, this towering wedding cake represented similar McMansions springing up in new subdivisions throughout the countryside. It seemed a lot of Yankees liked the old southern architecture when accompanied with modern amenities like swimming pools and sprinkler systems.

For that matter, so did rich southerners.

"Did you see the cannon?" Todd hopped from foot to foot, his hands shoved in the pockets of his cargo shorts. "Pretty cool, huh?"

I glanced at the flower bed where a normal rich person would have put a fountain or a fancy tree. Instead of water gurgling from angel's lips, a long cast iron barrel rested between oversized spoked wooden wheels.

"Looks like someone has an inferiority complex."

My eyes drifted from the canon to the immaculate drive marred by Todd's beat-up Civic. The tailored gardens and clipped

Bermuda grass looked worthy of the Masters Championship course in Augusta. Someone only needed to dig a few holes, stick flagged poles in them, and Max could charge locals for a three-holer.

"He must be mega-rich," said Todd.

"Don't you wonder how he got all this money?" I leaned into the doorbell. Adrenaline juiced my nerves. My finger retreated from the doorbell, but a gonging had already echoed inside the house.

Todd peeked in another window. "You think he's got a butler?"

"I thought you'd been here before."

"Not his house." Todd peered in a tall window. "I met him at a bar in Line Creek. That's where I introduced him to Pete. I believe he was looking for ringers."

"Ringers?"

"He talked kind of funny. Probably misunderstood him," Todd said quickly. His expression snapped from thoughtful to vapid. "So you think he's got a butler?"

Before I could respond, one of the double wooden doors swung open, and we jumped back. A shadowy figure paused in the dark foyer.

"Ah, the artist and, wait." Conjuring his memory, Max waved his hand at Todd. "The card sharp. The artist and the card sharp. To what do I owe this pleasure?"

His beefy hand grasped my fingers, and he swept my hand up to his lips. "*Ça me fait plaisir de te revoir.*"

"I'm not a shark," Todd mumbled, eyeing the kiss and my pink-cheeked response to the French. "I win fair and square."

"Sharp not shark. However, I do quarrel with you. You beat me without humility, my friend."

Max extended his hand, and Todd reluctantly accepted the handshake.

"But I forgive you." Max gave a short bow. "I am not used to your style of playing. During the game, you are a monolith. I would think you were asleep if it weren't for your open eyes. But at the end, after you have taken my money, your energy bursts forth into a mocking tirade of dancing like a chicken and what is it you scream? Boo Yes?"

"Booyah," Todd replied, whisking his hands into the pockets of his shorts.

"What is this booyah? Some rebel yell of your ancestors as they charge the battlefield?"

"Todd's ancestors were more likely taking bets on the outcome of a battle than participating in it," I said.

I glanced back at my ex-fiancé with mixed pity and annoyance before turning back to our host. "I apologize for his exuberance. His snarking is unsportsmanlike, and he realizes that now. You see, he's been playing with a rougher crowd who doesn't mind these antics. We're used to touchdown dancing and NASCAR donuts. Now that he's played with more respectable people, he understands the cock walk isn't appropriate."

Max waved off my concern. "It is of no wonder Todd is proud of his accomplishments. He is amazing to watch. I wished for him to teach me his card sense. He has no hesitation. To disarm your opponents with such speed and accuracy, it's a kind of genius. To read the bluffing so intuitively. Is it skill? Is he reading the cards?"

Todd stared, seemingly without comprehension.

I kicked him in the ankle to remind him to close his mouth. These were the times I doubted Todd's slips of brilliance.

"It's just a God given gift. Just like drumming. Although Todd practices the songs. Maybe he's just a good judge of character." I thought of his choice in Creepy Pete as a roommate. I doubled over my words. "I guess it's all instinct with Todd. I doubt he can teach that."

"So," Max repeated, "to what do I owe this pleasure? Are you selling cookies? Sometimes little girls in tiny fascist uniforms come to sell me cookies."

"I'm a little old for girl scouts."

"Just a joke. You are too serious, artist. Take the joke. But why are you here? Did I interest you in my collections? I hadn't thought you'd bring a friend."

I took a deep breath. "Can we come inside? We wanted to talk to you about getting Todd in on your next shindig."

"I am not familiar with the she-yin-dig. I can't help you."

"Todd's looking for a game." I dropped my voice. "We heard you host a fast company for high stakes."

"I don't know what you mean. My English is not so good."

"Maybe you could invite us in, and I could explain." I stared into the glacier depths of his eyes.

He looked back with detached calculation before flicking his glance toward Todd.

Todd flinched and inched closer to the door and me.

Max shrugged, and his good humor returned. "Sure, sure. Come inside. I will show you my collection. Who knows? Maybe I give you a commission someday. I very much liked your portrait of Dustin. It showed his confidence without revealing the blatant stupidity that often went with it."

He stumped through the open door. I exchanged an apprehensive glance with Todd. I got the feeling Todd wasn't getting good vibes from Max. Or maybe he still couldn't understand him.

I scooted through the door. A tugging slowed my pace. Feeling like a hooked fish at the end of its line, I spun around, dragging Todd with me. His finger remained crooked through my belt loop while I tried to shake him off.

"What's with the extra tail?"

"Huh?"

"Why're you hanging on to my jeans? You're going to rip them."

"Oh. I'm worried."

"Don't worry. We're just asking some questions. I've talked to him before. We seem to get along pretty well."

"It's just..." Todd covered my hand with his.

"Just what, hon?"

"If he gets out the cards I don't know if I'll be able to control myself. Nobody'll play with me anymore because I always win." He amended, "Not that that's the reason I don't play."

"We're just talking. There's no real game."

"I know, but he's talking poker. At least I think he is. What if he says 'How about a hand of short stud while you're here,' and I can't resist? I thought if I kept my hands on you, it'd keep me from reaching for the cards."

"I didn't realize how hard this was for you." Tenderness for Todd's struggle against his gambling addiction flooded through me. I stroked his shoulder with a sigh.

"Because if I start playing," Todd continued. "You'll probably haul off and hit me or something. Or throw something at me. Like you did in Vegas. Think about it. He's got real expensive stuff here, Cherry. You can't afford to break anything."

Jerking my hand off his shoulder, I clenched it to my side. "If that's the case, you just keep your hands to yourself. And I'll try to keep my hands off the china."

I stomped through the doorway and glared back at Todd. "And I think it's best if you just don't say anything else today."

"Baby, I was just thinking of you."

"I should have asked Ronny Price to drive me. He might be old, but at least he's a gentleman."

"He could afford the broken dishes, but he's a terrible poker player."

I marched past a wide staircase curling up and around the foyer to catch up with Max. He had disappeared through a doorway to the right of the staircase.

"Come on," I said, scurrying across the marble foyer and glanced back.

Todd still stood in the center of the large vestibule, staring at the ceiling in open-mouthed wonder. My eyes followed to the upper balcony where a massive chandelier caught the light pouring through the high porch windows. Rainbows danced across the walls and over the ceiling.

"Isn't that something?" Todd whispered. "I'd love to have a house like this."

"Quit gawking."

Cowed by the lavish surroundings, we slunk through the thick wooden door. Manly scents like leather, fresh kindling, and wood oil assaulted my senses. A carved marble fireplace faced by leather chairs caused a gasp of envy to escape my lips.

A colossal cherry desk with taloned feet sat across the room before the double porch windows shuttered with plantation blinds, keeping the library dim and protecting the furnishings.

The room would have oozed testosterone in a sexy, sumptuous, makes-you-want-a-sugar-daddy way except for all the glass cases covering all other available wall and floor space. All filled with junk. Old junk. Overpriced, boring War Between the States junk. And Max dying to tell us about every piece.

I hated history almost as much as I hated math. I readied myself for the opportunity to change the subject.

"Are those swords?" Todd leaped from the doorway to a large wall case decorated with a ripped and burned Union Jack and packed with gleaming swords. "Cool."

Max paced to the case to start the lecture while Todd looked on with eager admiration. "Of course. Most are the field officer swords, you know. But this you see, a little longer? Is the cavalry saber. These are all Confederate, of course. They're a bit smaller than the Union Army. Let me show you something better."

They strolled from case to case, while I half-listened with my hands stuck under my arms and toes tapping soundlessly on the oriental carpet. I eyed the leather chairs and thought about a nap.

"This is like a museum except in a house. I never thought anyone would want a bunch of old stuff if you're rich enough for new." Todd trotted to a suited dummy in full Confederate regalia standing in a corner behind the desk. "Wow, would you look at this."

"This, my friend, is the uniform of Colonel John S. Mosby, the Gray Ghost. I have gone to much expense to acquire this piece."

"Do you do those battle plays with this?"

"Reenactment?" Max stopped behind Todd. "No, I would not risk hurting this piece. It does not interest me to play the soldier because I know what it means to be a soldier. I collect because I have the fascination of people who want to separate from their government and determine their own fate."

"It didn't work out too well for the South," I said. "If you haven't noticed, we're still standing in the United States of America, and we're pretty proud of that down here."

"Yes, of course."

"And we don't agree with all the reasons our ancestors wanted to separate."

"Of course."

"Just making sure you understand that. I know you're foreign. You might have some funny ideas about Dixie. We don't sit around picking banjos and cotton anymore. We're like everyone else."

"Except we're better at football," added Todd.

"Yes, yes. You are so serious, Miss Tucker. Do you have some sensitivity about this? Does your family come from the sharecropper? There is no shame in poor beginnings. I, too, come from the proletariat. But look at me." He waved his arm around his lavish surroundings. "I have risen without the help of man or government. I pull myself up with the bootstrap."

I gave him a slow blink. I felt insulted on several levels, but couldn't put my finger on what they were.

Todd looked from Max to me. "You look like you want to throw something. Is it time to go?"

"We still haven't spoken your business. Miss Tucker and I like to butt the heads, eh?" He laughed and slapped Todd on the back. "Artist, I would love a portrait of myself in this suit. I will think about whom best to paint me, but it is very convenient to have a portraitist in Halo. Maybe we make deal. I pay big money. However, other business first."

I conjured the paycheck that would accompany that commission. Maybe it would buy a Camaro. Inferno Orange. With the black racing stripes, of course.

"Now would you look at all these belt buckles? Cherry, come see this. None of these are as nice as the ones you got."

Max's eyelids slid from widened interest to narrowed contemplation. "Do you collect the buckles?"

"No," I answered honestly.

I shuffled to the buckle case and peered around Todd. None looked similar to the buckles Dustin had squirreled away. Most of the plates appeared to be brass with war eagle insignias or letters. Dustin's belt buckles seemed contemporary. So had the other pieces of jewelry.

It didn't take a history scholar to know that a Rolex watch and diamond rings wouldn't appear in this room.

Circling past the buckle cases, I approached a thin, flat case on a pedestal stand in the middle of the den. Spotlights directed from the ceiling and the floor shone over the glass and mahogany case. Old coins abounded. I examined the small pieces looking for those that resembled the ones from the Pink Pig bank that now sat in plain view on my dresser. I recognized a few Indian Head pennies amongst many old, unrecognizable coins, but none like Dustin's.

A smaller Lucite case gleamed with high tech internal lighting. Two round indentations in the red felt bottom showed the case held two missing coins. With the elaborate display in the center of the room, these missing coins seemed to be the showpiece of the entire collection.

I glanced up.

Max watched me from the opposite side of the case. "You are interested in the coins? I like the Lady Liberty coins. That gold one is the dollar. Lady is head only. But seated, she is silver half-dollar. These are from more than one hundred years ago."

"That's pretty old."

Todd had returned to the sword case. I scooted toward him, bumping his hip with my elbow. This was our opportunity to question Max about Dustin's valuables. If I could get Max off the history tract.

"Actually, very old for your country, but not so old for mine." Max chuckled. "They are worth not so much, though. Just a few hundred dollars. That is nothing compared to my coins from the middle box. You probably noticed them missing."

"I saw the empty case."

"Those coins are also the Lady Liberty type coins I love so much. The face value is only one cent and fifty cents, though."

"Isn't that interesting, Todd?" I patted my carrier bag.

Todd shrugged. With a twitch of his broad shoulders, he turned back to the swords.

"My missing coins are C.S.A. coins. Confederate States of America money," said Max, intent on the lecture. "Both from original samples, 1861, ordered by Jefferson Davis himself. Very few were ever made. The one-cent is made from nickel, such a cheap metal. But the value is more than thirty-five thousand dollars. Can you believe? The half-dollar, she is made from an ordinary half-dollar and then restriking the coin with the C.S.A. motif. So simple, but it is priceless."

He grinned with the cunning ferocity of a man accustomed to impossible achievements. "But you steal from me, you pay a price."

Tingling with excitement, I felt goosebumps break over my skin. I had a lead. More than a lead. Max must have discovered Dustin had stolen his coins. Max killed Dustin, ransacked his apartment, then the Branson's house, looking for the missing coins.

"We can talk to you about your next poker session another time," I said. "I forgot I've got to do something."

"But what about—" said Todd.

"Don't worry about that, Todd," I caught his eye and tried to convey the urgency with an intense look. "We'll come back another time."

"I will find those coins," continued Max. "Everyone knows

they are mine. No one steals from the Bear without regard to his life."

Max stretched his stooped shoulders and slammed his hand on the glass case, shaking the stand. His accent deepened in anger. "The Bear is the great hunter. I use my dogs to track the thief and the coins. I make pay for betrayal."

"Did you say dogs?" said Todd. "What kind of dogs you got?"

"Have you reported the burglary?" I asked, elbowing Todd. Max's outburst accelerated my central nervous system into hyper-overdrive.

"I prefer to handle it my way."

"Good luck with that." I pushed Todd toward the door. "Thanks for the tour."

"You will not leave yet. I have so much I want to show you, Artist."

"I think we got what we needed," I whispered to Todd and yanked him from the sword case. "I didn't even have to break out the sketch pad. Let's go talk to Uncle Will."

"Where are you going Cherry and Todd?" Max blocked the door with his considerable size.

"Now's not such a good time, Bear," I said. "We do need to go. I told my Uncle Will I'd meet him. He's kind of expecting me. I told him I'd drop in after I swung by your house."

"So disappointing. Why don't you call him and tell him you will be late."

"Um," I said, while my mind screamed, "Get out. Get out. Get out."

"Where do y'all play poker?" asked Todd. "In there with the war stuff or in another room?"

"I have not said I host the poker. You are jumping the conclusions, my friend." His teeth glinted in the sunlight. "I'll show you my basement where I entertain only select peoples. It's impressive to have basement in this part of the country, no? Are you suitably impressed?"

A chuckle rumbled deep within his chest while his eyes narrowed, checking our reaction.

"Very impressed," I said. "We must've been misinformed about the poker. We'll just scoot."

"Go to my basement." The deep growl made me jump. He shepherded us toward a door beneath the spiral staircase.

"I'd love to see y'all's basement. I like basements," said Todd.

I schlepped behind Todd, my heart beating the rhythm of hummingbird's wings.

The Bear's bulk stalked my heels. His murky outline blotted out my shadow, cooling the heat pouring through the upper windows.

I shivered. I didn't have much experience with basements. As far as I knew, below Max's luscious mansion was a *Silence of the Lambs* hole.

And he seemed determined for us to descend underground.

"You know you're right." I planted myself before the open basement door and whipped my cell phone from my back pocket. "I should call Sheriff Thompson — you know, my uncle — and let him know I'll be late."

"The reception here is not so good," said Max. "You can use my house phone in the basement."

"He's right." Todd glanced up from his phone. "I'm not picking up any bars. You can't afford roaming."

"Quit telling me what I can't afford, Todd," I hissed and gasped as the Bear grabbed the phone from my hand.

"This phone is like Stone Age. It is garbage. I can get you good deal on better one." Before I could protest, he yanked Todd's from his hand and examined it. "This, too, is garbage. Come with me now."

Max shoved the two phones into his pants pocket and bumped Todd toward the door. "Come on, big guy. Go down the stairs."

SIXTEEN

OUR FOOTSTEPS RANG on wooden stairs finished with a dark cherry stain. In other circumstances, I would have admired the craftsmanship. The buff colored walls enclosing the stairs seemed sterile after the cluttered display in the library. Recessed light pooled at the bottom of the stairs and along a long, carpeted hallway lined with closed doors.

My eyes flicked to an alarm panel mounted on the wall near the light switch. The flat screen display was blank and dark.

I edged closer to Todd and took his hand in comfort.

He squeezed back.

When I looked up for his reaction, he remained focused on the long hall, his nostrils quivering and palms sweating. If I was going down, I couldn't ask for anyone more loyal than Todd.

Except maybe someone who could get me out of this mess.

Max pressed the alarm screen and pointed to a door at the end of the hall on our left.

"After you," he grunted.

Todd grabbed the knob and pulled me through the door. We blundered into a dark, windowless room.

Behind us, Max fumbled for the light switch. Light dimmed

from translucent sconces ringing a home theater. We stood near a curtained wall faced with two rows of recliner chairs. The back row had been raised on a short platform to create stadium-style seating. A popcorn machine stood near the door.

"Whoa," said Todd. "This is so cool. Way better than the old junk upstairs."

I spied a door near the back. Max guarded the exit to the hall.

His arms flexed and he planed his hands on his hips. "Sit down."

Todd leaped into the nearest chair and found a remote control stuck in the side of the seat. Pushing back in the seat, he popped the footrest and the lounger began to vibrate.

"Chhh-eee-rrr-yyy," Todd's voice pulsated with the chair. "You gotta try this."

"Sit, Artist. Enjoy the chair like your friend. I'll be back in a moment." Max strode out, slamming the door behind him.

I skipped to Todd, snatched the remote, and pushed the off button with more strength than necessary. "What are you doing? We've got to get out of here."

"I know. The door at the end of the hall is the garage. I could smell the motor oil. But it's probably locked up tight with all those expensive vehicles. You're best to try another room on the other side of the hall."

"Why the other side?"

"This side is the hill. You got to go to the other side for the walkout. It probably goes to the pool."

"How do you know that?"

"I deliver to houses with these kinds of basements all the time. The customers have me walk round to the back door. Usually, it's sliding glass. Sometimes they've got a pool room or a workshop, but I never saw anything this nice."

"Todd, you're a genius." My puppy had grown into a guard dog. A tall, muscular guard dog with gorgeous blue eyes and an amazing jaw line.

He yanked keys from his pocket and tossed them to me. "I

keep telling you that. You're always underestimating me. You take the Civic."

"I can't leave you."

"Go report to the sheriff. Maybe I can convince Mr. Max to play some hands or look at the swords again. I'll just tell him you're in the bathroom. Don't worry. I'm pretty good at distracting folks."

I leaned over to kiss his cheek. "I'll never underestimate you again. I promise to bring Uncle Will right away."

"Now that's what I'm talking about," he murmured and brushed my hair aside to place his hand on the back of my neck.

Before he could pull me into a kiss, I slid from his embrace and ran to the door. I grabbed the handle. The knob rotated beneath my palm. I scurried back to Todd.

The door swung open. Max walked in, carrying a folded table.

"We have business to discuss, Artist." He plunked the table on the ground before Todd's chair. "But first, young Todd will show me his tricks."

Sharing a long glance, Todd and I simultaneoulsy flinched at a loud crack.

Max popped out a leg, constructing the table with the speed of a Marine reassembling a gun. He pulled a deck of cards from his pocket to toss on the green felt.

"First you explain your method, Todd, then I will speak to Miss Tucker." His glance commanded me to wait. "A simpleton cannot defeat me. Todd must have a method. I don't believe his act for one minute."

Todd shrugged and slid forward in his seat, drumming the table with his open palms. "What's your game? Hold 'Em? Triple Draw? Crazy Pineapple?"

"Take off your bag and relax." Max pointed to the chair next to Todd.

I didn't move.

Max yanked the strap of my messenger bag over my head and slid it to the floor. "Try the massage chair."

Biting my lip, I stared at my bag holding the sketches of Dustin's stolen items lying at Max's feet.

"I'm going to the little girl's room," I said and strode to the door. The bag would have to stay with Todd. I hoped Max wouldn't think to peek in the sketchbook.

He jerked a thumb to the back wall. "Go there."

I hesitated. How long were we going to play this game?

"Up there," his low voice growled.

I slunk away from the door, squeezing Todd's shoulder on my way up the riser. Locking the bathroom door, I tried not to panic and checked the cupboards for anything useful.

Fluffy towels and pretty soaps in fine European packaging. No guns and ammo.

However, what I thought was the linen closet was another door, leading to another dark room. I hesitated before crossing the threshold. Either this pitch-black room was Max's inner lair of torture devices, waiting for our arrival. Or he had forgotten to reset the alarm when he got the card table.

I smacked the wall, searching for a light switch. Finding several, I hit them all. The room leaped to life. I blinked against the glare of the bulbs of a million colored lights winking from various signs on the walls.

Dadgum, the Bear had brought Vegas to Georgia.

A glittering chandelier hung over a felt covered table ringed in luscious dark stained wood. Ten leather armchairs circled the table. I stood next to a cashier's booth topped in lighted letters. Brass slot machines lined one long wall. A gaming table shaped like a figure eight faced a fully stocked mahogany bar at the far end.

I swept my eyes over the room searching for another exit and spotted a small door sandwiched between video gaming machines and a bank of slots.

Ducking into a long hallway, I heard a door creak. I darted through a doorway on the opposite side of the hall. Light poured through French doors leading to the pool. I dashed to the glass door, fumbled with the lock, and sped through. Behind me, the locks tumbled.

Lord Almighty, the Bear must have finally reset the alarm. I stared at the sky and thought about blowing a kiss. But we weren't out of the woods yet.

My poor Todd remained locked in a windowless room, forced to bluff his way through a card game. Waiting on me to save his life.

WHILE MY BRAIN fixated on Todd in that basement playing cards with the devil himself, my body drove Todd's Civic on muscle memory. My driving felt worthy of Talladega on the open country stretches as I raced toward rescue.

My first thought was to find the closest phone but didn't want to waste time knocking on the doors of all the little houses sprinkled along the highway.

The Sheriff's Office was too far away in Line Creek, but JB's dealership was on the edge of town. Cody wasn't working, but salesmen cultivated shoppers on Saturday. I could snatch a phone in one of the little offices in the cinder block hall, call the sheriff. Maybe talk someone into returning to Max's house with me.

I pushed the little red vehicle to its limits, screeching into the parking lot at 60 mph. The Civic took the corner loose. I slammed the brakes to halt at the edge of the lot. No one milled around the stretch of pre-owned vehicles, so I ran for the building.

Ronny Price hung outside the glass doors, sunning his oily features in the spring sunshine. His salesman radar perked at my jog to the showroom, and he met me between a line of sedans.

"I sure am glad to see you," he said. "Finally ready to let go of that truck? You look hot. Step into the shade. Can I get you a water or a Coke?"

"Ronny, I need a phone." I panted, bent over Ronny's tasseled loafers. "Quickly."

"You're in luck. My car's parked just down this line. You can have a seat in total luxury and talk in privacy."

"Don't try to sell me a car. I have an emergency."

"Let's get going then."

We sped down the line of sedans to a polished silver Town Car.

"Hop in." Ronny opened the passenger door for me.

I scrambled inside.

"How do you like the Lincoln?" Preening, he ran his hands over the leather and wood dash. "Not as large as the F-150, but a classic. Beautiful, isn't she?"

"Does it have a phone?" I spoke sharply, hurrying Ronny along.

"Of course, this beauty comes with a top-of-the line navigation and security system. Hands-free voice control for the phone, too."

"I've got hands. I just need to talk. Please, hurry."

He popped the glove compartment door, pulled out a cell phone, and handed it to me. "Here, use this one."

I pushed the numbers for Will's private line.

Ronny cracked the driver door and slid in beside me.

As Will's ringer flipped over to voicemail, I smiled at Ronny and risked a crazy-sounding question. "Would you drive me to Max Avtaikin's house while I call the police?"

"Avtaikin's? Why?"

I jammed 911 with my thumb. "Mr. Max has my friend locked in his basement. And I think he killed Dustin and Pete. He pretty much admitted Dustin stole some old coins from him."

"He did?" Ronny's voice climbed with excitement and his eyes nearly popped from his skull. "Call the police. We're on our way."

I put the phone to my ear and spoke to the dispatcher. "Hey, who is this? Mindy? Cherry Tucker. I've got something to report to Sheriff Will. Can you patch me through?"

Mindy squawked a reply in my ear.

Ronny pulled through the parking space and turned toward the far end of the lot.

"He's busy? Listen, Mindy, this is important." I paused, listening. "I know, but this time it's important for real. Tell Uncle Will I'm returning to Max Avtaikin's house... That's right I said returning. And Max has Todd locked in the basement...Yes, I said locked. They're playing poker, but I don't know how long Todd will last."

I pulled the phone from my ear and glared at the receiver before slipping it back. "What do you mean you've got another call? Dammit, Mindy. Tell Uncle Will that Max killed Dustin and Pete and I have proof. I escaped the basement, but Todd's still there, and I'm going back to save him...Hello?"

I hung up with a frustrated scream.

"Sounds like she had trouble believing you." The engine revved. Ronny turned onto Oakleaf and slowed.

I fastened my seatbelt. "I'm going to try Uncle Will again. Mindy Carroll is an idiot. This thing's got a V8, right? Can't you go faster?"

"We're still in town. Hand me the phone, and I'll call for you. They're more likely to believe me." He turned right with cautious precision and made another left onto the state road. Never taking his eyes off the road, Ronny grabbed the phone with one hand and dropped it in his lap. "Maybe you should have been more patient with Mindy."

"You're right." I smacked the leather door rest and cursed under my breath.

"You seem to be having a bad day."

"You don't know the half of it. Can you try calling now?"

My legs jiggled with nervous energy while I massaged my temples until the vibration made me nauseous. The car felt heavy and slow. I longed to thrust my foot on top of Ronny's loafers, squeezing those little tassels flat to push his ridiculous Lincoln to the limits.

I sniffed the air, and my stomach flipped over at a familiar odor. Scotch.

We rolled to a stop at a four-way. Ronny stared at the stop sign like he was trying to read Sanskrit.

"Ronny?" Did JB know Ronny carried a flask during work

hours? "I need the sheriff at Mr. Max's house like ten minutes ago. If we get there before the police, I'm going to need you to distract Max while I rescue Todd."

The vehicle jerked forward, turned in a gentle ninety-degree arc, then accelerated. Ronny rolled his window down.

A breeze whipped my hair around my face. "Aren't we going the wrong way?"

"I thought we'd go someplace quiet and work this all out. Could you hand me a tissue? In the center console."

I pulled open the console, yanked a tissue from a little box, and held it out. It fluttered in the wind and Ronny snatched it. Holding the tissue, Ronny picked up the phone, wiped it off, and tossed it out the window.

My jaw dropped. "What did you do that for?"

"It wasn't my phone."

"Who's phone was it?"

"Dustin's."

SEVENTEEN

"HOW COULD that be Dustin's phone?" I stared at Ronny. This is what I got for being nice to lonely middle-aged men. "Is this about last night? I'm sorry we were interrupted by Luke, and then I got all riled up about Todd's songs—"

"This is not about last night." He peered out the window. His eyes roamed over the cars in the parking lot of a landscaping nursery. "But now that you mention it, I did buy you a lot of drinks. You were supposed to leave with me."

Ronny's voice climbed like the reedy yap of a small dog. Beads of sweat dotted his brow. "Now I'm driving you around in the middle of the day where all of Halo can see us."

"You're embarrassed to be seen with me? I haven't even agreed to go out with you."

"Just shut up a minute. I'm trying to think, and you keep yammering."

"Excuse me? You did not just tell me to shut up. I need Sheriff Thompson, Ronny. And there's no way in hell that I'm going out with you."

"You think I want to date you? Christ Almighty, Cherry Tucker. Why would I be interested in a little nothing like you?"

I opened my mouth and clamped it shut.

Ronny laughed. "You are just like your momma. Did anyone tell you that? Thought the world revolved around her and every man was hers for the taking. She was no more than a bitch in heat. All blonde hair and boobs. And you only got the blonde hair." He laughed harder.

I slid closer to the door and curled my fingers around the handle. "You are a genuine asshole, Ronny Price."

"Tell me something I don't know." He flicked a glance at me. "Don't think about getting out of this car."

His left hand pressed the lock then dropped toward the floor. He fumbled beside his door for a moment, his eyes on the road and right hand gripping the wheel. Jerking his left hand up, he pulled my Remington Wingmaster into his lap and slid his finger through the trigger guard. The barrel jutted around the center console, aimed at my knees.

I pulled my knees toward my chest. "What are you doing?"

"Getting something back that was stolen from me that I took from someone else." Ronny accelerated past the town limits toward the countryside.

The blacktop felt extraordinarily bumpy. I slid my legs underneath me. "What did you steal?"

"What do you think? The C.S.A. coins. Which you will produce because I know you have them. You have to have them. You have Dustin's stuff. Everybody in town knows that."

I swore under my breath and tightened the hug on my knees.

"You just saved me a lot of trouble. I've been trying to get you to help me one way or another. Now when they find your body, everyone will think Avtaikin shot you."

"But," I stuttered. I had unwittingly set up a semi-innocent man.

For once in my life, my mind didn't spin in all different directions. It had slowed to cold molasses, my thoughts dribbling into a dark puddle dimly reflecting Ronny Price and my gun in his lap.

I watched the low-rent houses on the outside of town dwindle.

The cleared land turned to sweeps of spindly Loblolly pine and scruffy hardwoods. "You're telling me you stole the coins from the Bear?"

"He probably stole them himself, the Ruskie bastard. He's been robbing me blind with his stupid house accounts in that dungeon hell hole. Didn't even want to let me play because I wasn't 'the right type.' What a snob."

I choked back a pot-calling-the-kettle-black remark and let him continue.

"When Dustin guessed I took the coins, he broke into my house and stole them. Which means Avtaikin already knows I have them or will figure it out soon. He's already breathing down my neck for payment. That good-for-nothing Dustin tried to blackmail me. And after all, I've done for JB. Years of service with crappy commissions."

"So you killed Dustin?"

I still could not believe this was Ronny Price holding a gun on me and speeding off into the sunset. Ronny Price did not seem capable of murder. Gambling? Yes. Robbery? Absolutely. He ripped people off at the dealership all the time, so stealing the coins were probably not that far out of his wheelhouse. But murder? Ronny didn't seem to have the backbone for murder.

I studied Ronny's trembling grip on the rifle and the sweat dripping under his slick sideburns. "What about Creepy Pete?"

"Who? The other guy who works for Avtaikin?" Ronny jerked the car onto a gravel road hidden between copses of trees. "Pete was watching your house the other night, probably waiting to search for the coins. Maybe he's just a peeping tom, but I can't take chances. When he cornered me behind Cooper's, I shot him. I was feeling jumpy. That's the problem with guns."

Ronny focused on the bumpy, narrow road.

I winced and curled between the console and seat back, not wanting to be in the line of fire if the gun accidentally went off. Of course, if he shot a load through the dash, he would probably blow us both up.

"Look, I'm not going anywhere," I said. "Can you put the gun away while we're on this road? You'll kill us both if it goes off."

"Shut up." He slid his finger from the guard and settled the gun between the seat and door.

We bumped along a road squeezed between pines and bracken. Gravel had long dispersed from the logging passage, compressed into the clay or sprayed into the undergrowth hugging the road. Hunters used this lane all the time during the season. Unfortunately, we were five or six months off hunting much of anything, except maybe wild turkey, so I didn't feel too hopeful on meeting anybody in these trees.

"Where are we?"

"Behind Avtaikin's property. Now shut up."

Ronny's face wore a sheet of perspiration. His eyes flicked over the landscape with the agitated vexation of a mother sparrow.

I held my tongue as we drove deeper into the wood, winding up and down a ridge. Trying to think of anything to save my life.

"Aren't you worried about this beautiful car?"

Ronny jerked. "What?"

"You're going to get it covered in dirt, and you know how hard it is to wash off clay."

He stared at me, and I could tell I pointed out an obvious fact he hadn't considered. "If Uncle Will can match traces of this mud to the same dirt from my body — assuming you plan to shoot me in these woods – he's got you."

His forehead began work out new wrinkles and his right hand slipped to his hair, smoothing the pompadour with trembling fingers. The left hand kept a white-knuckle grip on the leather steering wheel.

"Besides that," I continued, "how are you expecting to find the coins if you shoot me in these woods? And what about my gun? Why would Mr. Max break into my house to steal my old hunting shotgun when he's probably got a nice armory collection at home?"

Ronny's face reddened.

"I'm sorry," I said, knowing I pushed my luck. "But I just don't think you put enough thought into this crime. Uncle Will says that's the problem with most criminals. They're just not smart enough to consider all their options."

"Shut up," Ronny exploded. "Just shut the hell up, or I will shoot you right now."

He grabbed the gun with his left hand, swung it up in his lap, and braked. The car jerked forward. Our backs hit the seat with a soft thud. Ronny grasped the keys and wrenched them from the ignition.

"Slide over the console and don't try anything funny."

Tucking the gun under his left arm, he grabbed my wrist with his right hand, and yanked. We tumbled from the car.

"Walk." Ronny shoved the barrel of the gun into my back.

My boots scuffled against the red dirt road, kicking an occasional piece of gravel. I squinted into the woods, wondering how far we were from civilization. There was nothing to see but the colors of the forest: dull browns, grays, the dark evergreen of native holly, and the bright green of emerging leaves. If I concentrated, I could have picked out a wider variety of hue.

However my mind, for once, refused to stray from the matter at hand. Which was the crazy man holding my daddy's gun on my back.

"Dammit, you know I'm right. Give up this idiotic plan and turn yourself in before you add more years to your sentence. Shooting me is not going to solve your problems."

"Shooting you will solve one of my problems." His voice rasped behind my right ear, his breath hot on my neck. "It'll keep your jaw from flapping."

His desperation and anger curdled inside my stomach. I wasn't going to be talking much longer.

"Come on, Ronny," I whispered. "I'm not like Dustin. I'm not trying to blackmail you or steal from you. You know my family. We're not bad people."

"The way I figure it, you're the only person who knows about me, except maybe Avtaikin. He's not one to talk to the police."

I shook my head and tried to plant my feet, but he nudged me forward.

"I saw your little drawings on those napkins last night. Didn't see my picture on one of them, but I saw the bear and the cow, which is probably Avtaikin and that piece of trash, Virginia. You even had a little sketch of JB's stepson, Mr. Luke. Nice group of suspects. And not a coin drawn there, either. You seemed a little obsessed with belt buckles."

I felt queasy. From fear and foolishness and sheer stupidity. I had overlooked the obvious money for the artistic bling of those belt buckles.

Ronny chuckled. "Don't worry. I made sure those drawings are safe. Your Uncle Will Will get them. And by the time he starts looking at those little pictures, you'll be dead, and I'll be in Mexico. I put in for a vacation the day I took those coins. Wanted it to look natural when I left for my condo across the border."

Ronny jerked my arm and spun me around. "Now, are the coins at your house?"

I swallowed and nodded.

"Where? I tore through that rickety house pretty good."

"I can't tell you. I have to show you."

"Tell me, or I start shooting body parts. Those paint-stained hands are first. Or maybe I'll shoot those old boots off your feet. You think I care? Those coins are worth millions."

"Millions? Max said they're only worth thousands."

"You think you can trick me?"

I stared into his crazed eyes and knew Ronny Price was completely delusional. Which meant I was never getting out of this forest alive.

"You play games with me. I'll play with you." Seizing my arms, he jerked together and taped my wrists.

A hard shove on my shoulders sent me sprawling on the

ground. Pain shot through my tailbone while my brain scrambled over various pleas and plans.

"Won't need these." Ronny yanked off my boots and hurled them into the forest along with Todd's keys. They thudded into the blanket of dead leaves and pine straw. He wrapped my ankles with the silver tape.

"You are making a huge mistake. This is never going to work."

"Just shut up."

Ronny clenched his teeth over the tape and tore a shorter piece. He waved the tape at me. "This is for your mouth."

A slight breeze blew the free end of the tape toward his hand. The tape stuck to itself.

"Dammit," he cried and ripped off another piece. With eyes gleaming, he bent toward me. "Now tell me where those coins are. I'm warning you. I don't want to hear anything else come out of your mouth."

"No way in hell."

Ronny tossed the tape and slapped my face.

My ears rang. Stars lit my vision.

His grin revealed his pleasure in battering people. Ronny Price popped me with the flashlight, killed Dustin with a torque wrench, and completely enjoyed it.

His next slap was nearly a punch.

I pulled my knees toward my chest and thrust them at Ronny, knocking him backward. Throwing myself over the gun, I tried to pin it beneath me.

Ronny pitched on to his feet. Leaning over, he pushed me to the side.

My knees straddled the gun. I heaved myself back on top. Ronny kicked me. Hard. The kick sent me rolling. My knees drew into my stomach. My eyes and nose ran. I inhaled the dirt and bits of leaves lying under my face.

"If I don't find those coins, I am coming back to kill you." He snatched the gun. Gripping the barrel, he raised it high above me.

I felt a light rush of air stir my hair. The glossy walnut stock crashed down. I rolled to the side. The gun caught my hair as it slammed into the ground. I continued the roll and found myself staring into Ronny's astonished face.

Before he could think to raise the gun, I drew in my legs. My feet shot out and smashed into his groin. He turned an astonishing shade of green-tinged white and buckled. I kicked again, this time slamming my heels against his nose. Blood spurted.

Ronny tipped forward, cursing, and the gun fell sideways.

The recovery period from getting kicked in the jewels wouldn't take long. And he'd be pretty ticked about that broken nose. I threw my body on top of that gun and shuffled inchworm style.

My only thought was to get my daddy's gun out of Ronny's reach.

With my fingers curled around the gun stock grip and my chest flattened against the barrel, my Remington scraped across the ground below me. Weeds and vines whacked my swelling cheek. One tear trickled out my puffy eye.

"Get back here," Ronny shouted hoarsely. "Or as soon as I get up, I'm going to make you wish you had."

Crawling to escape wasn't an option. And I sure as hell wasn't going to keep my back to him. I halted my creep forward and shuffled in a wide pivot to face him.

Ronny sat with his knees pulled up, tentatively feeling his nose. Spattered blood besmirched his apricot shirt and tasseled loafers. His face looked none too good, but I feared it was a sight better than mine.

With an undignified half-roll, I hauled myself to sitting and scooted backward until my back hit a tree. I wedged the gunstock between my thighs and aimed the muzzle at Ronny.

His laugh, short and brittle, sent a new flurry of goosebumps to prickle my skin.

"This is how it's going down," he said. "You're going to give me that gun, and I'm going to leave you here. By the time you get to town, I'll be on my way to Mexico."

"You must think I'm pretty stupid." I panted, fighting the

nauseating clenching in my belly. I couldn't catch a breath with the piercing pain in my side.

He pushed himself off the ground.

I slid my hands off the grip and to the trigger guard, feeling for the safety.

"You're not going to shoot me."

"Guess you'll find out."

I waited a tic, watching his feet for a change in direction. I prayed he would take the smarter option and drive away. Approach me, and he'd make a pretty big target. I couldn't let him take my gun. My finger slipped around the trigger. I held my breath.

"I need those coins, Cherry."

Pressing myself against the tree, I slid my knees higher. If he didn't take off, this would hurt. Real bad.

"This is your last chance. Give me the gun." He stepped forward.

"Stop where you are."

A bird cawed. Ronny lurched at me.

I pulled the trigger and screamed at the burn. Then I pulled off another shot. The scorching pain knocked me sideways. My head smacked the earth. An avalanche of sticks and leaves showered me. Out of the corner of my eye, I registered a large branch falling.

I took that crack to the noggin as blessed relief.

EIGHTEEN

WHEN I WOKE to the sound of birdcalls, I was taken back to summer campfires in high school. I always woke the next day in a hazy state of hangover, just shy of food poisoning.

The cutting ache in my side and throbbing head made me want to barf up non-existent BBQ. I lay still, fighting the dry heaves, confused as to why my arms and legs refused to work. After my head cleared, I remembered.

Ronny Price and my daddy's gun.

I flipped around to sitting and surveyed the damage. My lace shirt had ripped in several places and sported a rusty toe print from where Ronny's dirty shoe created the sharp pain in my side. Silver tape still strapped my bootless ankles.

Ronny lay a few feet away, bleeding from a gash in his leg where I winged him. He looked unconscious, but my shot had gone wide. Otherwise, he'd have a much bigger hole.

However, I wasn't sticking around to resuscitate a crazy man. And no way was I searching his body for the keys to his car with bound hands and feet.

My legs flailed to no avail. The tape wouldn't give. Neither would the tape around my wrists. I tried rubbing the tape against the raspy bark of a sweetgum and only succeeded in scraping off skin from my arms.

I struggled to my feet, ignoring the blinding pain pulsing in my temples. Resolve and anger mixed with the pain as I steadied myself. I glanced down at the gun with regret. It would already take a miracle to shuffle out of the woods without having to juggle a shotgun between taped hands. Using small hops, I pushed it under the fallen debris and hoped Ronny wouldn't look too hard.

By the time I reached the second ridge, every part of my body hurt. When I wasn't cursing Ronny — and Dustin for blackmailing him — I began a rant on duct tape and the makers of my cheap socks that couldn't withstand the wriggling, hopping movement I had mastered after numerous falls. When my knees bit the dirt, I cursed Georgia for her hills, forests, and hard packed clay that felt like granite.

Knowing anger was the only steam to fuel my engine, I continued to find fault in the world around me. The logging road was much longer and had more hills than I remembered. I didn't want to think about the long trek down the county highway.

When the sound of a V8 engine reached me, I panicked and hopped into the woods for cover. My cursing turned to pleading at the thought of Ronny's crazed anger when he found me missing. The time it took me to creep to this point in the lane would take him but seconds in his car.

I inched into the tree line and bumped against a fallen limb. The engine's growl grew. Pitching myself over the log, I bent my knees to save my face. My forehead plopped into the weeds and dead leaves at the edge of a clump of seedlings.

The vehicle roared past, taking the narrow, rutty road too quick for safety.

I wriggled forward, pushing with my shoulders and squinting my eyes against the weeds and stems that snapped and flapped against my face, hoping to hide.

A thicket of sprouting honeysuckle looped and twined among the seedlings, tying them to the nearby trees in a tangled mess of vine. My head worked through the vines, perfuming the air with their sweet scent.

The rumble approached.

All of my moveable parts were writhing and scrabbling.

This time the vehicle crawled along the road. He was looking for me now.

I froze, flattened, and waited.

The tires crunched over bits of gravel in the road. Dust kicked up from the dirty lane and floated in the air, mixing with the saccharine smell of honeysuckle. A squirrel chattered, angry at my abuse of his territory.

A twig popped under a tire and the car stopped.

I held my breath, willing my body to disappear into the undergrowth. And desperately wished I had worn camo instead of teal.

A door opened with a metallic groan. Feet smacked the dirt road. Squeaky shocks absorbed the release of body weight. The door slammed shut.

Footsteps stirred more dust as they tracked across the road, plodding closer.

I squeezed my eyes shut and tried to lie still, but my body began trembling all the while my brain screamed to cut it out.

The footsteps stopped, retreated, and stopped again.

I took a minuscule gasp of honeysuckle air.

The feet pounded hard and fast across the compacted dirt.

A tiny tear tracked down my cheek and stuck on my lip.

Lord, my inner voice screamed, I do not want to go out like this.

"Gotcha."

My body began to writhe, wriggle, and buck with an uncontrollable desire for freedom. I managed to get my knees under my chest and push off with my toes when a hand snagged my waistband.

"Quit squirming!"

"Screw you, Ronny Price," I screamed. "You kill me, and I'll haunt you every night, you scumbag!"

His hand tore out the vines around my shoulders.

I kicked my legs with the intensity of a pissed-off mule.

"Just lay still."

"Hands tied or no, I knew I should've tried to shoot you again."
I kicked again and felt my feet smack against something firm.

He grunted in pain and then spoke. "You shot him?"

I prepared to bellow my answer just as the question actualized
in my brain. "Ronny Price?" I squeaked and tried to crane my neck
to see behind me, but couldn't.

"Just calm down and lie still."

"Oh my Lord, who is that? Can you cut the tape, please? Thank
you. Oh Lord Jesus, thank you." I stopped flopping but continued
to jabber into the crushed weeds. "You need to hurry. Ronny Price
is still out there. He did this to me. He murdered Dustin and Pete
and stole from Mr. Max. He's crazy."

I heard the snick of a knife opening and the ripping of the tape
at my ankles. My legs collapsed apart. "Oh, thank you. I don't
know how to thank you."

"I could think of something."

I turned my head to the side, but only saw trampled weeds and
an end of the honeysuckle vine. Tiny leaves tickled my nose as a
curling tendril waved before my face.

"Luke?" I twisted to my side.

"I'm damned sure I'm not Ronny Price." He ripped his knife
through the tape at my wrists.

My arms fell apart in painful relief.

"You're going to be just fine. Don't worry about anything. Sher-
iff's up there now. He and his boys took the logging lane near
Avtaikin's place when they located the Lincoln with the LoJack.
They found Price but didn't find you."

I lay on my stomach staring into the pine straw, spent.

Luke's hands ran over my legs, up my back, and down my
arms, checking for injuries.

My eyes squeezed shut while he gently prodded my
head. "Ouch."

"You've got another goose egg," he murmured. "I'm going to roll you over now. Tell me if it hurts too much. Sheriff Thompson's got the ambulance coming."

He placed one hand on my neck and turned me slowly toward his body. Another wave of nausea wafted over me as my back collapsed onto the forest floor.

"What hurts?" Luke smoothed my hair from my forehead and attempted a smile that appeared more of a grimace.

"Pretty much everything. What are you doing here?" I closed my eyes.

His hands drifted down the length of my body, gently bending my joints. I gasped as he prodded my side.

"Did he kick you?" I strained to hear Luke's low rumble, then shrank back when he touched my tender cheek.

"In the face, too?" His rumble crept to a growl.

"Is my face messed up?" My hands flew to my face, but it made my shoulders ache, so I let them drift to the ground once again.

"Don't worry, you'll do. Can't mess up that pretty face too bad."

"You think I'm pretty?" My voice cracked. "Ronny said I was a little nothing."

"You're too much of a mess to be nothing. Now, your hair is interesting. You got little flowers stuck all in it. And some dirt and grass, too. You look like a blonde hedgehog."

"Thanks a lot," I mumbled and heard him snort. "You want to tell me how you found me?"

"Wasn't too hard to spot with your tail stuck in the air, pointing straight to heaven."

"No, how did you know I was out here?"

"Long story, hon."

I threaded my fingers through his. "It's not like I'm going anywhere."

"The Sheriff used the vehicle's LoJack system JB installs on every expensive dealer car. The LoJack uses radio waves for the police to track stolen vehicles. That part was a piece of cake." Luke spoke to the trees.

I searched his face for some glimmer of emotion within the deadpan delivery.

"Lucky for you Maksim Avtaikin reported your disappearance from his house. Said some drawings and a chat with Todd McIntosh tipped him off you might be in trouble. They located McIntosh's Civic in the dealership parking lot. Video surveillance showed you and Ronny leaving together in the Lincoln."

"I guess I owe the Bear an apology."

A smug look hovered beneath Luke's serious profile. "The apprehension was successful thanks to a concussion and injury to the perp's leg, which looked like buckshot graze. I volunteered to find you, which Sheriff Thompson allowed..."

He muttered the final two words, "for once."

"Why are you talking like a cop?" I struggled to sit up, but Luke gave me a gentle shove back to the ground.

"Five years as a Military Police Investigator will do that to you." He fixed his eyes back on the forest and shrugged off the statement.

"Why didn't you tell me?"

"I don't know." He leaned forward, letting his arms dangle over bent knees. His long fingers picked at a crushed flower.

With a need to steady my nerves and clear my head, I stared at the pines above me, swaying in the slight breezes. When wind pushed through the waving thin columns, the whooshing sound always reminded me of the ocean. Which made me think of Tybee Island, Savannah's local beach, and some rollicking Luke and I had done there.

"I think you like secrets, that's what I think," I said. "You never want to tell me anything. If you keep your thoughts to yourself, you don't have to get close to anyone."

"You watch too much daytime TV. I just know when to keep my mouth shut. As soon as Sheriff Thompson heard I was looking for a job, he was all over me to apply for deputy in Forks County."

"Work around Halo? Why didn't you tell me?"

"Forget I even mentioned it. It's bad enough I spent all those years pushing papers in the Army for petty theft violations when I wanted to do CID — Criminal Investigation Special Agent. Then I got out and learned I had to go through the Police Academy and start all over again. I'm going to be forty before I get to detective."

He slapped his boots. "You think I wanted to move back to this crappy town to throw my step-brother and his buddies in the can every other weekend?"

"We would be proud to have you serve in Forks County. Halo's a great town to live in."

"I don't want to work in the boondocks. I'm going to apply in a city, maybe Atlanta."

"There's nothing wrong with Halo. We had two murders in the last couple weeks. That's as good as Atlanta." I glanced at my battered body. "Almost three murders, actually."

Luke's jaw tightened.

"Anyway," I continued."I think you're afraid that working in Halo means settling down. Or just settling. You need to forgive your momma and JB and find some peace."

"Stop analyzing me. Do you really want to get into this now? Can't you just act like a normal victim and lay here until the ambulance arrives?"

"I am not a victim," I said, ignoring my body's obvious distress. "I just helped the sheriff catch a criminal."

"A minute ago you were trussed up like a hog ready for slaughter. I have never met anybody so foolhardy in my life. Shooting someone with your hands tied like that? You're lucky you didn't kill yourself."

His eyes held the color of a thunderstorm. "It was easier to be half a world away, trying to remain ignorant to what went on in your crazy life."

The wail of an ambulance siren startled me.

Luke stood, brushing pine needles off his pants.

"My life is none of your business," I mumbled.

"Don't I know it. I don't know why that idiot stood you up in Vegas, but I wished he had married you and taken you out of the picture. It would make my life a hell of a lot simpler."

He leaned over and kissed me. Hopping up, he spun toward the road and waved to flag down the ambulance.

I can't say my jaw didn't drop, my toes didn't curl, and my insides didn't heat enough to fire pottery. But I did recover enough from the flip-flop of my emotions to turn toward his retreating back.

"For the last flippin' time. I was not stood up in Vegas!"

NINETEEN

I SMILED WIDE, hoping I didn't have "Everlasting Ruby Red" lipstick on my teeth.

My hair looked good for once and not flying around my head like an electroshock case. Casey had straightened and shellacked it into submission. I yanked the straps of my bra back to my shoulders and took a final peek at my aquamarine toenails for chips in the polish.

Casey pushed me through the door. "Let's get this done. I want some of that champagne."

We entered an open room of waiting guests in a beautiful gallery in Virginia Highlands, one of Atlanta's funkier old neighborhoods. My old classmate Shelia worked at this studio, host to a collection of Georgia illustrators and artists I admired.

When Shelia learned of my recent misadventures, she asked me to join her collective show. Fascinated by the strange tale and quick to see a marketing gimmick, she made use of my unfortunate incidents. With her magical gallery girl abilities and a strange sense of humor, she concocted a hip theme blending me with the edgier pieces by other emerging artists.

Now my work was for sale under the collective title, "Transcending Permanence."

Whatever the hell that meant.

Scanning the room for Shelia, I spotted Uncle Will, Grandpa, and Cody languishing next to an angel-themed assemblage. They appeared one beer from tearing off their ties and tossing suit jackets over the sculpture.

A few steps away, Todd strummed a rhythm on his pants leg to an internal melody. I sensed the eyes of the locals flicking over the three bumpkins and the beefcake that is Todd.

I scurried to placate my entourage before our redneck roots became too evident.

"How much longer?" Cody whined. "You said there would be girls here, but they're not exactly my type."

"Be supportive, son," said Uncle Will. "This is a big deal for Cherry."

"Come on. Let's get some drinks." Casey drifted toward the makeshift bar. Cody followed Casey, pulling off his tie to shove into his jacket pocket.

I steered Todd toward *Dustin*, the portrait. "Because of the exhibition I didn't have time to do this properly, but I wanted to thank you for your help during…" I paused, hunting for an easy phrase to describe my investigation of Dustin's murder. "The Ronny Price thing."

"No problem, baby." Grasping my waist, Todd lifted me until my toes dragged the floor, then planted a soft kiss on my mouth.

Once I found my footing, I punched him in the arm.

"Don't blame a guy. You looked like you wanted me to kiss you."

"I was trying to express my thanks."

"I appreciate your gratitude. It's a little unusual, so I thought I'd test the situation." He grinned, and again I wondered if I misjudged his intelligence.

Before I could remark, Sheila sauntered to my side.

"Cherry," said Shelia, her voice full of gallery flair. "You'll be glad to know your buyer for Dustin is a friend. Let me find some champagne so we can celebrate."

"Say again?" I called, but Shelia had slipped into the crowd, leaving the "friend" next to the painting.

"It is an odd subject, but I'm glad you found good use for Dustin's portrait." Max ran a finger down the edge of the frame. "And the quality is exceptional."

"Hey, Mr. Max," Todd said, then turned to me. "I invited him. Dude's really into art. I'll let y'all catch up while I grab a beer. I'm not into champagne."

"Bear, thank you for coming," I said trying to hide my embarrassment. It's not every day I accuse a man of murder and kidnapping.

I quickly started to babble. "And yes, after all that happened, JB and Wanda turned it down. They said it was in poor taste. Luckily, when Shelia saw the painting, she insisted on putting it in the show. Sometimes the art crowd can be a little strange."

"Strange, but one of personal significance to me. If you continue painting, perhaps one day your earlier works will acquire financial relevance."

"Personal significance?"

"I gambled on two young men whose scruples I thought I could cultivate. I misjudged Dustin's eagerness to assist me when he steals from my clients to blackmail them. With the help of his mother, no less. And I misjudged the depth of Ronny Price's greed and desperation. Because I did, those young men lost their lives."

"So your gambling days are over?"

"Does that disappoint you?" A small smile quirked his mouth. "I received the feeling you enjoyed trying to catch me as the villain."

"I noticed you didn't answer the question."

"Neither did you."

"Touché."

He retrieved a shopping bag from the floor and handed it to me. "This is yours, I think."

"How wonderful," Shelia mock-squealed, returning with three champagne flutes and forcing them into our hands.

"A gift from your newest collector." Shelia tapped our glasses with hers in a quick, rehearsed move. "To a long and prosperous relationship between the two of you."

Max tossed the champagne down the back of his throat and handed the glass back to Shelia. With another strange, short bow, he growled "Artist" and strode from the gallery.

Traipsing after him, Sheila clutched the glasses while delivering a quick speech about payment and delivery.

"Still intent on harassing Max Avtaikin, I see," said a voice over my shoulder. He chuckled. "But the look on your face was priceless."

A hand snaked around my body and grasped the champagne glass.

I dropped the bag on the floor and spun around, bumping into Luke's arm as he brought the glass to his mouth.

Champagne rained over the two of us.

"When are you going to stop sneaking over my —" My voice choked off and I stared. All those beautiful curls. Gone. I forced my open mouthed shock into a friendlier expression.

"I've got a towel in the truck," he said and gave me a gentle shove toward the door. "I've got something to show you anyway."

"What are you doing here?"

"I'm done for the day and thought I'd come see the show. Mom told me about it." He ran his hand over his shorn head. "Come on, before the sheriff spots me."

Why the hell not, I thought, and picked up the bag to trot after Luke. We wandered down the sidewalk and around the building to a small lot where he parked his black pickup.

Two seconds later, Luke pinned me against the passenger door.

I clutched the shopping bag with one hand and the back of his prickly, shaved head with the other. We kissed as if he was going off to war and might never return. When we finally pulled apart, I slid down the door.

Luke caught me before my ankles collapsed in my too high heels.

"What did you want to show me?" I choked out.

"That. And I really like those shoes." Luke sighed and rested his lips on my temple.

I pressed my cheek against his shoulder, savoring the pounding pulse that matched mine. My palm ached, and I realized I still gripped the shopping bag. I opened my hand and allowed the bag to drop to the ground.

"What's that?"

"It's from Bear," I said. "I mean Mr. Max. My newest patron slash old nemesis."

Luke tore open the bag. "It's your green purse. Why did he have that?"

I grabbed the chartreuse messenger bag and yanked out my sketchpad. My fingers flipped the pages. "Where are my drawings of Dustin's swag and the stolen coins?" All that remained were the paper entrails left on the spiral. "Sumbitch. I knew that stuff was related to his gambling den. It's still on."

"What's still on? Pictures of the evidence you withheld?"

I waved him off and shoved the sketch pad back into my duffel. "I was going to turn the stuff in eventually. Nobody asked me for it."

"I did."

"You weren't part of the sheriff's team anymore than I was. You're lucky I didn't report you to Uncle Will. I bet he warned you to stay clear of your step-brother's murder."

"Of course he did." His mouth didn't turn up, but his eyes smiled. He took a step closer, fixing me back against the truck.

I pushed against his chest. "Are you staying in Atlanta?"

Luke sighed. "Atlanta Police are making cutbacks. Sheriff Thompson got me into the new academy class anyway. You're looking at Forks County's newest deputy. I need a job. Sheriff promised me if another opportunity in the city came up, he'd let me go. He'd already done the background checks and everything. My mom's thrilled to pieces."

His sigh deepened. "I guess you were right. I need to spend some time with her. She lost Dustin after trying her best. JB isn't going to be much of a comfort."

"Checking for skeletons," I murmured, remembering Luke's argument with Uncle Will. I slid my hands around his waist to palm his back. "I'm proud of you."

A kiss landed against my ear. "He already knows my skeletons. Everybody knows everybody's skeletons in Halo."

"We didn't know Ronny Price's." I blinked slowly so he could get the full effect of my Shimmer-Glow eyeshadow in Hellacious Heliotrope.

"Guess I've got my work cut out for me then." He grinned and nudged my leg with his knee. "So what's going on with you and the drummer?"

"His name is Todd."

"I know. Todd McIntosh. You still seeing him? I saw him kissing you in the gallery."

"Like you care. Why're you making out with me in a parking lot if you're worried about Todd McIntosh?"

The dimples flashed. He gave me one of those sizzling, lazy grins that does a number on all women over fifteen with eyes in their head.

"I thought that if I were working in the county, maybe you'd give me another chance."

"You going to hang your hat up in Halo then?"

"I'm not making promises to stay in Halo forever." His lips hovered millimeters over mine. "But I promise to pay the check at the Waffle Hut."

I closed my eyes, escaping the intensity of his smoky gaze, and reexamined the risks and rewards that rode along with dating Luke Harper.

"Cherry, tell your brain to shut up so I can kiss you."

His lips descended, and an explosion of color rioted in my brain, cutting off my internal monitor.

It took me a few minutes to find words again, but I worked them out along with a sly smile. "I was thinking about getting a dog, but I guess you'll do for now."

If I could have captured Luke's grin on canvas at that moment, I'd have sold it as a masterpiece. But we got back to business instead.

And by business, I'm not talking about selling paintings.

THANK YOU FOR READING PORTRAIT OF A DEAD GUY

Thank you for choosing Cherry Tucker's first caper, my debut novel. If you enjoyed it, please leave a short review for it's a great help to both readers and authors. You'll always have my gratitude. And if you let me know you reviewed -- by email (larissa@larissareinhart.com) or by social media message -- I'd love to send you a Cherry Tucker bookplate or other swag with my thanks. <3!

——————

I've had a writing career full of blessings and strange luck. This story, *Portrait of a Dead Guy*, occurred to me as I coped with the funeral for my father. It was an unexpected death. At the time, I was living in Japan with my family and received the shocking call on a Friday morning, just as I was dropping my first-grader off at school. Because of the peculiarities of time zones and trans-Pacific flights, the Lord amazingly got me to my mother's home that same Friday night.

My young daughters and I stayed with my mother for nearly a month. Cherry Tucker and friends had been playing around in my head previously, but I didn't know what to do with her. And for some reason — maybe due to grief, maybe because I'm just odd — while staying with my mother, I got the idea for an artist painting a death portrait. The portrait of a murdered man. After I returned to Japan, I started writing.

I'll always be grateful to Kendel Flaum and Henery Press for giving me my first break into publishing. I returned from Japan with the manuscript for *Portrait of a Dead Guy*, the second manuscript I'd ever written — the first of which will never see the light of day — and submitted it to Henery Press after encouraging advice from writer friends like Debby Giusti and Donnell Bell. Kendel said she liked my voice, although it needed work. Boy did it. Her notes were my first editorial experience. I think the stars were aligned for that submission for I hadn't yet done the typical slog of queries most authors go through.

Five years have passed since *Portrait's* first publication. Now she's in her second edition with five more Cherry Tucker novels and three novellas published between 2012 and 2017. I can't believe it!

When I was a child, I wanted to become a writer, but I didn't think people like me could do something as great as that. I didn't live in a big city (my hometown's population hovers around 600 on a good day). I wasn't sophisticated. I wasn't particularly smart or talented. I wasn't even particularly creative. Although my writing teachers saw my potential, they told me, "write what you know."

I knew nothing. So I didn't write.

But I loved books and words. I loved making up stories. Twenty years later (after my husband's urging), I let all those characters spill down on paper. Now I do this every day, and I've never known such fulfillment (and stress. lol).

If you love to make up stories, too, write them down and see what can happen. Don't give up. Then write me a note and tell me. Nothing would make me happier than knowing you dared to do the same.

Happy reading!
Larissa <3!

THE MAIZIE ALBRIGHT STAR DETECTIVE SEIRES

15 MINUTES

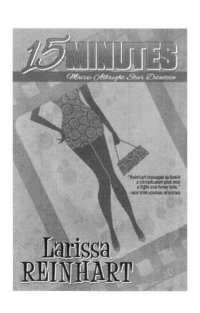

#10Days
#FindTheWoman
#GetTheJob
#DoNOTFallinLove

"Child star and hilarious hot mess Maizie Albright trades Hollywood for the backwoods of Georgia and pure delight ensues. Maizie's my new favorite escape from reality."

— Gretchen Archer, *USA Today* bestselling author of the *Davis Way Crime Caper* series

#WannaBeDetective When ex-teen star Maizie Albright returns to her Southern hometown of Black Pine, Georgia, she hoped to rid herself of Hollywood tabloid and reality show hell for a new career as a private investigator. Instead, Hollyweird follows her home. Maizie's costar crushing, but now for her gumshoe boss. Her stage-monster mother still demands screen time. Her latest rival wants her kicked off the set, preferably back to a California prison.

By entangling herself in a missing person's case, she must reprise her most famous role. The job will demand a performance of a lifetime. But this time, the stakes are real and may prove deadly.

16 MILLIMETERS

#BabysitTheStarlet
#FindTheBody
#AvoidTheKiller
#StillAWannabeDetective

Look for Maizie Albright's third book, *NC-17*, in 2018. Maizie Albright also appears with Cherry Tucker in the December 2017 novella, " *A View to A Chill*," (for a limited time in the Christmas cozy mystery anthology, *THE 12 SLAYS OF CHRISTMAS* and later as a single).

THE CHERRY TUCKER MYSTERY SERIES

STILL LIFE IN BRUNSWICK STEW (#2)

"Reinhart's country-fried mystery is as much fun as a ride on the Tilt-a-Whirl at a state fair. Readers who like a little small-town charm with their mysteries will enjoy Reinhart's series." —Denise Swanson, New York Times Bestselling author of the *Scumble River* and *Devereaux's Dime Store* mysteries

Cherry Tucker's in a stew. Art commissions dried up after her nemesis became president of the County Arts Council. Desperate and broke, Cherry and her friend, Eloise, spend a sultry summer weekend hawking their art at the Sidewinder Annual Brunswick Stew Cook-Off. When a bad case of food poisoning breaks out and Eloise dies, the police brush off her death as accidental. However, Cherry suspects someone spiked the stew and killed her friend. As Cherry calls on cook-off competitors, bitter rivals, and crooked judges, the police get steamed while the killer prepares to cook Cherry's goose.

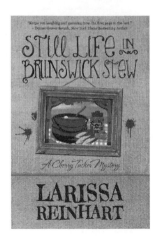

"Delightfully Southern, Surprisingly Edgy, and Deliciously Unpredictable." — award winning author, Hank Phillip Ryan

———

More Cherry Tucker Mysteries

Hijack in Abstract #3, Death in Perspective #4, The Body in the Landscape #5, A Composition in Murder #6, The Vigilante Vignette (novella), A View to a Chill (novella), and Quick Sketch in Heartache Motel

READER'S DISCUSSION GUIDE

1. LUKE ACCUSES Cherry of vigilantism. Do you agree with him? How do you feel about gun-toting heroines?

2. THROUGHOUT THE STORY, there is a theme of parental failure. Can you give examples of this theme using different characters? How does it affect their behavior and attitudes?

3. WHAT KIND of backstory can you imagine about Cherry's absentee mother? Toward what end do you see this storyline continuing?

4. CASEY SAYS ABOUT HALO, "appearances mean more than fact." How does this play into the murder?

5. IS Shawna a kind of character you love to hate or did you have sympathy for her?

6. IF YOU could have a talent of any character in the book, it would be...

7. CHERRY SUSPECTS Todd of pulling a "dumb blonde" act on her. Do you think he's smarter than he lets on? If yes, what would be his reasoning?

8. AS A HALO OUTSIDER, Max Avtaikin appears respected by some, looked down upon by others. He also appears both brutish and sophisticated at various times during the story. Do you see him as a criminal? Where does he fall in the roles of villains and heroes?

9. WHO WAS your favorite character and why? Which character can you relate to the most?

10. Were you glad Cherry ended up with Luke or would you have liked to see her with someone else? Do you think they'll be able to sustain their relationship?

11. Which scenes made you laugh the most? Could any have happened in your family (hopefully aside from murder, kidnapping, and burglary)?

ACKNOWLEDGMENTS

Second Edition (2017):

I'd like to add a huge thank you to the following:

Ritter Ames for her help and advice. Dru Ann Love for her continual support. Kim Killion of The Killion Group Inc., for the illustration and adorable cover. And to my Mystery Minions, Advanced Reader team, and all my readers out there for all the support and love for Cherry Tucker.

And Tater says thanks for all the goat pictures you send me, too!

First Edition (2012):

First of all, I know I'm going to forget somebody. Forgive me and thank you!

Thank you to all the fabulous writers at GRW and KOD from whom I learned so much. Particularly to Debby Giusti, who didn't know she would become my mentor a year ago, Pamela Mason, Leslie Tentler, Bente Gallagher, and Donnell Bell for their support, and to Denise Plumart, my fabulous critique partner. Also in that group belongs my fellow Hen House chicks, Terri L. Austin and Susan M. Boyer. Thank God Twitter doesn't charge by the tweet.

Gratitude to Cheryl Crowder for your goat stories and information. And to the talented writer, Jennifer Tanner, for being a good sport about letting me steal your fictional horse's name.

Thanks to Elbert Nieves for all the scoop on MPIs and CIDs and cool stories about the army. Good luck to you!

Thanks to Michelle, Nate and Maizie for their expert advice, time and effort (and cuteness).

A very special thanks to all my cheerleaders in Peachtree City, Andover, Orion, New Bern, Highland, St. Louis, and Nagoya, Japan. Y'all rock!

Thanks to Ann & Linda for your support and helping me dress and do my hair for a professional picture. To the Metzler-Concepcions and Johnstons for their encouragement. Plus all the Funks, Reinharts, and Hoffmans for their love and for spreading me around Facebook.

Special thanks to my best readers, Gina and Mom, who read all the early drafts and put up with character and plot changes halfway through the stories.

A super duper, extra special thank you to my genius editor, Kendel Flaum. I am so lucky to have you as an editor & for you tolerating all my questions. Your words "I like your voice" are in my top 5 best things I've ever heard. Unfortunately, I can't remember anything else you said in that original conversation.

And my undying gratitude to Trey and my girls. Telling me to write down my stories is the second best gift you gave me. Giving me the time to do it is the third. Your love is the first.

ABOUT THE AUTHOR

Larissa is a 2015 Georgia Author of the Year Best Mystery finalist, 2014 finalist for the Silver Falchion and Georgia Author of the Year, 2012 Daphne du Maurier finalist, 2012 The Emily finalist, and 2011 Dixie Kane Memorial winner. Her work also appeared in the 2017 Silver Falchion Reader's Choice winner, *Eight Mystery Writers You Should Be Reading Now*.

Larissa, her family, and Cairn Terrier, Biscuit, have been living in Nagoya, Japan, but once again call Georgia home. See them on **HGTV**'s *House Hunters International* "Living for the Weekend in Nagoya" episode. Visit her website, LarissaReinhart.com, find her chatting on Facebook, Instagram, and Goodreads, and be sure to join her newsletter for a free short story: http://smarturl.it/larissanewsletter.

56585306R00158

Made in the USA
Middletown, DE
22 July 2019